Whispers of Chernobyl

Lyla Lynn

Simon Publishing LLC

Text copyright ©2022 Lyla Lynn
Cover Design by Joanne Simon Tailele
Photo credits for cover included:
Shutterstock #1420904579
Shutterstock # 1582540216
Shutterstock # 1951751095
All Right Reserved.
ISBN: Trade Paperback: 978-1-7376246-6-0
ISBN: eBook: 979-8-9861221-0-6
Library of Congress Control Number: 2022909533
Published by Simon Publishing LLC, Naples, Florida

Second Edition

2 0 2 2 0 6 0 1 0

Whispers of Chernobyl

Lyla Lynn

Florida Authors and Publisheers Association
Book Award was presented on August 3, 2023.
Hosted by the Florida Authors and Publishers Association, this prestigious national award was open
to books published between 2021 and 2023. The
judges for this national competition are
librarians, educators, and publishing professionals.

The FAPA President's Book Awards recognizes
book publishing excellence and creativity in design,
content, and production for authors, illustrators,
cover designers, and publishers. This contest isn't
limited to Florida; it is open to anyone worldwide,
as long as the book is written in English.

Dedication

**This book is dedicated to Clean Futures Fund
and all those who assist in taking care of
the animals after the Chernobyl explosion.**

One

When I reflect upon my life, impressions appear in my consciousness as dreams. They are all I am left with. The whispers in my dreams drag me down and squeeze my heart to the point where I can't breathe. I gasp for air.

I was ten years old, living in the city of Cherynobyl in the Soviet Union when the tragedy of the Chernobyl nuclear power plant happened. The sadness of the destruction in the Exclusion Zone will resonate within me forever. I will never forget. *I will never forget.* That's what brought me to New York where I was introduced to my Aunt Olga and my twin cousins. My brother, Aleksei, was left behind. He was forced to join the Soviet military and work for them. He was only fifteen years old.

Now, flying back for the first time, as I look out the airplane window, I clutch my chest.

"Are you okay?" a flight attendant asks.

I struggle to find my voice. "I'm fine. I

was only a child in Chernobyl when I witnessed the explosion of the nuclear reactor. I'm going back as a volunteer to assist the feral dogs and cats that are stranded near the plant and to find a descendant of my beautiful dog, Sasha. We had to leave our pets behind when we were forced to leave."

She pauses, a coffee pot poised in her hand. "Oh, I'm sorry. Wasn't that a long time ago?"

"Yes." I nod. "1986. But now I've joined a team of medical volunteers with a five-year mission to go back every year to assist the now feral dogs and cats left behind and who have been breeding for all these years. This is my first trip. I am scared, nervous, and excited."

She smiles softly and wishes me luck. She tells me to buckle up as we will be leaving shortly.

I do. As we take off, I still feel anxious. Maybe I should have taken a Xanax or something. I twirl my fingers through my wavy chestnut hair over and over. It doesn't calm me. What will this trip bring me? Will I find closure for my childhood nightmare in Chernobyl? Will I be able to face my fears once and for all? I hope I'll find peace. I have suffered for many years with PTSD, which I attribute to the trauma of Chernobyl.

Two

While we rise through the clouds and come out above them to clear blue skies, I reminisce about my neighbor and best friend, Pavlov Bonder, from so long ago. He was tall with straight dark hair, his eyes so dark they were almost black. Dimples on his cheeks close to the corners of his pink lips peeked out when he smiled — which wasn't often. We met outside almost every night. We were in the same grade at school. I felt bad for him even though he was a bully. He had so much anger inside that I was almost afraid of him although I knew he would never really hurt me. He picked on the weaker kids in school.

His anger came from a history with his father who was an alcoholic and drank every night. Through the white see-through curtains of their living room window, I'd watch his father drinking and hitting Pavlov. I'd wait patiently for Pavlov to come outside after his brutal beating.

Once when I tried to speak to him about his abuse, he grew angry. He didn't want to talk about it. I was sad for him because he couldn't hide the bruises on his frail body. The abuse made him callous. That's probably why he was a bully in school. He needed to have a sense of control he didn't have at home. Why didn't his mother ever defend him? She just looked the other way. She must have been afraid of her husband and knew Pavlov could take it. I let him have power over me; I gave into his every whim.

"Come on, Nini!" Pavlov yelled one night. "Let's go sit under the bridge. It's going to rain, and I don't want to go back inside."

Pavlov called me Nini, his special nickname for me. I loved it. It made me feel special. We ran through the tall, scratchy grass until we got to the broken cement bridge. It began to rain. "We made it," he said gasping for air.

I liked the smell of rain. When it rained, I always felt it was a new beginning, a clean slate, a fresh tomorrow.

We sat in silence, watching the water fall from the dark sky. We could hear the crickets singing from afar. The glow from the moon shone over the Chernobyl plant, which resembled a giant beast. Smoke billowed from the plant's tall metal smokestacks that glistened through the rain. Sometimes I'd catch Pavlov looking at me. I stared back, trying to look deeply into his shiny dark eyes. I wanted to know his thoughts, his fears, and his goals. We didn't speak much; we just liked being together in the evenings. "Pavlov?"

He looked back at me.

"Do you remember that my birthday is coming up? I hope you'll come."

"Yes, I'll be there. So will my parents."

Mother and Father were good friends with the Bonders. Not only were they our neighbors but our fathers worked at the Chernobyl plant. Mr. Bonder was a maintenance worker. Father was the manager and oversaw the temperatures of the reactors. But I could never understand how my gentle father could be friends with such a mean man.

"Do you want something special for your birthday? I'll get you anything you want," said Pavlov.

I knew Mr. Bonder didn't make much money. "Only for you to be there."

"Do you know what your parents are getting you?"

"No, but every year I ask the same thing, a puppy that I can love and take care of. Maybe this year I'll get my wish."

"I hope so," he said.

I looked at the gray sky. The rain stopped, and it was getting late. "Well, I guess we'd better get back."

"Yeah," Pavlov said with a sad voice barely above a whisper.

We slowly walked back in silence.

We reached our homes. "I'll see you tomorrow," I said.

"duh VSTRIE-chi, catch you later, Nini," he said in Russian. He said that phrase to me every time we parted.

The next day, as usual we walked to school with a group of other children who lived in the same neighborhood. I loved school, I loved learning, and I had a great fondness for my teacher, Ms. Babin. She was very pretty. She had long, dark, shiny hair and glistening blue eyes. She was soft spoken and always kind to us. I could tell she really enjoyed teaching, and she appreciated her students. She made us feel special, writing exceptional positive quotes on our papers when she returned them with our grades. Even if we didn't do well, she always made us feel extraordinary.

"Pavlov?" I asked while walking home from school. "What do you think of our teacher?"

"I don't know," he replied, kicking a small stone. "I don't care."

That was Pavlov's typical response to questions about people and things. It made me sad to think he didn't care.

He asked, "Will I see you tonight after dinner?"

"Yes." I replied. "Let's go back to the bridge. I love it there."

We met outside our front houses and ran to the bridge. Pavlov loved to run. Maybe it gave him a sense of freedom.

He yelled, "Come on, Nini! Keep up!"

I always let him go ahead of me. I wanted him to feel a sense of accomplishment.

"Your birthday party is tomorrow," he said.

"Yes. I'm so excited," I said as I trailed behind. "I hope Mother makes me a fluffy chocolate cake. I love chocolate. Do you think I'll finally get the puppy of my dreams?"

"Perhaps, Nini," he said. "Perhaps." He giggled like a little girl.

I hadn't heard Pavlov giggle in a long time. Did he know something I didn't? Well, I wasn't spoiling my surprise by probing for information. While we sat watching the stars, I pointed to the dark sky. "Look, it's a shooting star."

We watched it until we couldn't see it anymore. "Does that mean good luck? Maybe it does," I wondered out loud. "Maybe it's a hint I'll finally get my puppy tomorrow. Well, I'm tired, Pavlov. Can we go back now? I want to sleep so I can wake up to my big birthday party."

"Sure." He grunted as he rose to his feet.

When I got home, I went straight to bed and prayed at my bedside, kneeling with my hands together, just like Mother taught me. "Please, please, please! I really want a puppy this year. I promise I'll take good care of it."

When I opened my eyes, I caught my mother and father watching through the crack of my bedroom door. I heard them chuckle. They slowly closed the door and went to the living room. I could hear them wrapping my birthday presents. Finally, I crawled into bed and fell asleep.

My brother, Aleksei woke me the next morning. He repeatedly sang "Happy Birthday" to me in a soft whisper close to my ear until I was fully awake then he howled, "It's your birthday! It's a beautiful Saturday, Mother is making a huge breakfast for us. Get dressed."

I rolled over and smiled at him. "It smells wonderful. I'll be there in a bit."

When I ran into the large kitchen, everyone was waiting for me. I ran around the table giving everyone a big kiss. I loved our house. It wasn't huge, but still the largest in the neighborhood with a big backyard. Its siding was a soft yellow with black shutters and a black front door. Mother had decorated the large front porch with wicker rocking chairs painted black and potted plants. She had impeccable taste for dressing and decorating.

"Happy Birthday, my love." Father whispered in my ear and gave me a big hug.

"Happy Birthday, sweetness," Mother said as she caressed my cheek.

"Breakfast smells great," I said.

Mother sat a steaming plate in front of

me. "I made all your favorites. Eggs, ham, sweet cheese fritters, and fresh cold orange juice."

After I gobbled my breakfast without even tasting it, I grew a little impatient. Were Mother and Father hiding a puppy somewhere in the house? I pretended not to be excited. I hunted through each room of the house looking for any evidence of a doggy. Nothing. I felt the disappointment deep in my belly. I heard soft laughter and whispering from Mother and Father who were still sitting at the breakfast table.

"What are you looking for, dear?" Mother asked.

"Oh, nothing! What time is my party again?"

Mother gave an exasperated sigh. "It's three o'clock, dear. You know that. The Bonders will be coming. I'm getting ready to make your birthday cake. Chocolate, right?"

"Yes, Mother. Can I help?"

"Of course, you can."

As I helped Mother with the cake, I worried I wouldn't get the puppy I longed for. Maybe next year. Well, if I don't get my birthday wish, I'll think positively about the other gifts I'll receive and be grateful to have such a loving mother and father.

At three o'clock, there was a knock at the door. Father answered. It was the Bonders, including my friend Pavlov.

"Hello, Mr. Kravets," Mr. Bonder said

formally. They both chuckled.

Father escorted them to the living room and offered them a cool beverage. Mother came from the kitchen to greet everyone. When I joined them, everyone wished me a happy birthday. Pavlov handed me a present. I thanked him. I squeezed the gift; it felt like a doll. How sweet of Pavlov. I loved dolls. I'd know for sure when it was time to open my presents. I hoped it would be soon.

I sat on the soft carpeting and listened to Mother and Mrs. Bonder talk about recipes and Father and Mr. Bonder discuss issues about the plant for about thirty minutes. I kept looking back at the clock near the front door. It was so hard to be patient. I looked over at Pavlov and caught his twinkly eyes as if he was enjoying my fidgeting. Mother finally invited everyone to the large dining room where she had my cake and presents laid perfectly across the table.

"Everyone, please sit down," she said. "It's time to sing happy birthday to Antoniya."

They all sang happy birthday to me.

I felt heat creep to my face and ears; I didn't care much for attention. I couldn't wait for the singing to stop. I just wanted to open my presents. After the singing, Mother prompted me to blow out the candles. "Make a wish."

I closed my eyes and wished.

"What did you wish for?" Pavlov asked.

"It's bad luck to tell your wish," I replied. "Then it won't come true."

I could tell by the smirk on his face he didn't believe in wishes.

Then, it was time to open my gifts. The first was from Mother and Father, a beautiful yellow and white dress with arnicas on it. I loved it. Arnicas were my favorite flower. They looked like daisies which were native in America, where I hoped to visit one day. I couldn't wait to wear it to school.

My brother handed me his present. I opened it up carefully since I could tell he'd wrapped it with care. Every crease was perfect, and the wrapping paper was beautiful. I opened it to find beautiful colored pencils. He knew I loved to sketch. They came with a pouch. On the cover was a dog playing in a field of arnicas. I gave Aleksei a big hug. Maybe that was the dog I was getting for my birthday. Everyone chuckled and looked at me. I hoped I hadn't said that out loud.

I moved on to Pavlov's present. He handed it to me with a half-smile. I opened it thinking it was a doll, but it wasn't. It was a little black, brown, and white stuffed animal puppy. Just like the one I dreamed of. I wanted to give him a big kiss, but I knew he wouldn't like that. Instead, I gave him a warm smile and thanked him and his parents.

As Mother was cutting the cake, Mrs. Bonder excused herself saying she left something at her house. Mr. Bonder and my father continued to talk about work. Aleksei, Pavlov, and I sat patiently as my mother handed us each a piece of cake. I heard the squeaky kitchen door, and Mrs. Bonder came back through the back porch. I thought that was strange. Why did she leave and come back so suddenly? Mrs. Bonder called for Mother. "Natalia, can you come here? I need some help."

Mother greeted her in the kitchen. I could hear them whispering. Then Mrs. Bonder returned to the dining room table and ate some of her chocolatey slice of cake.

Then Mother asked Father to join her in the kitchen.

My head was spinning from curiosity. What was going on? A minute later, I felt something cold and wet on the back of my neck. I gasped. I turned around ... and there she was. My beautiful puppy! I cried profusely. I held her close to my chest and rocked her as if she was a human baby; I was so happy. I looked at Pavlov and a smile appeared on his lips, just for a second.

My beautiful puppy looked like the stuffed puppy that Pavlov had given me. Tears filled my eyes. She was perfect; I loved her so much. She was shiny black with brown and cream and a little bit of soft white on her chest. I analyzed the white marking.

"Look at her chest! Do you see the white marking? It looks like a heart. Do you all see that?"

"What will you name her, Antoniya?"

Aleksei asked.

"I'm not sure. I'll have to get to know her a bit first. What kind of dog is she, Father? I love how she's so smooth and shiny."

"She's a smooth coated Russkiy Toy Terrier."

"So, she'll stay small? That's perfect. Then I can carry her around with me after school and on the weekends. I'm so excited! Thank you all so much for the best birthday party and presents ever."

Pavlov and I met outside that evening and ran to the bridge. It was our forever place to go. For the first time, I brought my new puppy.

"I figured you'd bring her," Pavlov said.

"Of course. You're good with secrets. I didn't know she was at your house. Did you take care of her?"

"Yeah," he replied. "She stayed in my room last night."

I looked at him in surprise. "Did you snuggle with her?"

"No, Nini," he shouted. "I did not snuggle with your stupid little dog." He turned away from me.

I knew he wasn't telling the truth, but I decided not to talk about it anymore, because it would only upset him. "Will you help me think of a name for her?"

"No!" He yelled as he forcefully kicked a small rock in the grass.

I began to think of names for my sweet little puppy. I shouted some names aloud to see if he would lend a hand anyway.

"I'm thinking about Karina." I looked over to see if Pavlov would respond.

He just kept looking up at the sky. As I held my little baby, I looked down to see if maybe she liked it. She just stared at me, panting. It looked like she was smiling at me.

"How about Bella?" I got nothing from either one of them. "Anna? Valentina?" Still nothing. "How about Dasha?" I asked, pleading for some assistance. My little puppy's left ear rose. She looked at me. "I'm getting close, aren't I?" Then it hit me. "How about Sasha?" She jumped to my face and gave me a big, wet lick. Sasha means defender of mankind. Just like my brother, Aleksei. I remembered the meaning of my brother's name from a school project about a favorite family member. I had picked my brother. We had to define names, so I learned that Sasha was a form of Aleksei. This was perfect. I loved both my brother and my little puppy whose name was now officially Sasha. "What do you think, Pavlov?"

"I don't really care." He shrugged his shoulders.

We walked back to our houses for the night.

Three

Weeks went by, and I enjoyed taking care of my Sasha. We didn't go outside much. She didn't like the cold. We stayed in the house and played. I missed my nights with Pavlov. We only saw each other when we walked to and from school. The winter months were too frigid to hang around outside.

Spring arrived, and all the wetness and dirt of winter disappeared. I missed Sasha so much when I was at school. I frequently gazed out my classroom window and dreamed of her. I loved taking care of her and playing with her. My teacher, Ms. Babin, often caught me and redirected me to my schoolwork. I'd catch myself twirling my wavy dark hair absentmindedly. Sasha and I relished going outside again to play after school. Pavlov and I resumed our nightly visits to the bridge. I took Sasha with me every night.

One day while walking home from school together, Pavlov and I talked about the amusement park that was opening in a few days.

"Do you want to go together when it opens?" I asked.

"Sure."

"Hey, I have an idea. Let's go see it tonight. It's not far, right?"

"How far do you think it is, Nini?"

I had no idea. "I don't know. What do you think?"

"It's about a mile from the plant. Not too far from the bridge, though."

"Okay, so can we go? I'm curious about the rides. I want to plan which ones I'll ride when it opens."

"Sure. Let's meet up a little earlier. duh VSTRIE-chi, Nini."

"All right. See you later."

After dinner, we met outside. I had Sasha with me. I knew at some point I would have to carry her. I figured a mile each way would be too much for her. We began to walk, and it started to get dark, but we made it in time to walk around a bit.

"Wow. This is exciting. Look at all the rides. They're all so colorful like a box of crayons. I think my favorite is the Ferris wheel. Look at how big and tall it is. I didn't know they could make rides that large. It's beautiful, so bright." The Ferris wheel was so tall, my neck began to ache, and I started to get dizzy looking up at it. "It'd be kind of scary to be that high in the sky. But I can't wait to ride on it. Will you ride on it with me?" I asked.

"Sure."

"Which ride do you think will be your favorite, Pavlov?"

"I like the electric go-karts. I can't wait to crash into other karts and the walls."

Why was I not surprised this would be his favorite?

"Look at all the food trailers. Cotton Candy!" I yelled. "Yum. I can't wait. What do you think Sasha? Anything for you here?"

She looked up at me and put her two paws on my knees so I would pick her up.

"You must be tired, my little girl. Let's head back, Pavlov."

"Okay."

We walked back a mile in the dark. I held Sasha the entire time.

One evening when Pavlov, Sasha and I went for a walk to the bridge, I noticed larger than usual bruises on Pavlov. It sickened me to know that he was being abused physically and probably emotionally by his father, but I didn't know what to do about it. Should I get him to talk to me or should I leave him be?

I took a chance. I went for it.

"Pavlov?"

"Yes?"

"Please tell me that you are all right."

He knew what I was getting at. "Yes!" he bellowed. "Mind your own beeswax and leave me alone!"

"But I worry about you. I see your slender body with bruises. I know it's your father. Why does he hurt you? Why?" I twisted my hair. "Does your mother know?" I knew she did, but I was curious how he'd respond.

"Nini, my father works hard at the plant. He comes home angry and tired and likes to pick on me. My mother always complains about not having enough money. It makes him angry. Father doesn't make as much money as your father. You must have it easy in your house." His face turned red. "This discussion is over!" he roared and ran back to his house.

I threw myself on the ground and sobbed big, ugly, racking tears.

Sasha crawled into my lap and licked at my tears with her cold, soft tongue.

I hadn't wanted to make Pavlov angry. He was my best friend. I only wanted him to be safe. Sasha and I stayed a little while longer so I could collect my thoughts and wipe the tears from my face.

April 26, 1986

The next evening, I went to the bridge without Pavlov. Sasha and I left a little earlier than usual, so we didn't have to spend the evening with him. I hoped he would take the hint and stay home. I needed a little break from last night's drama.

On the weekends, I often went to the bridge alone after breakfast with Sasha. I loved looking at the blue sky, feeling the warm sun, and dreaming. I fantasized a lot about how I would look, who I would become, and if I would find the man of my dreams when I grew up. If I did get married, I wanted him to be like Father, kind and gentle.

I said goodnight to Mother and Father and told them that I wanted to go to bed early.

"Are you feeling all right?" Mother asked. "You're not going out with Pavlov this evening?"

"Not tonight. I want to go to bed early. I'm feeling fine but a little tired." I felt bad fibbing to Mother and Father, but I didn't want to go to the bridge with Pavlov. My only way out of the house, other than the main doors, was through my bedroom window. It was in the opposite direction of Pavlov's house. That way he wouldn't see me leaving. I gave them both a goodnight kiss and went to my bedroom.

I wouldn't stay out very long. I'd be back before Mother and Father realized I was gone. I went to the window and pulled back my white curtains which were adorned by arnicas. I slowly lifted my heavy bedroom window, grabbed Sasha, and snuck out. I ran as fast as I could away from the house in case Sasha barked. I didn't want to get caught. I brought

Sasha's favorite toy and played with her under the bridge. It was a beautiful night. The dark blue sky twinkled with bright, shiny stars. I grew drowsy, sat, and leaned against the cool stone bridge. I yawned.

"A few more minutes and then we will have to leave. It's getting late, and I'm exhausted." I said to Sasha. My eyes got heavy. I closed them and fell asleep.

BOOM! BOOM! I woke quickly. I looked up and saw the plant. It had exploded and filled the sky with bright yellow and red rockets that shot high in the air. A large pink glow floated over the plant. The heat from the flames warmed my cool body. I watched the plant burn for several minutes. It smelled bad. So bad, it was indescribable. I was shaking and biting my lower lip. I thought of Father. He sometimes went back to work late at night. Was he in the plant when the explosion went off?

I looked down and didn't see my beautiful Sasha. I looked at my watch. "Oh, no. It's 1:30 a.m. I'd been asleep for hours. Mother and Father would be worried if they learned I snuck out." Nevertheless, I had to find my Sasha.

I stood and screamed her name. "Sasha! Sasha! Where are you?" She must have run off when she heard the loud explosion. While I was running in the scratchy field and calling for her, I began to cry. I decided to go back to the bridge in hopes that she would return. I sat weeping and twirling my hair. I brought my knees up to my panting chest and started to rock. Nothing calmed me. I waited for hours. Sasha never returned.

Suddenly Pavlov came running up. "Nini! What are you doing here? Your parents are looking for you!"

"I fell asleep, and I can't find Sasha."

"Forget about her," he screamed. "You have to go home."

He grabbed my hand, and we began to run. He looked at me and said, "No matter where you go, no matter what you do, you will always be my best friend."

What did that mean?

When we arrived home, he let go of my hand slowly until our fingertips parted and said, "duh VSTRIE-chi, Nini," and ran into his house.

I ran into my house.

Mother was waiting. She grabbed me tight and gave me a huge hug. "Where have you been, Antoniya?" she howled and started to cry. "Your father and brother have been outside looking for you."

"I'm so sorry, Mother, but I went to the bridge with Sasha last night and fell asleep."

"Yes, we know you left. I checked on you before I went to bed. We have been looking for you for hours. Did you climb out your window?"

"Yes, I'm sorry. I just wanted to watch the

stars for a bit. I fell asleep, and then there was a loud boom and Sasha ran off. I can't find her. I'm so scared for her. She's all alone. We need to find her. Please!"

"There's no time. Pack a small suitcase of clothes. We must go!" she screeched.

Mother raced around the house packing Father and Aleksei's clothes and some food. I didn't understand what was happening, but I did what I was told. As I packed, I saw the stuffed animal puppy that Pavlov gave me for my birthday. I shoved it in my suitcase and began to sob. My little Sasha was lost, and I didn't know what to do.

While packing, I heard Father and Aleksei in the living room.

"Did she return yet?" Father yelled to Mother.

"Yes, just now."

Father rushed in my room, gave me a big hug. "I'm so glad you're safe. We need to go quickly." He placed his hand in his pocket and pulled out his antique shiny gold pocket watch and looked at it. "We're losing time. We need to go now."

"Why? Go where? I don't understand," I pleaded. "Father, I fell asleep under the bridge and when I woke to the loud explosion from the plant, Sasha was gone. I'm afraid the loud noise scared her, and I can't find her." I couldn't wipe my tears fast enough. The front of my shirt was wet. I knew she must be scared. "Can we go back and try to find her? Please?"

"No, Antoniya! There is no time. Just do as you are told."

He rushed around the house grabbing things and throwing them in bags. "Are we ready? Natalia, did you grab the passports and visas?" Father looked all around the house as if it would be the last time.

I started spinning my finger around my mane. Why were we leaving? What was a passport? We rushed to the car with our suitcases and bags and Father zoomed away.

Aleksei sat in the back seat with me and grabbed my hand, too tightly.

I pulled away, and then wished I had his hand again.

"Don't worry, Antoniya, Sasha will be fine." He looked the other way outside the car window as if everyone had a secret and I was out of the loop. Everyone looked numb. I was too afraid to ask where we were going. I sat in the backseat and watched out the window. It was now 6:00 a.m. and the sun was beginning to rise. I could see snow-like flakes falling from the sky. But it wasn't wintertime. It was spring. What was falling from the sky? I didn't ask. The car was silent. I could feel the stress from Father and Mother.

Thirty minutes later, we arrived at the train station and got out of the car. Mother, Father, and my brother were quiet. Everyone looked exhausted and tired. Father purchased tickets. I heard him ask for four to Kiev. Why were we going to the next town? We boarded the train.

I overheard Father speaking softly to Mother, "When we get to Kiev, I'll purchase airplane tickets to New York City in America. We can stay with your sister until we figure this out."

Mother nodded. She looked dazed.

I whispered to my brother, "Please tell me what is going on? Why are we leaving? Will we ever come back?"

"We aren't coming back, Antoniya," he whispered. "Don't you understand what's happening here?"

"No."

"Something bad happened to the plant. I don't know if you will understand, but Father thinks one of the reactors got too hot, and the pressure made it explode. In the explosion, radiation was released."

I nodded. "I saw it from the bridge. That's what woke me when I fell asleep."

"Well, radiation can make you sick, really sick, like sick enough to die. The whole town is full of it now, and it will spread. Did you see the snow-like flakes while we were driving here? Those are the ashes from the explosion, and they're contaminated with radiation. Father thinks it will spread even more. So, we are fleeing the Soviet Union to save ourselves. We're going to America to stay with Aunt Olga and our cousins."

My head was spinning. "I understand now. What about my precious Sasha?"

"Sorry, Antoniya. I'm afraid you will never see her again." He placed his arm around me.

I only had the strength to weep. My beautiful little doggy was lost. She was probably looking for me and hungry. I'd never forget her beautiful face and the heart shaped marking on her chest. I laid my head on Aleksei's shoulder and fell asleep.

Four

I woke up to arguing outside the train. Father was yelling at soldiers from the Armed Forces of the Soviet military. Two men were holding him back. I could see Mother from the window outside, crying and holding onto Aleksei's arm. She was screaming at the Armed Forces guards who grabbed my brother and tried to push him into a van. He freed himself and ran back to Mother. They were taking Aleksei? I began to sob. I started rocking in my seat of the train. I was paralyzed and couldn't get up. I pivoted my finger around a strand of my hair. My legs were shaking. I watched Mother finally let go of Aleksei.

The guards released Father and pushed him to the ground. Mother crumpled to the ground in a heap and screamed, "We love you! We love you!"

My eyes followed the van until I couldn't see it anymore. What was going on? Father lifted Mother off the ground and embraced her. They pulled themselves together and got back on the train. What happened to Aleksei?

Mother knelt close to my seat. "Aleksei had to go back to Chernobyl," she said. "The Armed Forces are taking all unmarried men from fifteen to thirty to join the Soviet military to assist with the Chernobyl explosion."

"Assist with what?" I asked.

"We don't know. Probably cleaning it up."

"Will we ever see him again?"

"We hope so, Antoniya." Mother wiped a tear from her face.

I was still in shock. Too much was happening and too fast. I had lost my brother, Aleksei and my beautiful Sasha. I remembered what Aleksei said about the radiation.

We took a cab to the airport where Father purchased tickets to New York City. I watched as he showed them several pieces of our ID.

The woman behind the counter scanned us with piercing eyes. We had to walk through security. All our items went through a conveyer belt into a large box where they could see our personal items in a screen that looked like a television. I wasn't sure what all of this meant. After collecting our things, we walked through several terminals to get to ours. We waited patiently for our turn to get on the plane. After boarding, I watched Father fuss with our luggage and bags in the overhead compartments while Mother and I settled in our seats.

"May I have the window seat?" I asked.

Mother nodded without speaking. Father finally sat down next to her.

We were speechless and very tired. I heard the engines roaring and saw men with sticks outside waving toward the front of the plane. The plane moved backwards. I started rocking and twirling my hair with a shaky finger. My whole body was shaking.

Mother caressed my knee. She knew I was terrified, too.

After the plane took off, I saw the orange glow from the explosion. It was huge. My eyelids grew heavy, all I could do was think of my Sasha. Would someone find her and take care of her as if she were their own? I wanted her to be safe. I'd never forget her beautiful face, her gentle body, and the birth mark on her chest.

I woke to the screeching noise from the airplane tires and the pressure of being pulled forward.

Mother saw that I was awake and took my hand. We had arrived in America.

Through a speaker, a flight attendant welcomed everyone to the United States. We were in New York where I would meet my Aunt Olga and twin cousins, Mandy and Margo. Sadly, not under the circumstances that I'd hoped for. Mother gave me a sandwich she'd saved when the flight attendant handed them out while I was asleep.

I was starved, and it was good. I never tasted a sandwich like it before. I didn't know what kind it was, nor did I care.

When the flight attendant announced it was safe to get up, I watched Father fuss with the luggage again. He looked so tired and weary. I was worried, too. What was in store for us?

We left the plane and walked outside the airport. People rushed about everywhere, getting in and out of cars and hailing cabs. It made me dizzy. I grabbed my hair.

Finally, Father hailed us a cab.

I got in and pressed my nose to the window watching everything as we drove away. We went through New York City where hundreds of people rushed on the streets, looking like they were on a mission. I looked up as far as I could at the tall buildings. So tall that I couldn't see where they ended in the sky. Each building had many windows. Mother was watching me, she leaned over and whispered, "Those are called skyscrapers."

"Mother, they are so tall. I can't see where they end. They reach through the sky all the way to the bright sun."

When we got out of the bustle of the noisy city, the road grew quiet.

"Where does Aunt Olga live?" I asked.

"She lives in a small house outside the city in a borough called Brooklyn. Everything will look a little different in this country. You'll get used to it."

We arrived at my aunt's house in the afternoon. I got out of the cab and stared at her house while Father was getting our things out of the cab. Her house was very small compared to our house in Chernobyl. It was yellow with white shutters. The front porch had stairs with a clay pot on the top step with a big leafed green plant inside. Aunt Olga greeted us on the porch. She gave Mother a big hug. It lasted several minutes. Both of their eyes filled with tears.

"It's so good to see you. I missed you so much," my aunt said.

She looked a lot like Mother except she had straight blonde hair and looked a little older. She had creases on her forehead. They were both tall and slender with blue eyes. She was soft-spoken like Mother too.

When Father reached the porch, they too embraced.

Then Mother introduced me.

"Hello, sweet girl," Aunt Olga said. "You are very pretty." She bent down and placed a soft kiss on the top of my head.

"Thank you. It's nice to meet you." Mother had explained on the plane that my aunt was a divorced single mother, so I knew not to ask for an uncle.

"Oh, Natalia, she looks just like you. Well, come in. Viktor, put everything down here for now."

Once inside, she pointed to an open space

next to the sofa. "You must be exhausted. Is anyone hungry? Let's go to the kitchen."

We walked through the small living room, which had a light green couch and a matching chair. The wooden coffee table was shaped like a cube. The curtains were a soft yellow that matched the walls. There were pictures of two young girls on the wall before we entered the kitchen. I quickly glanced at them. I assumed they were my cousins.

I was anxious to meet them, but they were still in school.

We entered the shiny white kitchen, which had a table that sat four. There was a window above the kitchen sink. I could see trees out in her backyard. The kitchen had a back door and another with a screen. Aunt Olga offered me cookies and milk. I sat at the table eating.

Father, Mother, and Aunt Olga left me in the kitchen while they walked outside on the back porch. I waited until the door closed. I tiptoed to the small kitchen window but couldn't see anyone. I pushed a chair over to the sink so I could see better. They were sitting on the back porch that had beautiful white wicker chairs with soft green cushions. Lots of pretty flowers and plants framed the porch.

I listened as they spoke softly. My aunt asked exactly what happened. They lowered their voices even more, so I put the chair back and crawled to the door quietly so they wouldn't see me eavesdropping. I pulled the door open just enough for me to peek at them.

Father said, "The Chernobyl plant exploded, possibly due to overheating. The reactors were very sensitive and required continual monitoring. Somebody made a big mistake that night. They probably weren't checking. That's always been one of my big issues with the workers."

Aunt Olga gasped and placed her hand over her mouth.

Father continued. "I knew what that meant. Radiation would cover the entire city and perhaps the adjacent cities too. Maybe even the entire country. I'm not sure. All I know is we needed to leave as soon as possible so we wouldn't be affected by the radiation. I knew they would eventually evacuate everyone, but I wanted to be the first to protect my family."

"Why did it take you so long?" Aunt Olga asked.

"Well, we couldn't find Antoniya. She was out late with her dog, Sasha. Aleksei and I hunted and hunted for her. I ran next door to see if she was with her friend, Pavlov. He said he knew where she might be. He ran out of the house without telling us where he was going. I told Aleksei to stay put. I ran after Pavlov but didn't get too far. I had to stop. You couldn't smell it, but I knew the air was toxic. I was having a hard time breathing. I walked back to the house and sat on the porch. Pavlov found her and brought her back, but without her little dog. Sadly, we'll never see Sasha again."

"Oh, that's so sad."

"Yes, Antoniya is very sad. We're all upset."

"What happened to Aleksei? Where is he?"

As he told her what happened to his son, Father choked on his words.

My aunt began to cry. So did Mother.

My tears matched theirs as I sat on the cool floor near the door.

"We gave Aleksei your phone number, and we hope to hear from him soon. I'm worried he'll be exposed to the radiation for days. The Soviet military will give him a job. I'm assuming to assist with the evacuation or cleaning the plant up."

The phone rang. I quickly crawled back to my kitchen chair. My aunt came in from outside to answer the phone.

"Aleksei!" she yelled. "Hold on. I'm getting your father."

"Viktor!" My aunt shouted. "It's Aleksei! Come quick in case there is a disconnection."

Father ran inside and grasped the phone tightly. "How are you, son? Are you all right?"

Mother came through the back door slowly. She wiped tears from her eyes and held her arms around herself.

"Did they give you a job yet?" Father asked. "Not yet? What does that mean? Oh, I understand. I'm going to hand the phone to your mother so she can say hello." He passed the phone to Mother.

"Hello, dear. How are you? Are they feeding you? Did you sleep?" There was a long pause, then Mother said, "I love you and keep in touch."

She handed the phone back to Father, and he said the same thing.

"I love you, son."

Mother said she wanted to clean up and rest. She asked her sister Olga where we would be staying. My aunt only had one bedroom for us upstairs. It was a loft. She lived in a three-bedroom bungalow. The other two bedrooms were downstairs. My cousins each had their own bedroom, but now they would share a room.

Mother appeared thankful.

"I'm sorry this is all I have for you," Aunt Olga said.

"We are grateful for anything, and it is lovely," Mother said softly.

"Yes, thank you, Olga," Father replied.

I was too tired to say anything. We walked upstairs to our bedroom. The room was small but doable. The ceiling peaked high in the middle of the room and then sloped down on two sides. It had a double bed for my parents and a small wooden cot with a thin mattress for me in the corner. My aunt had placed a bouquet of beautiful yellow flowers on the dresser next to the bed. The room smelled of fresh flow-ers. We unpacked and placed what clothes we brought in the dresser and hung some clothes in the small closet. Mother made my cot with fresh linens, and I curled up on it with my stuffed animal puppy.

Five

I woke when the twins, Mandy and Margo arrived home from school. I heard Mother and Father greeting them and boasting on how big and beautiful they were. My cousins were my age and the same grade level in school.

I was still exhausted and couldn't get myself out of bed. It took every ounce of energy to sit up with my newly named stuffed animal, Sasha. Finally, I dragged myself slowly down the stairs. I caught myself twirling my hair, dropped my hand, and tucked it behind my back. I was a little nervous about meeting them. I hoped they'd like me.

I reached the bottom step.

They turned when I came into the room and scrolled their eyes up and down as if they were sizing me up. I did the same. Mandy and Margo were a little taller than me. They both had long, stiff, blonde hair and blue eyes like Aunt Olga. They were thin like me. I felt we strangely looked a little bit alike. The only difference was that I had long wavy chestnut brown hair.

We introduced ourselves to each other. Mandy began to giggle and pointed to Sasha clutched tightly to my chest. She whispered to her sister. I could hear her say that I was a big baby. I pulled Sasha closer to me and squeezed her tighter.

Aunt Olga called us to the kitchen for an afterschool snack. I followed my cousins.

"I have pizza bites for a snack," Aunt Olga said. "And soda."

I had no idea what that was. I'd never had pizza. I tried it, and I really liked it. It was a little spicy for me, but I still enjoyed the warm bread, cheese, and pepperoni. I also liked the soda; it was very sweet and bubbly. Food was certainly different from back home.

Mother was a great cook back home. We always had big dinners. My favorite meal was Beef Stroganoff over egg noodles. She made everything from scratch, even the noodles. I loved to watch her cook. Sometimes she would let me help, and we would have innocent flour fights. We had a lot of fun in the kitchen.

Mother made the best desserts too. My favorite dessert was chocolate salami. When rations were low in the Soviet Union, as they often were, she would treat us to this chocolatey delight. I watched her crush milk biscuits and toasted almonds and stir them into a chocolatey sauce. She'd roll it like a log and place it in the refrigerator to get hard. It was always yummy. I hoped my Aunt Olga would let Mother make some of her delicious meals.

After snack time, my cousins invited me to play with them outside. They had an old rusty swing set in their backyard. The twins played jump rope while I sat on one of the swings, dangling my legs while holding onto the corroded chains.

They looked at me and laughed.

I started to twist my hair again with my finger.

Mandy gave me a stare and turned her lip up.

I heard whispers of her having to give up her bedroom for my family. I got it. They were upset about having to share a room. I supposed I didn't blame them for being angry at us. We intruded on their privacy. I hoped we wouldn't have to stay there long.

Aunt Olga called us and told the twins to start their homework.

I went upstairs and cuddled with my toy Sasha on the cot. Mother came in with fresh linens and asked if I was okay.

"Mandy and Margo aren't very nice to me. They laugh and give me dirty looks. I heard them whispering about us staying in their bedroom, and now they must share. Mother, they are not happy with us." I bit my bottom lip to stop myself from crying.

"Well, your father and I will try to find jobs tomorrow after we enroll you in school. When we do and we have some savings, we'll find our own place to live. For right now, we need to stay here with my sister. Don't let the twins bother you."

So, this wasn't just a short visit. I'd thought we'd be leaving right away, maybe even the next day. I caught myself twirling my hair, again. I remembered what Aleksei said when we were leaving Chernobyl. We were staying here indefinitely. I wanted to ask if we would ever go back to the Soviet Union, but I was afraid of the answer. I could see the stress on Mother's and Father's faces. I missed Aleksei. What kind of job would the Soviet military give him? I hoped he would call again soon.

The next day, I was enrolled in school. They placed me with a different teacher than my cousins. I was glad. I didn't want to spend too much time with them. It was going to be hard enough living with them. The only time I'd see them at school was during recess and lunch. I was hoping to make new friends in my new school.

I liked my new teacher, Mrs. Smith. She welcomed me with a warm smile and introduced me to the class. She asked me to say hello and tell them where I came from and a little bit about myself. I stood and walked to the front of the classroom. My stomach had jellybeans jumping around inside me. I twisted my hair with my finger, realized it, and dropped my hand to my side. I felt heat rush to my face.

"Hello, my name is Antoniya Kravets. I am from Chernobyl, in the Soviet Union. My father, mother, and I moved here due to an accident that happened in my hometown. We are living with my Aunt Olga and cousins for a short time until Father and Mother get jobs."

Some of my classmates began to giggle. I didn't understand.

Mrs. Smith chimed in, "Class, doesn't Antoniya have a beautiful accent?" She gave me a warm smile. "Did I say your name right, dear?"

"Yes." I went back to my seat with my head down. I heard some girls laughing behind me.

"Let's give her a nickname," one said.

"Let's call her Ant," said another.

A third girl scooted behind me and whispered in my ear, "You're just a small little ant. You're nothing and stupid. You can't even talk normally."

I held back my tears and stared at my teacher. I couldn't wait until recess so I could go outside and catch my breath. Mrs. Smith had a little shiny brass bell on her desk. She rang it and told the class to line up for recess. I went to the back of the line so I wouldn't take anyone's favorite spot. Apparently, I already had enemies just for introducing myself. I decided to lay low.

While I was out at recess, I saw my cousins. I don't know why I decided to walk toward them, but I did.

"Go away, Antoniya!" Margo shouted.

"Yeah, we don't want to be associated with you and your fancy name and accent at school," shouted Mandy.

Now I knew what they were giggling about when we first met. Not only were they mad about sharing their bedrooms, but they didn't like my name and accent. Well, I couldn't change the situation or who I was.

Tears blurred my vision. I slowly walked away with my head down. I found a tree and sat under it. There was a little breeze which helped me calm down. I twirled my hair and took deep breaths. Soon I heard the brass bell ring. I looked up, and Mrs. Smith was yelling for everyone to line up. I walked up slowly and placed myself last in line again. I finished my first day with my head down, trying to ignore the ignorant, mean girls of the class.

As I walked back to my temporary new home, I remembered my dear friend, Pavlov, who used to walk with me after school and to the bridge. What had happened to him? Did his family escape the infected snowflakes which had filled the skies of Chernobyl? I hoped he and his family were safe. "I miss you, Pavlov," I said under my breath.

When I arrived at my aunt's house, Mother was waiting for me at the front porch sitting on the cool cement steps. "Hello, my beautiful Antoniya. How was your first day of school? Where are your cousins? Why didn't you walk home with them?"

I tried to be brave, but I couldn't hold back my tears that spilled onto my cheeks. I told her about the girls in class and my cousins teasing me. I begged her not to send me again.

"Antoniya, I am so sorry for your bad day. Tomorrow will bring sunshine and another new beginning. Ignore the girls who are not kind to you. Find some friends who you like. Give it time." She kissed the top of my head. "Come inside for a snack."

"Mother, did you find a job?"

"Not today. But tomorrow will be bright with joy, and a new day will bring new promises."

Mother was always positive and served as a great role model for me. When Father came home shortly after my snack, Mother told me to go outside so they could talk in private.

I went in the backyard and swung on the rusty swing. I waited for one of them to summon me to come back in.

"Mother?" I asked after they called me. "Did Father get a job today?"

"Maybe, Antoniya. He has an interview tomorrow."

"That's wonderful!" I jumped for joy.

"Yes, it is. Keep your fingers crossed."

That evening after dinner, the phone rang. My aunt ran to the kitchen and answered it and immediately called for my father. We all ran to the phone.

"Who is it? Is it Aleksei?" Father asked.

"Yes," she said.

He grabbed the phone from her. "Aleksei? How are you, my son?" His voice quivered with excitement. "Are they treating you well? That's good, that's good. What kind of job did they give you? WHAT?" he bellowed. "Hold on. Everyone, please go to the other room. I would like to have a private conversation with my son."

We obeyed and waited. A few minutes went by.

Father then called Mother.

She went to the phone and spoke to my brother for a few minutes. She came back with tears in her eyes.

"Mother? "I asked. "Is everything all right? Why are you so sad?"

"I miss your brother very much, and he has a very hard job to accomplish in Chernobyl."

"Well, what is it?" I asked.

"Antoniya, you are too young to understand the importance of his job. Please do not ask me anymore."

I walked slowly up the stairs to the confinement of our bedroom. As I lay in my cot, I wondered all night what kind of job could be so bad. I kissed my Sasha goodnight and fell asleep.

The next morning Mother assured me that today would be a better day at school. I left a little earlier than my cousins so I wouldn't have to walk with them. I kept my fingers crossed all day for Father so he would get the job. I prayed that his interview would go well. I also prayed I would have a better day than yesterday. I would be strong and try not to let the mean girls get to me.

RING, RING, RING! I was awakened by the school bell. Oh, my goodness. I'd fallen asleep in class. I was so tired. Probably because I worried about Father and Aleksei all night. Thank goodness I didn't get caught by Mrs. Smith. I grabbed my lunch pail, backpack, and raced home.

Mother greeted me again on the front porch. "How was your day, dear?"

"Better," I replied. Even though it wasn't. I didn't want her to worry. She had enough to be concerned about.

Father arrived home with a smile on his face.

Mother and I were still outside enjoying the spring fresh air, sitting on the front porch steps.

He picked me up, swung me in the air,

and hugged me. "Hello, my sweet little girl. How was your day today?" He put me down and kissed Mother on top of her head. "How was your day, my dear?"

"It was good. I cooked some of your favorite foods for dinner tonight."

"Me too, Mother? Did you cook my favorite foods too?"

"Yes, you too, Antoniya. I cooked everyone's favorite; Beef Stroganoff, and your favorite desert, Antoniya. Can you guess what it may be?"

"I hope it's chocolate salami!"

"Of course it is, my dear." She turned to my father. "Viktor, did you get the job today?"

"Well, yes, I did great in my interview, and I got the job. I am the new assistant manager at the nuclear power plant, Pony Point Energy Center."

"Father, that's wonderful. Does that mean we can move soon?" I asked.

He chuckled. "Well not right away, Antoniya. We need to save some money first."

"Okay," I replied. My happiness sunk back to the bottom of my stomach. I didn't like it there.

We walked into the house. My father sniffed the air. "Mm, it smells great in here. I can't wait for dinner. Let me wash up and relax a bit. It was a stressful day interviewing. I had a lot of competition for this job."

I went upstairs to our room and lay on

my squeaky cot.

Mother and Father stayed to visit with Aunt Olga.

I could hear my cousins playing out back. My eyes grew heavy. I squeezed my toy Sasha and fell asleep.

Twenty minutes later I woke and went downstairs. I stopped. Everyone was talking about Aleksei. They spoke softly, so I crouched down on the steps and stuck my head between the stair railings. I could see them, but they couldn't see me.

"I don't know if Aleksei can handle such an emotional job," Mother said. "Shooting the animals that were affected by the explosion and radiation? It's too much for him. He's so young. I worry so."

I could hear her crying again. I gasped and reached for a lock of my hair. My hair-twirling habit wasn't working. My eyes began to swell. Was my Sasha running around the streets of Chernobyl trying to find me? Would she be shot?

Father comforted Mother by holding her hand. Aunt Olga looked dazed about the entire situation.

I ran back upstairs. I needed to cry hard, and I didn't want them to know that I'd heard. I flopped on to my cot face down on my stuffy pillow so I could get it all out and cry harder. My poor brother. My poor Sasha. Aleksei was in such a difficult predicament. He loved animals too much to hurt them, let alone kill them. How could he do this horrible job? I needed to talk to him about Sasha the next time he called.

After eating what was supposed to be the glorious meal Mother had made, the phone rang. Aunt Olga answered and called for Father.

I knew it was my brother.

Father went in the kitchen to speak to Aleksei. I motioned to Mother. "Can I speak to Aleksei this time? Please, Mother. Just for a short time. I miss him too."

"Okay, but make it short," she said. "Phone calls overseas are expensive."

Mother spoke to him first. When she was finished, she called for me to come to the kitchen to speak with Aleksei. She handed me the phone and went to the living room.

I whispered, "Hello, Aleksei. I miss you very much. I miss you."

"Hello, my favorite sister." His voice trembled. "How are you? Are you enjoying New York? I wish I could be there with you. I miss you all."

"We miss you too, Aleksei. Is it true? Are they making you shoot the dogs?"

"How did you find out?"

"I overheard Mother and Father talking about it. They don't think I know. How are you able to do it? Are you really killing the animals left behind? Why were they left behind?"

"Antoniya, are you sure you wish to know?" His voice quivered. He sounded so sad.

"Yes, please," I said.

"Well, the government began to evacuate everyone the day after the explosion. Remember when I told you about those radioactive snowflakes? They promised the pet owners they could come back in a few days for their pets. They told them to leave enough food and water until they could return. They lied to everyone. No one is allowed to return. There's too much radiation now. The dogs and cats wandering the streets are now full of radiation. We wear gas masks and a team of us are assigned to kill them all. They don't want them to spread the radiation if they escape the town. Antoniya, it is the hardest thing I have ever done. I haven't shot too many. I try to hide, but when they're watching me, I have no choice. I cry with each shot. I don't know how much more of this I can take."

I heard him sobbing. "I'm so sorry, Aleksei. Have you seen Sasha?"

"No, I haven't, but I've been looking for her. She's so small; I'm sure she's hiding somewhere. Most of the dogs and cats are hiding. The noise from the gunshots scare them. They know what's going on."

"Okay, please watch out for her. I miss you so much. Please come to us when you're finished. I love you." I hung up the phone and raced to my room. I grabbed my toy Sasha and lay on my cot, twisting my hair until I fell asleep.

Six

Every few days we would hear from Aleksei. Mother and Father let me speak with him for short conversations and all I could do was ask about Sasha. My heart was heavy with sadness.

School was getting a little better, or maybe I was getting used to the mean girls and my cousins being jealous of me. They still teased me about my accent and my name.

One day Margo came up to me at recess and roared, "We're changing your name to Nina. After all, that is your name in America. Not fancy Antoniya. We are sick of your fanciness. Your mother dresses you in fancy clothes and fancy shoes. You always look perfect. Even your long fudgesicle-dark hair." She stuck her bright red tongue out at me.

I learned to ignore my cousins and the mean girls. I was no longer afraid. Mrs. Smith watched out for me. When she witnessed their meanness, she'd motion for them to stop.

Sometimes I saw her scolding them.

I went home from school that day, crying to Mother and telling her I was going to be called Nina from now on.

"I love it," she said. "What a beautiful nickname. I'll call you Nina, too."

She always had a knack for turning a negative into something beautiful. From that point on, my name in America was Nina. I kind of liked it. It was very close to what Pavlov called me, Nini.

At school each day, when the mean girls and my cousins chanted, "Nina Nina," I smiled back because I liked my new name. Little did they ever know. Ha!

Life started to settle into a new type of normalcy. Father loved his manager position at the plant. Since my mother was always good at making clothes at home, she became a seamstress for a local dry cleaner. She contracted out her work so she could stay at home and be there when I came home from school.

Every night we prayed for the phone to ring, hoping to hear from Aleksei. One evening, the phone rang, and it was him. When it was my turn to speak to him, I whispered to him the same question. "Aleksei, did you see Sasha?"

"Yes, I did."

Something was wrong. I could hear the sadness in his voice.

"She saw me from a distance, ran up to

me, and jumped in my arms. She was shaking, probably from the loud gunshot noises and being on her own. I gave her a big hug and kiss. I told her to run and hide. I put her down on the ground and tried to walk away. She kept following me. The only thing I could think to do is shoot my gun in the air so she would run off."

"Did she? Did she run?"

"Yes, it scared her. I doubt I'll ever see her again. At least we know she's still alive."

I cried for joy knowing she was all right, yet my heart hurt from sadness. I knew I would never see my Sasha again. I could only hope she made friends with the other animals left behind and would live a long life on the streets. "Thank you, Aleksei, and I love you."

Father was not happy with Aleksei's situation. He had many friends who stayed behind. He contacted them often, offering money to get Aleksei out. But everyone's hands were tied. They were all being watched by the Federation.

Several days later, a letter arrived for my father. When he returned from work, my aunt pointed at the letter on the table near the door. It was from the Soviet military. Father read the letter and walked out into the backyard slowly, tears filling his eyes.

I ran to the back door. "What is it, Father?"

"Nina, please ask your mother to come out here and then go upstairs."

I wanted to know what was going on, but I did as I was told.

Mother went out back.

I rushed to the bedroom window which faced the backyard and cracked open the window. I watched through the sheer curtains. I could barely hear.

"Viktor, what is it?" Mother asked.

He looked at her with disbelief in his blood shot eyes. He threw the letter down and stomped on it. "Natalia, he is gone. He is gone."

"What happened? What happened to my son?"

"He is gone."

I was so confused. Did he say that Aleksei was gone? Gone where? My heart pounded in my ears. Something was very bad. What was in the letter?

Father collapsed to his knees in the damp, dirty grass.

Mother held his head close to her, and they rocked back and forth and bawled. They stayed outside for a long time sobbing in each other's arms.

Aunt Olga came outside, and my mother told her about Aleksei in a whisper.

Olga sucked in her breath and clamped a hand over her mouth, like she was stifling a scream. Tears flowed down her face. She turned and went back inside.

A chill ran down my back, and I twirled my hair while watching out the window. It didn't calm me. I went to my cot and rocked. While twisting my hair so much, my fingers got caught in it. I clutched my chest. What was happening to me? I could barely breathe. I lay back on the cot and held my toy Sasha tight. I took slow and deep breaths like Mother taught me.

The bedroom door opened. My parents stood in the doorway, clutching each other, dried tears streaking their faces.

I sat up. Mother and Father took me to their bed and sat on either side of me. They hugged me. Mother whispered in my ear that Aleksei was gone.

"I don't understand. What do you mean gone? Is he lost?"

"No, my love," she said, her voice breaking.

"The stress was too much for him. Your brother took his own life," cried Father.

I burst into tears, blinding me, choking me. I fought to find the words, to force them out of my mouth. "Why would they give such a hard job to my brother who is so young? WHY?" I couldn't see through the tears running down my face and I couldn't catch my breath. This couldn't be real. Was Aleksei really dead? I wouldn't believe it. "No, no, no."

Mother rocked me and rubbed my back, trying to calm me. We sat on the bed in distress and shock for a long time.

I no longer heard sounds, banging of pots, no blaring advertisements on the TV or music coming from my cousins' room. My aunt must have told my cousins. She gave a gentle knock and walked away.

Mother went to the door, opened it, and picked up a tray of food.

Even though we lived in America, my mother and father still lived with our country's traditions. The next day they displayed ornate pictures of saints in the corner of my aunt's living room on her shelf that rested in the corner against a wall. They placed crosses and lit a candle on the shelves, too. I just watched intensely. I made sure to stay out of their way. Then, when Mother made sure everything was perfect, Father read from the Book of Psalms. Psalms 118 said, "Give thanks to the Lord, for he is good; his love endures forever."

We all prayed together, holding hands facing the pictures, on the third, ninth, and fortieth day after learning of Aleksei's death. This was to formally remember Aleksei.

Souls wandered for forty days after their death. My aunt placed a towel and cup of water on the windowsill in the living room. This allowed my brother's soul to revisit to rest and wash. After the fortieth day, Father took the towel to the backyard, and my aunt placed it in a silver tin bucket. Father poured kerosene on it and lit it with a match. I had to pinch my nose from the smell. My eyes burned. This was to release Aleksei's soul forever.

The house became stale and quiet for months. I walked slowly to school each day by myself. I gazed out my classroom windows still horrified. All I thought of was how much I missed Aleksei and Sasha. We all tried to resume our normal daily activities. But it was difficult.

Everyone changed with the death of my brother. My aunt was still polite but a little quiet. My cousins laid off me for a short time, but they eventually resumed their rudeness.

My clothes were getting big on me. They didn't fit right. I noticed after I brushed my long wavy hair that something would tickle my feet. I'd look down and see globs of my hair on the bathroom floor.

Mother and I frequented the local Russian Orthodox Church. She'd have me sit a few pews behind her thinking I couldn't hear her. But I could still hear her telling God she would do anything for my brother's return.

She murmured, "It's a mistake. It was a different boy. Not my Aleksei. If I promise to be more devout, will you give me back my son? I promise. I'll do better." She sobbed.

I didn't know how to help her. I'd clench my hands on the edge of the seat of the pew and rock back and forth.

Father also struggled. I used to hear him with Mother in the bedroom. He'd holler, "Why did I let them take my son? Why? Why didn't I fight harder? It's because of me my son is dead!

What kind of father am I?"

Mother's sobbing only got louder.

This went on for months.

Finally, it was summer, and I only had a few days left before school break. I'd be going into sixth grade in the fall. Junior High School. I did my best to get excited about a new school. However, I still reminisced about Aleksei and Sasha. I would always have fond memories of both.

I knew I'd also miss Mrs. Smith who always protected me from the mean girls. Would I make new friends? I really hadn't had a chance with the excitement and sadness of moving to America.

When school finished, my parents decided that it was time to move. They had saved enough money and found a small house to rent close to my aunt and cousins. Yay. I could finally be away from the relentless teasing of my cousins. I couldn't wait to get out of their house. Too many bad memories.

The day of the move was easy. I didn't have a lot to pack. I couldn't find my toy Sasha. I looked all over the bedroom. I went downstairs. I looked in closets. Where could she be? In my heart, I knew my cousins must have done something to her. I snuck into their room and prowled in hopes to find Sasha—nothing. My last hope was to check the garbage. I ran to the kitchen. There she was, smashed on the bottom of the pail soiled with food. I took her upstairs to the bathroom, bathed her, and tried my best to get the stains out. She wasn't perfect, but I'd saved her.

I wanted to scream at my cousins, but I knew they'd laugh at me. I wouldn't give them the pleasure. I just wanted to leave the house forever. I couldn't get down the stairs and into the car fast enough.

We pulled up to the new-to-us house. My eyes grew big. I quickly jumped out of the car, slammed the door, and leaned against it. The house was beautiful. It was white with blue shutters and had a quaint front porch with a matching blue swing and chairs.

I ran to the front door and waited for Mother and Father. "Hurry. I'm so excited. I can't wait to see my bedroom."

We entered the house. It already had furniture. It was gorgeous. The couch and chair were a soft shade of green. It matched the rug which was laid over dark hardwood floors. The coffee table was a dark wicker and a piece of glass lay on top. The walls were white, and the curtains were soft green which matched the furniture. I asked Mother if she'd made the curtains. Of course, she had. "Did this furniture come with the house?"

"Yes," said Mother.

Wow. I'd never heard of such a thing. Mother had made a few adjustments though.

Her personal touch showed through in little things she added, like fresh flowers which she placed on the dining room table.

"That's great," I said. "Where's my bedroom?"

"Hold on, my sweet," she said. "I'll take you. It's to the back of the house."

"Which door is it?" I ran past her, twirling around in the hall looking at the closed doors. "Which one?"

She stepped to the second door on the left and slowly opened it. "Surprise. I hope you like it. I made the curtains and a matching bedspread just for you, darling."

"I love it, Mother. Thank you so much. It's beautiful." I ran to the curtains and fingered the soft fabric. Then I did the same to the bedspread. They were soft white with bright yellow daisies, which looked like arnicas. She'd remembered that I liked arnicas. A little white desk and matching chair were next to the bed so I could do my homework. My cheeks were hurting from smiling. I hadn't smiled since the news of Aleksei. My heart stopped, and I looked at Mother. We stared at each other for a minute.

"I know, dear. I know. I wish he was here, too." She kissed the top of my head. "Now get yourself settled and ready for lunch."

I unpacked my clothes, placed them in the dresser, and hung some dresses in the closet. I gazed at my beautiful room. My own room again! And I still had my Sasha with me.

I placed her under the covers with her head on the pillow and raced to the kitchen for some lunch.

As my mother, father and I ate our lunch, the conversation dwindled down to nothing. I could hear the cars passing from the street in front of the house. I was thinking about Aleksei and missing him. I'm sure they were too. Aleksei should have been sitting at the table for the first time in our new home with us. Like hundreds of times in the Soviet Union.

In my mind's eye, I saw us sitting around the old table in our house in Chernobyl. Mother put fresh arnicas in a small vase in the center of the table. The sunlight cast a halo around Aleksei's head, and I teased him about looking like a ghost.

"No, an angel," Mother said.

And then the vision was gone.

Those days would never happen again. I was just grateful for my parents who always took great care of me.

We spent many days getting adjusted to our new home. Father went to work during the week and Mother stayed home and sewed. There was a park in the neighborhood to which I enjoyed walking, I kept Sasha at home as I was getting a little too old to be hanging out in public with a stuffed animal. No one would understand what she represented. So, I kept her safely tucked away in my bedroom.

"Good morning, Nina. How was your

night?," she asked in a sing-song voice, then chuckled.

Summer days were quiet and relaxing. Thankfully, I didn't have to see my cousins too often anymore. I couldn't wait to start school again and make some new friends. My accent was slowly going away, so I hoped I wouldn't get teased about it anymore. I liked the idea of being more independent going from class to class with new teachers and classmates.

As Father came home from work daily, he grew more and more quiet and withdrawn. He started to go to bed earlier than usual. I thought he was depressed from the loss of Aleksei.

"Mother? What's wrong with Father? He's not himself."

"Yes, Nina," she said. "I noticed that too, but he works hard all day. With everything we have been through, I believe it's just catching up to him."

"Okay," I said with a deep sigh.

It was only a few more days before school started and I was thrilled about it. Summer had been good but a little boring without Aleksei and Sasha. Mother made some of my school clothes. I loved the personal touch she placed on each piece of clothing she made. I liked to shop for school supplies, too. All my folders had a picture of a doggy. That way I would always be reminded of my Sasha.

The evening before school started, I heard Father in his bedroom coughing hard. I pressed my ear to their bedroom door to listen. Mother was begging him to go to the doctors. "You've been coughing for quite some time now, weeks even," she whispered.

She was right. I remembered hearing him cough a lot recently. I was so caught up with the excitement of school, I hadn't payed enough attention. I thought he had a cold or allergies. I hoped it wasn't something more serious.

"I'll call and make an appointment tomorrow, and you're going, my dear!" Mother said sternly.

"Yes, dear," my father replied.

I tiptoed back to my room. Tomorrow was going to be a big day for me. So happy!

Seven

My alarm went off, and I couldn't wait to try on my new dress that Mother had made for me. I rushed to my closet and pulled out the dress. I stood in front of the mirror next to my desk and held it to my skinny body. It was soft yellow, lined with a green hem around the neck and on the bottom. I really liked it.

When I finished dressing, I stood in the mirror again for a few minutes examining myself. Was my brown wavy hair too long? I pulled it back and put it in a ponytail. There, that was better. I hoped my new classmates would accept me.

I dashed out of my room and ate my breakfast hastily so I could run off to school. Mother and Father kissed me on the top of my head and wished me luck. My mother handed me my backpack which held my lunch and school supplies. I scurried out the door and jumped high in the air off the front porch. I could feel Mother and Father watching me from the front door. I turned and waved as I walked briskly to school.

As I got closer to my new school, I saw lots of new faces. I pulled my schedule out of my backpack to see where my first class was. I had a hard time reading it due to my hands shaking with excitement. I saw the room numbers and teachers' names and headed to my first class. Suddenly, I heard familiar voices. Who was it? Mandy and Margo were walking right behind me. My heart sank. I didn't turn around. Did they see me? I found my first room number and rushed in and sat in the back, hoping neither of them would enter. I held my breath. *Whew, they must be in a different class. Thank goodness*. I rode out my entire day, which felt like a lifetime, hoping I wouldn't have a class with them. The day ended with no more signs of Mandy or Margo.

I rushed home to share my day with Mother. I told her how happy I was with all my teachers. I also told her how glad I was I didn't have classes with Mandy and Margo.

Mother chuckled. "Remember, they will always be your cousins."

"I know. I just don't want to see them daily. That's all."

I went to my bedroom and changed out of my school clothes. I put on shorts and a t-shirt and went to the kitchen where my mother made me a snack.

"Do you have homework today?" she asked.

"No, I guess it's because it was the first day. Today was all about getting our books and getting settled with school rules and policies."

"Good, so you have the entire evening to relax. Your father will be home shortly."

That night I overheard my parents talking in their bedroom.

"I made an appointment with a doctor tomorrow for you. Can you get the time off?" Mother asked softly.

"Yes dear." He started in a coughing fit.

I came home from school happy as ever on Monday. I loved my classes and made new friends who lived in our neighborhood. I knew it was going to be a great school year.

Father came home from work earlier than usual. He'd had a doctor's appointment, but since I wasn't supposed to know, I didn't say anything. I greeted him with a big hug and kiss in the living room.

He kissed me back and told me to get ready for dinner. I ran to my room to get ready.

Mother was in the kitchen cooking.

I came out of my bedroom and pranced toward the kitchen. I stopped when I overheard them talking softly. I positioned myself close to the squeaky kitchen door so I could hear. Father said they took blood work and did a chest x-ray.

The results would come back soon.

Mother called, "Nina, please come for dinner."

I ran quietly back to my room and called back, "Coming, Mother." I came into the kitchen smashing my shoes on the floor as hard as I could with each step to make sure they heard. We began to eat. Nobody said anything. You could have heard a pin drop.

I pretended I didn't know what was going on, so I started a conversation by talking about school. "So school was good today. I love my teachers. They were very kind." I babbled throughout dinner about school and making some friends.

The phone rang that evening after I had gone to bed. I tiptoed to the kitchen to listen. It was the doctor requesting my father come back for a visit to talk about his results. Mother wanted to accompany him, and Father agreed to go in tomorrow while I was in school.

I came out of my bedroom in my pajamas and gave both my parents a kiss goodnight.

Mother murmured in my ear, "Have a good day tomorrow at school."

"I will." I placed my hand and mouth up to her ear and whispered back. "I love school this year." I went back to my room and crawled into bed for the night. Again, I heard whispering. I decided to let it go and not be so nosy. I was sure they would tell me all about it in good time when they were ready. I prayed for Father that his results would be positive. I thought it was wonderful that the doctor wanted to see him again tomorrow. Could be good news.

The next day, I was so happy about school that I skipped home to tell Mother what a great day I'd had. As I got close to the house, I saw her sitting on the steps of the front porch. Her face looked red and blotchy. As I reached the sidewalk of the house, I noticed she was holding a tissue. I slowly walked closer. She was holding back tears.

"Mother?" I asked. "What happened? Is everyone all right?"

"No, Nina," she replied while reaching her hand out to me. "Come sit next to me. I need to tell you something about your father."

I sat down with both of my hands holding on to the edge of the porch steps, squeezing them for support.

"Your father has been coughing a lot lately. I'm sure you've noticed. He went to the doctors yesterday for some tests. We received the results today. Your father must undergo more detailed tests, but I'm afraid he has cancer."

I looked up. Cancer? I'd heard that word before but what did it mean? Was Father going to die? I twisted my hair around my finger.

"They found masses on his lungs. I know you're too young to understand, but it's called lung cancer."

I felt tears stinging my eyes. "I don't understand." I wailed. "How did he get cancer?"

Mother's voice suddenly turned cold and bitter. "Probably from the radiation at the Chernobyl explosion. That's why we tried to leave as soon as we could. Your father must have been exposed too long. They took more tests today and will determine how to treat him. We will know more in the next few days."

She stood and walked back in the house, slamming the screen door. She turned back at me, "Come inside when you're ready. Your father is resting right now. Don't disturb him," she said in a stern voice.

I was a little taken back how bitterly she'd spoken. I quickly brushed it off and blamed her tone on the stress of the situation. I wiped my tears with the hem of my dress, went inside, and ran straight to my room. I wasn't hungry for my after-school snack. I grabbed Sasha and lay down on my bed. I prayed for Father to be well and fell asleep.

I heard Mother calling me for dinner. "Nina!" she hollered toward my bedroom. "Please come out. It's time to eat."

"Coming, Mother." I quickly changed and freshened up.

I ran to the kitchen and saw Father sitting at the table.

"Hello, Sunshine," he said softly. "How's my sweet girl? How was school today?"

"It was good, Father."

"Your mother told me that she explained about my health. I don't want you to worry. They'll find a good treatment for me. I'm strong, and I can beat this disease. Please don't worry."

I got up from my chair and sat on his lap just like I did when I was a little girl. I loved to cuddle with him.

"Let's eat now," Mother said.

She served us dinner, and we ate in silence. I didn't understand cancer, but I knew it was bad. When I finished eating, I asked to be excused and I went to my bedroom to do my homework. The stress of the news made me tired. I rested my head on my books. I guess I fell asleep.

I woke in the morning when my mother opened my door and saw me still in my clothes from yesterday. "Nina, it's almost time for school. Did you fall asleep like this?"

"Yes, Mother. I'm sorry."

"Well, hurry up and shower and get ready for school. I'll get your breakfast ready."

I took the fastest shower and dressed quickly. I ran to the kitchen, and Mother gave me breakfast to go — a warm, toasted bagel with egg and cheese sandwich. Yum!

Even though I was running late for school, I couldn't bring myself to walk fast. I kept thinking of my father. I thought about him all day at school. I didn't even listen to my teachers. I just sat in the back of each class and looked out the windows.

In my last class, I slouched in my chair twirling my hair. A friend sitting next to me tapped me on my shoulder, leaned over, and whispered to me. "You know you're going to twist your pretty hair right out of your head."

I pulled my hands into my lap. Then I started biting my bottom lip. I hadn't realized I'd bitten my lip so hard it bled. A drop of blood splashed on my paper. I found a napkin in my lunch pail and pressed it to my bottom lip. Thank goodness I liked to sit in the back of each of my classes. I didn't like to draw attention to myself.

Eight

It was now fall, and I loved seeing the leaves turn such vibrant red, orange, and yellow colors. I loved the crunch of the fallen leaves as I walked home from school. I liked my classes and school mates, but each day as I walked home, I was saddened by thoughts of my father. He was undergoing chemotherapy and had lost all his walnut brown hair. My mother sat with him every night on the floor of the bathroom as she held a cool rag over his forehead while he vomited the intravenous poison he had to withstand. His arms were black and blue from the needles.

Mother worked more to assist with the bills. Sometimes she was so tired she forgot to make my lunch for school or my after-school snack. I'd been taking care of myself.

One day, I came home from school to find my Aunt Olga visiting. I ran over to her and gave her a big hug.

She kissed me on my cheek. "Hello, Nina. How are you, dear? We were just talking about you."

"You were?"

"Yes, would you like to come to our house for a few nights?"

I looked at Mother and glared at her. "No, thank you, Aunt Olga. I'm good here."

"Well, dear, it might be nice for your mother and father to spend some time alone."

I squinted my eyes and stared at Mother. She knew how I felt being around my cousins. Why would she send me there?

"Nina!" Mother barked. "It would help us. I'm not able to take care of you the way I'd like. It's just for a few days."

"No, Mother." I began to weep.

Mother stood, "You will do as you are told. Now go to your room and pack a bag."

She spoke with such bitterness in her voice. I didn't understand. Why she was so short with me all the time? Her rudeness had started when Father was diagnosed with cancer. I understood that his illness could cause her stress, but why was she taking it out on me?

I relented and went to my room and packed. I gave Sasha a kiss goodbye. There was no way I was taking her where my cousins could destroy her. I trudged into the living room with my luggage and backpack.

Mother kissed me on top of my head.

We didn't speak to each other.

I walked outside with my aunt and got in her car without looking back. "It's just for a few days, Nina. You'll get to see Mandy and Margo."

I looked at her in the mirror from the back seat. She had no idea how mean her daughters were.

She glanced back at me from the rear-view mirror and smiled.

I gave her a half-smile with my top lip pursed up. I turned and stared out the window.

"It's almost dinner time," Aunt Olga said. "Mandy and Margo will sleep in one bedroom together just like before. They'll be happy to see you."

I kept looking out the window and bit down on my lip. I didn't want to be tempted to tell her what I thought of her daughters.

We arrived at her house. My aunt encouraged me to go inside and get ready for dinner. "I'll get your bag, dear."

My cousins were looking at me through the sheer curtains while they knelt backwards on the couch. I walked in through the front door. They turned around and began to chant my name.

"Nina, Nina, Nina. I guess we'll be seeing you for a few days," they said in a teasing manner. "Where's your stupid little dog, Sasha? Did you bring her so we can play with her, too?"

They giggled.

I ignored them and went straight to my room.

A few minutes later, Aunt Olga came up with my luggage.

I went to the bathroom, washed up, and went back downstairs.

My cousins were outside in the back.

I sat at the kitchen table and waited patiently. "Can I help?" I asked my aunt.

"Yes, dear," she replied. "Can you set the table? You know where everything is."

I set the table while Mandy and Margo came in. We sat down and ate dinner. We had something new called meatloaf. Yum. I really enjoyed American cuisine. Was I becoming a real American? I was working hard to pronounce my words like Americans. My accent seemed almost gone. My clothes were store bought. Mother didn't have time to make my clothes anymore. It was okay. I liked store-bought clothes. They made me fit in a little better at school.

After dinner, I sat outside on the back porch and watched the sunset. I loved the fall season. The weather was brisk, and I pulled my jacket closer to me.

Mandy and Margo came out and joined me. They stared at me with their evil eyes.

I turned away.

Mandy was always the leader, and the nastiest. "It's your fault, you know," she whispered in my ear.

I looked back at her. "What are you talking about? What's my fault?"

"Your father, stupid," she snarled as she turned up her nose.

"What about Father?"

"He's sick because of you and your stupid little dog."

What was she talking about?

The back door opened, and Aunt Olga asked us to come inside. It was getting cold and late. She told us to get ready for bed and school for the next day.

My cousins ran inside ahead of me, almost pushing me down. Margo's coat brushed against me as she rushed by.

I didn't move. Why was I at fault for Father being sick? I tried to rationalize it. I finally went in the house with my head still spinning from such a disturbing statement. As I walked up the stairs, I bit my lower lip until I tasted copper.

A few days later, my aunt took me back home. Mother looked exhausted. I went to Father's bedroom and watched from the doorway as he slept. I crept over, gave him a kiss on his forehead, and crawled into bed with him. I lay next to him and held his hand. He stirred, took my hand, kissed the back of it, and gave it a delicate squeeze. He tried to smile at me. As I lay next to him, I thought about Mandy's comment. I tried my best to process what she'd said, but I still didn't understand. I tried to let it go, but I thought of it for several days and I couldn't stop perseverating about it.

Days turned into weeks as I watched my father's body dwindle, getting frailer by the day. He was so weak. Mother always looked drained. She barely spoke to me. We were like two ships passing in the night. She was busy working and taking care of Father. I continued to take care of myself.

The leaves from the big, beautiful trees were gone. It was bitterly cold outside. This was a signal that winter had arrived. I pulled my winter clothes from the closet, but they didn't fit anymore. Mother hadn't even noticed I needed new clothes, but I didn't complain. I understood her focus had to be on Father.

One day when I got home from school, there was no one there. I combed the house. Not one sign of my parents. I rushed to their bedroom. The closet door was open. I peered inside. Some of Father's clothes were gone. Then I heard a car pull up into the driveway. I rushed to the living room and looked out the window and saw my Aunt Olga. She came to the door, and I let her in.

"Hello, my dear," she said, her voice quaking. "Your mother asked me to stop to talk to you."

"About what? Where is everyone?"

"Well, your father wasn't breathing very well. Your mother called, and I came over. We took your father to the hospital so he could get help."

"Oh, my. Is he okay?" Tears welled in my eyes.

"Yes, he's better, but he's on a ventilator now to help him breath."

"Can I go see him?" I asked.

"Not today, perhaps tomorrow. Your mother is tired and suggested you come to my house. She'll be home later this evening. Do you want to go back with me for dinner at my house with the girls?"

"No, thank you. I prefer to stay here and wait for Mother. I'll find something to eat here."

Aunt Olga looked at me with a frown, but she didn't argue. "Okay. Well, I'm going to leave you be. Don't forget to do your homework."

As she walked out the door, she stopped and looked back me. Her eyes scanned my body. "Nina? Do you need some new clothes? Everything looks small on you."

"Yes, but I didn't want to bother Mother about it. I'm making do with what I have."

"Hey," she said. "How about I take all of you girls shopping this weekend? Would you like that?"

It would be nice to get fresh new clothes, but I didn't really wish to spend time with my cousins. My aunt worked in a department store in New York City and since she got discounts, we'd probably shop there.

"No, thank you, Aunt Olga. That's very kind of you, but I'd rather go see Father and stay with him this weekend." I tried to put a warm smile on my face. I really liked my aunt. She was always so kind to me. So, where did my cousins get their meanness? It definitely didn't come from their mother.

"Okay, dear. I understand. Please stay inside the house, lock the door, do your homework, and get some dinner. I'm sure your mother will be home soon."

"Thank you." I gave her a big hug.

Mother came home late that evening. She looked exhausted. I was already in my pajamas. I watched her tug off her coat and hang it in the hallway closet.

"Hello, Mother."

"Hello, Nina. How was your day?" Her voice was monotone, as if the very effort of talking was too much for her.

"Fine. Aunt Olga came over and told me about Father. Is he better now?"

"Yes, but he has to stay in the hospital for a while. He can no longer breathe on his own."

"I'm sorry to hear that, Mother," I said as my eyes filled with tears. "I made you dinner. Would you like me to heat it up for you?"

"No, Nina. I'm going to bed. Did you do all your homework?"

"Of course I did."

Mother walked right by me and said goodnight without even looking at me, no hug, and no kiss. I watched her walk by me and close her bedroom door.

The next few days, I came home to an empty house. It was dark and cold as if no life existed in it anymore.

Mother and I went to the hospital to see Father the following weekend. As we opened the door, I heard the ventilator machine pumping up and down to assist Father's breathing. How could he rest with all the loud and strange noises? I guess the sounds would change if something was wrong, and that would alert the nurses.

As I stepped closer to Father, I saw how fragile and pale he was. I bit my lip to keep from crying out. He looked so different from the last time I saw him, just a few days ago. Was Father dying? I sat on the side of his bed and took his hand. He opened his eyes and tried to squeeze my hand. He was too weak. I raised his hand to my cheek and rubbed the side of my face so he could touch me. He just stared at me with his glassy blue eyes. I looked over at Mother who was staring out the window. She too looked pale. I lay next to Father for a while and watched him sleep.

When Mother and I arrived home that evening, I went to my bedroom to change clothes. I opened the door and saw a surprise lying on my bed—bags of clothing. I was so excited that I couldn't contain myself. There was a beautiful navy-blue velvet dress. It was simply gorgeous. There were several pairs of jeans and some soft, fluffy sweaters. I couldn't wait to try them on to make sure they fit. Yes, they all fit. I found a pair of scissors in my desk drawer and cut the tags off. I took my dress to the closet, hung it up, and placed my jeans and sweaters in my dresser drawer. I freshened up and rushed to the kitchen to help Mother make dinner and phone my aunt. I knew she had purchased the clothes for me. I wanted to thank her.

As I entered the kitchen, Mother had her back to me as I watched her hang up the phone. She turned around slowly, tears streaming down her frail face. She just looked at me. I knew what that meant.

Father had passed.

Nine

A few days before Father's funeral, I walked by my mother's bedroom. She was sobbing and clutching Father's best suite tightly to her chest. It was black and tailored to fit his physique. She laid it gently across the top of her bed and picked out a tie and handkerchief. She stroked the fabric of the tie through her fingers. Those were the clothes for him to be buried in. She had loved to see him in the aqua blues that matched his sparkly blue eyes. He had been so handsome.

The day of the funeral, I opened my closet to pick something out to wear. I scrolled my tense fingers across the fabric of my wardrobe and come across the velvet navy blue dress. I realized why my aunt wanted to take me shopping. She must have known that Father would be passing soon. This was what she wanted me to wear to his funeral. I plucked it from the closet, pulled it up to my body, and looked in the mirror. I gave a soft smile. Father would love to see me in this beautiful outfit. I dressed and waited for Mother in the living room.

It was chilly outside. I got my coat from the closet and placed it on my lap while I waited patiently on the couch for Mother. She moved ghost-like from her bedroom, pulled her coat from the closet, and walked out the door. She said nothing. I followed silently. She drove down the street. Mother never spoke a word.

We arrived first. I looked around as I was getting out of the car. We were at a funeral home. I didn't understand. Why weren't we at the Orthodox Church that Mother and I went to many times after the death of Aleksei? Maybe she didn't want to be reminded of him.

I remembered seeing funerals in the church when we passed sometimes. I saw people crying as they walked in. I asked Father about the big box with six people carrying it into the church. Why did the people look so sad? Father explained that was a funeral. Inside the box was the person they were mourning. So, I'd assumed all funerals were in churches.

We waited in the lobby, bravely keeping our chins up with perfect posture. I didn't know what to expect. I'd never been to a funeral before. I started to coil my hair around my finger.

My aunt and cousins arrived. They also wore pretty dresses. Mandy and Margo gave me a break and left me alone. My aunt kissed my forehead and commented on how beautiful I looked in the dress.

With my hand partially covering my mouth, I whispered in her ear, "Thank you for the clothes. I love them all."

"You're quite welcome, my dear." She brushed my hair back with her soft warm fingers and gave me a hug.

Other guests arrived from Father's work. Mother greeted each one with a forced smile as they offered their condolences. I stood tall beside my mother and tried to look poised and did my best to smile.

Then it was time. We were directed to a room with many chairs. In the front of the room, Father lay in a shiny dark walnut casket. The interior had a soft white silk material that lined the entire casket. Only half of his body was visible through the half-open lid. Strange. I guessed people didn't need to see legs and feet.

Mother and I sat in the front row with my aunt and cousins.

The priest appeared and gave a lovely service and spoke highly of Father. Some of his co-workers came up to the podium and gave nice speeches. Mother sobbed uncontrollably. She couldn't hold back her tears. I caressed her back to comfort her.

When everyone was finished speaking, they left the room. Only Mother and I remained with Father's body. I stood in the back and watched my mother give Father a final kiss on his forehead. She turned to me and walked slowly passed me to the door. I followed her to the car. I watched through the car window as they placed Father's casket in a large black car and drove off. Someone from Father's work offered to drive. Mother accepted. Our car followed behind the hearse with Father's body.

When we arrived at the cemetery, they pulled out Father's casket and carried it to a hole in the ground. I twirled my hair unconsciously. Was this where people go when they die? Were dead people put in the ground? The cemetery felt cold and distant. I didn't want to be there.

We walked through the dry crunchy grass. We stood around the casket. The priest gave a short prayer. As I watched Father slowly go down a dark dirty hole, people threw flowers on the casket. Mother dropped on her knees at the edge of the hole and sobbed. Aunt Olga ran up to her and pulled her back.

When it was over, Aunt Olga invited everyone to her house for lunch. I figured out this was when everyone socialized and reminisced about how truly wonderful Father was. She handed out cards with her address on it to everyone. We drove again in silence on the way to my aunts.

Quite a few people came. Everyone was very nice to Mother and me. We mingled with my aunt to make sure everyone was welcomed and expressed our gratitude for their coming.

My cousins were also being polite. I didn't think they had it in them to be as nice as they were.

After the last guest left, Mother and I helped Aunt Olga clean up after everyone.

"Olga," Mother said. "Thank you for everything. I'm so glad we came to America to be with you. You've been so much help to us. I'm so glad I have you as a sister."

My aunt replied, "I'm happy you are here, too." She gave Mother and me a big hug and walked us to the door. "Are you sure you won't stay here tonight?"

Mother shook her head. "Thank you, no. I need to get used to being in that house without him. I can use some alone time. I'm exhausted."

Mother and I arrived home and went our separate ways to our bedrooms. After I got ready for bed, I went to say goodnight to her. I started to knock on her door, but I heard her sobbing. Maybe it was best to leave her alone. I tiptoed back to my room, picked up Sasha, and crawled in bed.

As I lay there, I thought about all that I'd lost. I lost my dear friend, Pavlov, whom I thought of often. Where he was now and how was he doing? I lost my brother, Aleksei, who watched over me and was a great big brother. I'd lost my dog, Sasha, whom I loved caring for and who loved me unconditionally. Most of all, I'd lost my wonderful father who I'd miss tremendously. He was my guide and protector.

Ten

Several weeks went by and winter had arrived. The snow on the ground was sparkly and soft. The house had remained quiet since Father's passing. Memories consumed me as I walked to school each day. Mother worked longer and harder to supplement the loss of my father's income. Would she work herself to death? Then what would happen? Would I have to live with my aunt and my cousins again? I often worried about these things.

When the holidays came closer, Mother informed me that we wouldn't be getting a Christmas tree this year. We simply couldn't afford one. Our country followed the old Julian calendar, so Christmas was January seventh, but in America, it was December twenty-fifth. I assumed we would go to Aunt Olga's. We'd probably celebrate it in December since she'd lived in America for many years.

There would be no presents. Mother had such bitterness in her voice when she told me; her eyes were cold and dark. Whenever she spoke to me that way, I pinched my bottom lip with my front teeth to keep from crying. She always upset me with her attitude. I couldn't tell if it was personal or if she still ached from losing Father.

A few evenings later at the dinner table, I decided to break the silence between us.

"What will we do on Christmas day?" I asked.

She turned and glared at me. "We will go to Olga's."

I mustered the courage to ask why she was so harsh with me. I felt that I had enough of the mingy treatment. "Mother, I know you are sad about Father, but why are you so bitter towards me?"

She gave me a long, mean look and slammed her hand down hard on the table, so hard that everything on the table shifted. "It is because of you!" she shouted. "YOU! You are why my beautiful husband is dead and why we lost Aleksei."

My eyes filled with tears which coursed down my face. "I don't understand." I could barely catch my breath. I gasped for air.

"You were with Sasha the night of the explosion. Your father and brother were out looking for you for hours. He even went to the plant thinking that maybe you were there. We were all worried about you," she shouted.

"I don't understand," I repeated.

"He was exposed to too much radiation. We knew we needed to get out of town right away, and we couldn't find you. If your brother hadn't put a gun into his mouth, he too would have probably died from cancer by now!" She towered over me with her hands on her hips and hate in her eyes.

I froze. Aleksei killed himself? I was devastated to learn how my Aleksei had died. I hadn't known how he'd done that. My thoughts were scrambled. I felt sick. I clutched my stomach and began to rock. Sweat poured down my face. I felt flushed. I looked up at her. "I'm so sorry, Mother. I'm so sorry."

"All because you were out late with Sasha, and she ran off. We couldn't take her anyway. Aleksei was left behind because we didn't leave soon enough."

Mother's accent got stronger when she was upset. It felt like we were back in the Soviet Union. She stood so abruptly that her chair crashed backwards to the floor, and she stormed to her room, slamming her door. It felt like the entire house shook.

By then I was bawling, curled into a ball, rocking in my chair while I twirled my hair around my fingers. When the tears finally subsided enough for me to see, I rose from my chair and began to clean the table and wash the dishes. I was still crying. I dragged myself to my room and lay down on my bed trying to breathe. Was all this really my fault? I clenched Sasha and cried myself to sleep.

When I awoke the next morning, I pried off my clothes from yesterday and put on clean clothes for school. I didn't eat breakfast or pack a lunch. I just wanted to get out of the house. I stepped onto the front porch and took a deep breath of cool fresh air. It made me feel a little better. As I walked to school, my head was spinning from Mother's outburst. I felt like a zombie. She really believed I was to blame for Father and Aleksei's passing. That was why she acted so cold. Chills ran down my spine with the thought of it. I was sad and in total disbelief.

I couldn't concentrate at school. In every class, I stared out the frosted windows trying to rationalize what Mother had said. I remembered my cousin's statement months ago about something being my fault. Now I knew they had meant Father's illness. It was true. How did they know it was my fault? I clutched at my stomach; I was going to be sick.

How could I face Mother ever again? How could she face me? I felt awful. I would have to live with Mother's words for the rest of my life. *The rest of my life.*

That evening, Mother came home from dropping off some hemming that she'd done for the dry cleaner. I was in the kitchen making dinner. She placed her pocketbook and coat in the closet and came to the kitchen. I felt her piercing eyes glaring at me while I stirred hot beef stew from the pot on the stove. I was too afraid to look back and acknowledge her. She left the kitchen and went to her bedroom. She came back minutes later and began to set the kitchen table. I poured the steaming hot stew into two bowls, placed them on the table, and sat down. She gathered two glasses from the cabinet and poured our milk. We said nothing to each other. I didn't even look at her. I assumed by her silence that she had no remorse for her actions. She was now a bitter woman.

Christmas was here, and Mother and I were barely being cordial to each other. Our relationship would never be the same. We went to my aunts for the holiday. I wasn't excited to see my hostile cousins. At least my aunt would be pleasant to me. I knew Mother had said no to Christmas presents, but I made something from my art class for her. It was a sketch of Father. I wrapped it gently in tissue paper and took it to my aunts. I also made my aunt a sketch of Mandy and Margo. I liked to sketch. It gave me peace and helped me feel centered at times when I were grieving my loses—which was often.

We arrived at my aunt's house in the afternoon, and we greeted each other with hugs and kisses. Except my cousins. Mandy and Margo were relentless, continuing to silently torture me so the adults wouldn't catch on. I tried to ignore them as best as I could, however it was difficult on that special day. I was feeling melancholy missing Father.

As I entered the living room, I smelled a turkey roasting in the oven. It was a glorious smell of warmth and celebration. We'd never had turkey on Christmas Day, so it was a special treat for me. Mother assisted my aunt by boiling potatoes and cutting the stems off the green beans to be boiled. I heard Aunt Olga and Mother arguing affectionately over how to make the gravy. My aunt's specialty was the stuffing, which was already made and stuffed in the turkey. I could smell the onions and berries, which she added with the bread soaked with the chicken stock. It all smelled so delicious. I couldn't wait to eat and try these new American traditions.

My choices were to go in the kitchen with my rude mother or stay in the living room with my nasty cousins. First, I took my portraits out of my backpack and placed them under their tree. I could feel my cousins watching me. Their tree was beautiful, a Douglas fir with traditional twinkly white lights. It smelled glorious and fresh. The decorations were all handmade by my sinister cousins which they'd made through years of school projects. I knew that because our Christmas trees back home had looked the same, full of Aleksei's and my Christmas school projects. All gone now.

Then, I went into the kitchen and asked my aunt if she needed any help. She smiled and asked me to set the table. I agreed. She had fancy cloth napkins. I took them and aligned two corners in the opposite direction, making triangles out of them. I gently tucked each napkin to the left of the plates and placed the silverware on top. I brought out the glasses and placed them up top to the right of the plates.

Dinner was scrumptious. It was so good that I had seconds. Traditionally, our Christmas dinners consisted of meat dumplings, dried mushroom soup, deviled eggs, and Olivier's salad. For dessert, Mother baked spiced gingerbread cookies.

My aunt carried most of the conversation as I silently reminisced about Father, Aleksei, and Sasha. Mandy and Margo spoke very little either. They just stared at me with their evil eyes. When I'd look up, they'd giggle as if to taunt me.

After dessert, we all went to the living room to open presents. Aunt Olga passed out the gifts to us. I was sure she would get me something. She was always so kind. Mother was so cheap. She could have at least gone to the Dollar Store for something. My aunt worked hard too. She struggled just like us. I slowly opened my present from her, which was wrapped in shiny silver foil with white glitter snowflakes. The paper was beautiful. I opened it gently by removing the tape on each side without tearing the paper. Beneath the gift wrap was a brown wooden box. I folded the paper and placed it next to me. It was so pretty. I could use it for something else. I opened the box to find an art tool kit for my sketches. My aunt knew that I liked to sketch. There were multiple vibrant colors. I loved it. I got up and gave her a big hug. I whispered in her ear. "You're the best, Aunt Olga. I love you so much."

I went under the tree to retrieve my presents for Mother and Aunt Olga. They appeared to have already been opened. There were tears near the tape, and the tissue paper was wrinkled. I looked over at my cousins as they grinned at me with their squinty eyes. They must have opened the gifts that weren't for them. They'd done it to spite me.

I placed the gifts on Mother and Aunt Olga's laps. I said nothing about the already-opened wrapping. They acted as if they didn't notice.

Aunt Olga opened hers first. She loved it and gave me a kiss.

Mother opened hers next. She stared at the sketch of Father for a few minutes, and a tear trailed down her face. She looked at me and gave me a warm smile. "Thank you, Nina," she said in a soft whisper.

I looked up at her and gave back a warm smile. Had her armor finally broken?

Eleven

Several years passed and I was a senior in high school. Mother and I still didn't have a close bond; however, we remained civil.

On the last day of football season, I was both excited and sad. I had to retire my pom-pom outfit. I'd loved being a part of the band. I had made so many new friends in high school. After the last game, we planned to go out for pizza to celebrate. I usually didn't go out after games, but this time I was excited to be a part of the alliance.

After arriving at the pizza restaurant, I caught up with my friends and my best friend, Jennifer. We ate, drank soda, and laughed all night. It was amazing. Some of the football players were there too. I was particularly fond of one who kept on looking over at me.

Jennifer whispered in my ear. "That football player is looking at you. I think he likes you."

I blushed and looked away. I reached for my hair and bit my bottom lip.

"Do you want me to introduce him to you, Nina?" she asked.

I shook my head. "No, why would he be interested in me?"

"Well, he's looking at you, and you're beautiful."

"That doesn't mean anything." I giggled and looked back at him.

"Come on," she said. "His name is Paul, and he's a senior like us. I can't believe you haven't seen him before. You haven't had him in any of your classes these past years?"

"No, I don't think so."

"He's been in some of mine. He's really nice."

"I'm gonna go now. Maybe we can get together this weekend." I rushed out the front door and didn't look back. I could feel his eyes watching me leave. Luckily, I was not far from home, so I was able to walk.

The following day, Saturday, Jennifer picked me up, and we went to the mall, one of our favorite spots. It was where all the teenagers hung out on weekends. I didn't go too often. I preferred to stay home and draw. My favorite drawings were of my Sasha, Father, and Aleksei, which covered the walls of my bedroom.

As we strolled through the mall, a group of boys sat on the edge of the fountain, smack dab in the middle of the food court. They appeared to be people-watching.

Jennifer gasped. "Look, there are the football players from our school, and there's Paul."

"What?" I crunched my bottom lip. "Where?"

She pointed forward.

"I don't see them. It's crowded in here."

"They're sitting on the edge of the fountain. Let's go say hello." She grabbed my hand and pulled me forward.

I yanked away and stopped. "No, Jennifer. I'm not comfortable. I'm not beautiful like you."

"Nina, stop being so reserved. Get out of your shell. And you're beautiful, too. Why do you think he was staring at you last night?"

"I can't," I said. I wiped my forehead, where I could feel perspiration beading, with the back on my hand. "Let's just go, please."

I turned the other way and walked away from the boys.

She reluctantly followed.

We tried on some clothes, got a soft drink, and hung out in the parking lot talking.

Graduation

As high school ended, I was thrilled to graduate. I applied to several colleges and ended up accepting Columbia University which was close to home. Jennifer accepted the University of Michigan (U-M). Her career choice was not offered at Columbia University, and she had distant family near U-M. Living with them would assist with expenses. We had hoped we could go to school together, but it didn't work out. She wanted to be a physical therapist. I wanted to be a teacher. I remembered the positive influence of Ms. Babin back home in Chernobyl. She was always so kind to me. Mrs. Smith, my first teacher, in America was also kind to me and always protected me from the mean girls.

Graduation day was a blast. We wore our caps and gowns, and everyone looked smashing. Especially Jennifer. I took pictures of her as she crossed the stage to receive her diploma. Jennifer was beautiful and had a perfect body. She had sparkling green eyes and long blonde ringlets cascading down her back. Her creamy white complexion glowed. She was always the best dressed, fancy, and most stylish.

I was sad Mother didn't come to the ceremony. She claimed she had to work. I knew better. However, my aunt came for the twins and, of course, rooted me on as I crossed the stage and received my diploma.

That night some of my friends went out for pizza to celebrate. Jennifer picked me up in her new graduation car, and off we went. We joined several of our band member friends. We laughed and ate. Everyone talked about which college they would be attending.

Suddenly Jennifer widened her eyes and motioned for me to look over my shoulder.

I slowly turned.

There he was, Paul.

I quickly turned back. "Did he see me?"

"Yes, and he's walking over here with some friends. You can't run now," she said giggling.

"Not funny!" I whispered.

"Relax, I'm just going to introduce you. Wait." Her mouth gapped open. "You won't believe who just intercepted."

"Who?" I didn't turn to look.

"Your ugly cousins."

I ducked my head deeper into my shoulders. "Did they see me? Do they know I'm here? Do you think they stopped him on purpose?"

"No, I don't think they know you're here. It's too crowded. But they're flirting with him and his friends."

"Ugh! I can't stand those girls. I'm so glad they're going to a different college than me. It's hard enough being attached to them on the holidays. Can we go now? I'm tired, and I don't want to see my cousins."

"Don't you want to stay and see if he breaks free of the rats and comes over here? I truly believe he wants to meet you."

"No thanks. I just wanna go," I said, twining my hair.

We got into Jennifer's car and left. On the drive to my house, Jennifer and I talked serious.

"How are we going to build your confidence, Nina? I worry about you sometimes," she said. "I can't say that I know what you've been through, but I know you've been through a lot. But you need to move forward. Tell yourself when you start college that you'll be more outgoing so you can meet someone and fall in love."

I looked at Jennifer and gave her a warm smile. I was so appreciative of having a best friend. Jennifer knew everything about Father, Aleksei, and Sasha. I even shared with her what Mother had said on that awful day of blame.

I had to get a job during the summer to help me survive at school in the fall. I took out student loans, but it still wasn't enough for me to survive financially. Mother couldn't help. She barely made enough to pay her bills and buy groceries. She wanted me to start helping her financially. What else could I do? Columbia University was not far from our house, so I'd stay at home, go to school on public transportation, and work.

I filled out many job applications close enough to home that I could walk or take the bus. I finally got a job at the local drug store, which was walkable. I loved it. They even gave a discount on anything in the store to employees.

I spent most of my summer working and hanging out with Jennifer. We liked to cruise the mall. Jennifer was a shopaholic. She loved to buy new clothes. I couldn't afford it.

Traditionally, the summer closed with the local state fair. Jennifer and I loved to go on the rides and eat cotton candy. This would be our last get-together. Jennifer was leaving for her new school in a few days, so we decided to have the most fun ever.

As we were playing some games, I heard loud laughter coming from behind me. I turned and could see the backs of some boys as they were throwing darts at balloons. One was tall, thin, and had dark, toffee-colored hair in a perfect short cut. He slowly turned around to speak to one of his friends. It was Paul. I was stunned and had to take a deep breath. Had Jennifer seen him? I glanced at her. She hadn't. I breathed a sigh of relief. I still wasn't ready to meet him. How strange that I bumped into him everywhere. I turned around and waited for her to finish playing her game. After she lost, I steered her away from the boys and motioned for us to go by the animals.

When the evening ended, Jennifer dropped me off at my house. I gave her a huge hug and wished her good luck for her first year at the U-M. That the two of us were attending different schools in different states made me sad. Nevertheless, I knew we'd stay in touch through phone calls, emails, and holiday home visits.

Twelve

After several weeks of getting my routine perfected with work hours, school, and homework, I was feeling good. Mother worked many hours just like me, and we rarely saw each other. It was probably for the best. She was toxic to me. We simply coexisted in the house. I was pretty much on my own.

I made acquaintances at work and at school, but I missed Jennifer. We kept in touch weekly via phone calls and emails. She was having the time of her life going to footballs games and parties. She told me she even had a boyfriend. He sounded wonderful.

I didn't go out too much due to my busy schedules and poor finances. I grew to be so miserable at home that I wanted to get a second job, so I could get an apartment and get away from Mother's venomous attitude. She was the most stubborn person I knew.

One of the pharmacists at work took a

liking to me and offered to train me as a technician. It paid a little bit more than being a front cashier. I took him up on the offer, and my new role was approved by the owner.

The pharmacist took his time with me and explained the importance of being careful with medications. He eased me into the training and watched over me so I wouldn't make mistakes.

After a few weeks, I got the hang of it. I was thrilled to be making more money. Mother pretty much cut me off, no longer buying me food and personal items every woman required. She wanted me to start paying rent. I did the best I could to help, but I'd had enough of her bitterness. Soon I would save enough to move out.

One day while at work, the pharmacist recognized how hard I was working to make ends meet. He told me there was a technician position opening in the pharmacy in a hospital not too far from my house. He worked both places, full-time at the hospital and part-time at the drug store. He encouraged me to put in for it. It paid even more than my new position at the drug store. Wow, I was feeling lucky. If I got this new job, then I could finally move out.

He arranged an interview for me. I wore my favorite navy-blue dress and jacket. I gussied up my resume and interviewed with the head pharmacist. I got the job. I couldn't stop smiling. Soon, I could move out and finally be on my own and away from 'negative Natalia,' my mother. The hours were great too. I could work late in the evenings which would allow me to rest between classes.

I finally saved enough money to get my own place. I needed to find an apartment close to school and the hospital. I kept my plans from my mother. She didn't need to know how happy I was about moving out and living on my own. I didn't want her to rain on my parade.

Whenever I had a chance between school and work, I hunted for a place to live. It didn't take me long. There were not many choices within walking distance of school.

I signed a lease on a quaint little studio apartment, gave a deposit, and prepared to share my news with Mother two evenings before my move. I sat at the dining room table and began my uncomfortable conversation. "Well, Mother, I think it's best that I move on. I've saved some money, and I'm moving out the day after tomorrow."

She glared at me as if I was supposed to get her permission or something. After a long pause, she said, "You must do what you must do." She got up from the table, took her dishes to the sink, and exited the kitchen without another word.

I rose from my chair and cleaned the dishes and went to my room. I began to pack a bit. I was grateful that the apartment had some furniture to get me started.

The day of my move was bittersweet. I was happy to be on my own but stressed about leaving my home which at one time had been filled with happiness, excluding the thoughts of Father, Aleksei, and Sasha. I struggled with my box of clothes, my backpack, and Sasha and took one last look at my room. I shook my head as I slowly walked out for the last time. I closed the door gently. What a shame that my relationship with Mother would be tarnished forever. Would she always be bitter toward me? I stood outside of the door to her sewing room where she was working. She knew I was there. She had to have heard me on the other side of the door. Didn't she want to say goodbye or wish me luck? What was I thinking? Did I really expect a response? I walked to the front door in silence. No goodbyes.

The holidays were nearing. The idea of spending Thanksgiving with my mother and my cousins nauseated me. Aunt Olga was the exception. I signed up to work at the hospital for Thanksgiving. Most people wanted to be with their families, so those shifts were always available. As a bonus, I was able to work a double shift with double pay. I did this as often as I could when people called in sick or needed to take vacations. It helped me stay afloat financially. Even with two jobs there were many months that, like so many other people, I struggled. It made me think of Pavlov and how his family struggled financially. I was grateful for the taste of these endeavors as they helped me appreciate what little I had at times.

I often had to turn down the thermostat during the winter months when the electricity bills were the highest. Just to stay warm, I spent many evenings at the school library or a coffee shop near my apartment doing schoolwork just to stay warm. I would go back to my apartment when they closed. Many times, my landlord would turn off the heat because I just couldn't pay. He had total control of the building and wasn't very nice at times.

My aunt routinely checked on me. We'd meet privately for dinner at a restaurant near school. She was so kind. I was always polite and asked how Mandy and Margo were. Then I'd ask about my mother. Aunt Olga always replied with a positive answer and an upbeat tone. We never spoke of Mother's bitterness toward me, but Olga knew. I think that's why she kept in touch with me. She knew Mother didn't. It was always up to me to reach out to Mother, which I did on special occasions like her birthday or a holiday, and that was pretty much the extent of our relationship.

Whenever I got home after meeting my aunt, I'd open my purse and find money in an envelope. Sometimes she'd leave new colored pencils for my sketching. She remembered I had an artistic side. Sketching was meaningful for me; it allowed me to erase my problems and forget my conflicts temporarily. It also helped me to forget that my only family was my aunt.

Acquaintances at work and school tried to include me with their gatherings, but I never had the funds to join their activities. I'd make up some excuse like I had too much schoolwork.

I was still haunted with the memories of Father, Aleksei, and Sasha. On days I didn't work or have school, I enjoyed watching romance movies. I dreamed one day my Prince Charming would find me and take me away from my battles. Always a dreamer.

Christmas was close and I couldn't wait to see Jennifer who was coming home to spend the holidays with her family. Wait till she sees my adorable little apartment. I'd decorated it with blues, greens, and yellows. I took my daisy curtains and bedspread that Mother made for me years ago. I showered my apartment with synthetic flowers from a craft store because I couldn't afford real flowers. The walls of my apartment were decorated with sketches of Father, Aleksei, and Sasha. I placed a small artificial tree in the center of my coffee table and decorated it with popcorn. I'd sketched some stars and bells, then cut them out of cardboard.

I agreed to spend Christmas at my aunt's since I'd missed Thanksgiving. I couldn't be rude to her. A few days before Christmas my telephone rang. It was my aunt. "Hi, Aunt Olga. How are you?"

"I'm wonderful, dear. I just wanted to make sure you're coming for Christmas dinner."

"Of course, I'll be there. Can I bring anything?"

"No, dear. Just yourself. Shall I pick you up?"

"No, thank you. I'll take the bus. What time?"

"If you can come around 3:00, that would be great."

"I'll be there. I love you. See you soon." I hung up the phone and began to twist my hair with my index finger. My stomach churned at the thought of seeing my cousins and Mother again.

Precisely on time on Christmas day, I rapped on Aunt Olga's door. Her home was decorated beautifully with a large tree, three times the size of my little tree in my apartment and adorned with lights and colorful balls. The twins greeted me coolly. No one offered an embrace or a kiss. I rose above the stress twisting in my gut and held my head high. I'd drawn sketches for everyone, even Mandy and Margo. My aunt was always so kind to me. I really made the effort for her.

When it was time to open gifts, I received a beautiful fuzzy pink sweater from Aunt Olga. Of course, I received nothing from my mother.

When it was time to go, my aunt gave me a huge hug. I could feel her sliding something into my coat pocket. Probably cash. I gave her a warm smile. She knew how much I appreciated her. I waved a soft goodbye to my cousins and went over to Mother and gave her a limp hug. "Merry Christmas, Mother."

She didn't even put her arms around me to be polite in front of her sister.

I got on the bus and sat on the glacial seats. I couldn't wait to get home to my tiny little apartment for peace. As much as I loved spending time with Aunt Olga, it was a relief to be away from the others. My apartment was my sanctuary. I made myself some hot cocoa, put on three sweaters and two pairs of socks, and lay on the couch to watch a Christmas movie. My phone rang. Who would be calling so late? I rushed to the phone. "Hello?"

"Hello, best friend."

Jennifer. My heart leapt at hearing her voice. "Are you in town now?" I laughed and jumped around the tiny room.

"Yes, and I want to see you tomorrow. Do you have time? Are you working?"

"Yes, but you can come over afterwards. I want you to see my apartment, and I can't wait to hear more about your boyfriend and how your studies are."

"Great! Call me when you get home, and I'll come over."

Too excited to sleep, I watched another holiday movie until I fell asleep on the couch.

Luckily, in the morning, my noisy neighbor upstairs who walked on the heels of his large feet awakened me. The floors and walls were thin. You get what you pay for. Cheap rent means a cheaply-built apartment. I was glad for the first time for his racket, or I would've been late for work. I hurried and dressed, ran outside to the bus station, and made the bus just in time. The bus was unwelcomingly chilly, but I was grateful for the ride and got to work on time. My face ached from the smile I couldn't erase all day at work. I couldn't wait to see Jennifer.

Thirteen

When I returned home from work, I rushed to my phone to call Jennifer. "I'm home, I'm home, I'm home. Come on over I can't wait to see you!" I screamed.

"I'm on my way."

I turned on the television and sat patiently. I didn't have to clean or tighten the place up as I was a neurotic neat freak.

Knock, Knock. There she was. I ran to the door, opened it, and we both screamed and put our hands over our mouths, trying not to disturb the neighbors with our excitement.

"I'm so happy you're here."

"Me too. You look like you lost weight," she said as she held my cold hands and eyed me up and down.

"Probably, I don't have a scale. I do feel a little thinner, though."

"Are you eating?" she asked with concern.

"Of course, I am. I'm on my own, remember? I do my best. Times are a little rough financially right now. However, I have a great routine with work and school. Things are flowing nicely. I just want to get through school so I can get a great teaching job and make real money. Enough about my weight. How do you like my little studio apartment?"

"I love it." Jennifer said with a high-pitched voice. "You have good taste like your mother."

"Let's not talk about her, please. She's poison to me."

"Okay, we won't. How is school? How is work? Did you meet anyone yet?" Her eyes danced, and she winked.

"Of course not, I only want to focus on my studies and pay my bills. I never want to go back to you-know-where again."

"What am I going to do with you?" She offered a warm smile and squeezed my hands.

I tried to deflect the attention to her and off me. "Tell me about your new friend? Do you have pictures of him?"

"Yes, let's go out for coffee, and I'll tell you all about him."

"Great. Let me get my coat. There's a quaint little coffee shop around the corner where we can walk."

We walked together holding hands with our cozy, warm mittens. It was a blustery day. Jennifer offered to drive, but I was accustomed to walking. She didn't seem to mind. When we arrived, we hung our coats on the coat rack, took off our mittens, and placed them on the table where we sat near the frosty windows. A waiter came over and asked us what we wanted. Jennifer loved coffee, and I ordered hot cocoa.

"So, tell me all about him?"

"Well, his name is Mark, and he wants to be a physical therapist like me. We're in a lot of classes together; that's how we met. He's a whole head taller than me, with jet black hair, and a cute little bump on his nose where he broke it playing football. We hit it off instantly."

"That's wonderful, I'm so happy for you. Where's he from?"

"He's from Michigan in the Ann Arbor area close to U-M. I love it there. It's a great place to live. There's always something to do. It has great restaurants, cafés, and bars. They have museums, farmer markets, and art exhibits on the streets. It's very artsy. We never get bored."

"That sounds great."

"You should come and visit when the weather heats up, maybe for spring break?"

"I would love to, but I doubt I'll be able to afford it," I replied looking down. "I don't even have a car yet."

Jennifer placed her smooth perfectly manicured hand over my scrawny one. She understood me and I could always tell her about my true thoughts without embarrassment.

Our coffee and cocoa arrived piping hot.

I could see the steam floating in the air between us. My hot chocolate was slathered with crystal-white whipped cream. It was scrumptious. "Have you met his parents yet?"

"Yes, his entire family. He has two older sisters and grandparents, too. His sisters go to U-M, also. They all have scholarships."

"Wow, how wonderful. I wish I had a scholarship for school."

"You can apply each year, you know."

"No, I didn't know. I don't even know how," I said wistfully.

"Go to your guidance counselor at school."

"Okay, I'll do it as soon as I can for next school year." I could be forgetful at times, so I needed to write that down somewhere in my apartment.

Jennifer blew on her coffee. "So, let's talk about you. How's school going? Have you made friends?"

"Well, I have some acquaintances. I really wouldn't call them friends. I'm too busy working and studying to socialize much."

"I know, but you could make friends by studying with them."

"That's difficult with my work schedule."

"You hold a lot in, I get it." Jennifer patted the back my hand that rested on the table. "I know it's from your past, but it'd be nice if you tried to be a bit more outgoing. Not so intimidated and sheltered."

I said nothing. I started thinking about Father, Aleksei, and Sasha.

"Moving forward," Jennifer said in an upbeat tone. "How's your job at the hospital?"

I straightened my shoulders and looked up from my chocolate. "Oh, I really like it. Everyone is so kind and professional. I'm learning so much about medicine. I wonder at times if I should change my major to nursing, but I really want to be a teacher. I'm thinking kindergarten. Kids don't judge, and five-year-olds are so innocent."

"Any friends from there?" she asked as she raised one eyebrow. "Perhaps a handsome intern?"

I glared back at her with a smirk on my face. "No more lectures, please." I giggled. "How long are you here for?"

"Just a week. I want to get back to my sweetie and spend some time with him while we're on school break."

"I bet your parents were elated to see you."

"Yes, they were. We had a great Christmas. I'm not gonna ask about yours. I'll leave that one alone."

We both snickered, and I nodded in agreement. "Well, it's getting late. When can we get together again?"

"Let me know your work schedule."

"I'm working evenings all week, so we can get together during the days."

"Great, let's go shopping tomorrow. I'll pick you up around ten."

"That sounds wonderful." We briskly walked back to my apartment, and I waved goodbye as she drove away.

The next day, we went shopping. It was nice to ride in her car again. It was toasty warm all the way to the mall. After doing a little shopping, we sat at the food court for lunch.

Jennifer grew serious. "I worry about you, Nina."

"Why?"

"You don't seem yourself. You've changed."

"I've had to grow up quickly and have many responsibilities. What's wrong with that?"

"No, I mean you seem sad."

"Well, let's see. I have an awful relationship with Mother. I still detest my cousins. My only nice family member is my aunt. And I have a busy schedule."

"How often do you see your aunt?"

"We try to meet up once a month. It's our special time. I don't think Mother knows. Anyway, I won't deny that at times I am lonely and sad. The sadness can be palpable. All I can do is move forward and stay focused on work and school. I still like to sketch."

"You need to get out and have some fun. Not just work and school. Yes, I know it's a money thing, but there are still things to do that don't cost money."

"I know that. I just don't have confidence right now. I don't feel good about myself."

"I can see that. That's what I'm talking about. You don't realize how pretty you are, how smart you are, and how nice you are to everyone. Hey, I have an idea that will help your loneliness. Why don't you get a puppy? You loved Sasha so much. You can get another dog who'll keep you company. You're a nurturer. It'll be good for you."

"Oh, Jennifer, I can't adopt a dog right now. I can barely afford to feed myself and pay my bills. I can't afford a puppy. Besides, I'm not home enough to properly care for an animal."

"Okay, here's another idea. Why don't you volunteer at an animal shelter? It doesn't cost anything, and it doesn't have to take up a lot of your time. You can go on Saturdays you have off or in between classes. It might be fulfilling for you. You can find a local shelter. I'm sure there's one around here."

"Hm, I'll think about it."

"Promise?"

"Yes, I promise. Let's head back now. I have to get ready for work."

Jennifer drove up to my apartment. "I'm busy with family tomorrow, but let's get together the day after tomorrow?"

"Great! I'm free before work."

"Let's do breakfast."

I nodded as I got out of her car. As I was getting ready for work, I couldn't help but wonder what it would be like to volunteer at a shelter. Maybe I should.

The day after tomorrow came. Jennifer picked me up, and we went to our favorite café for breakfast. "Guess what? I have a surprise for you after we finish eating."

"Now what?" I asked.

"I think you're going to like it," she said with a smile.

When we finished eating, we drove toward my school. "Where are we going?" I asked.

"You'll see."

We drove into a parking lot, and I could hear dogs barking from the back of a building. I looked at the sign in front of the building: Animal Shelter.

"Surprise. We're here. Now before you say, no, I just want you to go inside and fill out the volunteer application. Can you do that for me? Look how close it is to school and your apartment. It's within walking distance."

"Well, to tell you the truth, I've thought about it ever since you mentioned it. Maybe I will. I have nothing to lose, right?"

"You go, girl! I think you'll really like it."

We walked inside. The reception area was crisp white and smelled like the hospital I worked in. I could hear the dogs barking in the back and the cats were in their kennels up front near the reception area. I supposed they placed the cats there to entice people who come in for possible adoptions. They were all so adorable.

I asked a girl sitting behind a computer in the reception area for a volunteer application and filled it out.

She explained that the next step was reviewing my application and then an interview.

I was getting a little excited about the idea. "Can we walk around and look at the animals?"

"Yes, I'll have one of our volunteers take you on a tour."

"Thank you," Jennifer and I said in unison. Jennifer grinned at me like the Cheshire Cat from Alice in Wonderland.

A volunteer came through the double doors and introduced himself. He walked us through the shelter. I saw a little dog that looked like Sasha and thought I heard her whispering to me. Now, I'm really losing it. The tour was enlightening, joyful, yet sad. It was hard to see the animals looking at you with their beautiful faces hoping you would take them home.

After the tour, Jennifer took me home.

"I hope you do it, Nina. I really think it's something for you. I really think you'll find joy in volunteering."

I gave her a big squeeze goodbye and thanked her for taking me. "Let's just get through the process first and see if they will even accept me."

"Of course, they will. You are a soft, kind-hearted person. Everyone can see that."

Did I really want to do this? I worried I'd fall in love with another pup only to have my heart broken again.

Fourteen

Spring arrived, and I started another semester of school. Work at the hospital was good. I was full-time and picked up extra hours as much as I could. I didn't keep my hours at the drug store. They were dwindling anyways because I accepted more hours from the hospital due to the higher wage. I passed the requirements for volunteering at the shelter and was thrilled. I volunteered as often as I could. Jennifer was right. Volunteering was fulfilling. The puppies, with their bright shiny eyes and floppy ears made me laugh, but sometimes, one in particular would have something that reminded me of Sasha, and it felt like a knife plunging into my heart.

I volunteered often with a law student from Columbia named John. He took a liking to me. I liked him, too. We were the same age and were both working our way through school. He shared that his parents helped financially with his classes, but he covered his living expenses by working at the local hardware store.

One day, he asked me out for a picnic in the park at school. I could almost hear Jennifer telling me to get out and mingle. I decided to go. Why not?

It was a Saturday afternoon. We'd finished volunteering at the shelter. We picked a time and met under a beautiful large oak tree near the school library. As I walked to him, I caught myself twisting my wavy hair around my index finger. I quickly dropped my hand so he wouldn't see. I watched him gently lay a blanket on the grass and take items out of a dark brown wicker basket.

"Hi John. This looks lovely. Can I help you set up?" I knelt on the soft blanket.

"No, I'm almost set. Wasn't it fun today being with the dogs? I love going to the shelter."

"Yes, I love it too. That little Yorkie mix with the black ears should get adopted soon. He's just too cute. How are your studies going? Is law school hard?"

"At times. I have to study a lot."

"What made you want to be a lawyer? Are you following in someone's footsteps?"

He reached for two sodas in the basket and handed me one. "I have an uncle I admire. He's a lawyer."

"Why Columbia?"

"To see the Big Apple. I come from a small

town. I want to experience life." He looked up at the sky and raised his hands. Then he turned to me. "How's your program. Didn't you say you wanted to be a teacher? What grade level are you interested in?"

"I was thinking kindergarten. I like the young kids. They're so sweet and innocent."

"You're probably right about that." He chuckled. "Tell me about your family. Do you have any siblings?"

I paused and looked down. I felt my face turn red, and my ears grew warm.

"Oh, Nina, I'm sorry. I hope I didn't open any wounds," he said softly. "We can talk about something else."

"It's okay. But I'd rather hear more about you."

John told me about his wonderful upbringing. As I listened, I made a point to give him constant eye contact. I didn't want him to realize I was really thinking about my childhood and the ensuing tragedies. I wasn't ready to share those with him.

Besides that one hiccup, we had a wonderful time together. We laughed a lot. He was quite a talker, which I was thankful for. I preferred to listen rather than talk about myself.

John and I got together frequently at school. He lived in the dorm close to the library. I liked how his head towered over mine, how his body fit into his jeans, how his hair blew like golden wheat into his robin's egg blue eyes. He had a warm smile with perfect straight teeth. I really enjoyed his company. We started scheduling our time together at the shelter so we could see each other more. We enjoyed walking the dogs on the twenty-acre property. The back had beautiful trees and benches for resting and watching the dog's play.

If John was too busy, I went in to play with the cats alone. He didn't care for the cats as much as the dogs. I loved both. Cats were calming to me. I'd take them out of their crates and place them in the cat playroom. They were so starved for attention that they'd rub their bodies on my legs and purr happiness. I thought some of that happiness rubbed off on me.

John and I volunteered together on Sunday afternoon. He seemed a little nervous. He stuttered a little and had a hard time looking at me. I giggled to myself because my stress relievers were hair twirling and lip biting. His were stuttering and looking away. I asked if he was all right.

"Yes, I'm fine," he said, looking down to the ground while holding a puppy.

The puppy kept licking his face with its bright red and wet tongue. John had slobber all over his face.

I couldn't help but giggle. I felt heat rush to my cheeks as I thought what it would be like if I licked his cheek.

"Nina?" he asked. "I really like you. You're bright, beautiful, and nice. I'd like to take you out on an official date if I may."

John had such wonderful manners.

"Yes," I said. "I'd love to."

"I mean a real date. Like dinner and a movie. Not just a picnic."

"John, I said yes." I replied with a soft chuckle. It was interesting to watch him squirm a little. I found his behavior endearing. I was usually the one having nervous twitches.

"Great, how about next Friday or Saturday night?"

"I'm working Friday night, but I'm free Saturday night."

"Awesome," he said. I'll pick the restaurant if you pick the movie."

"Okay. That sounds fun."

"Can I pick you up at six?"

"Yes, perfect."

"Let's finish up here, and I'll walk you home." He beamed through those beautiful eyes.

I thought about John all week at work and at school. It gave me a tingly feeling in my stomach. What was happening to me? I didn't understand what those feelings meant, or why they happened. But they felt kind of good, though.

I worked an extra shift at the hospital one evening so I could shop for a new outfit for my date. Between classes, I went to the mall on the bus from school. I loved shopping. It always reminded me of my good times with Jennifer. I wished she was there to help me pick out something new and fresh to wear. I decided to buy a soft pink dress that brought out the undertones of my skin.

Date night arrived. My stomach ached a bit. I examined my new clothes in the mirror. Not dressy enough? Should I have bought something fancier? I put my hair up in a bun, then pulled it out and brushed it on my shoulders. I applied eyeliner and shadow, then changed my mind, washed it all off, and settled for a light lip-gloss and a few strokes of mascara. After grooming myself, I waited not too patiently for John's arrival.

Ding Dong! The bell sounded so loudly that I jumped. I rushed to the hallway mirror and made one more check of my hair and makeup. I swung the door open, and there he was. He wore a warm blue shirt tucked into his khaki pants that just happened to match his sparkling eyes. His brown belt matched his shoes too. He looked like a slice of heaven.

He held something behind his back.

"What do you have there?" I asked. We walked in circles facing each other while I tried to see what it was. He finally pulled out his hand. A beautiful bouquet of daisies which resembled my favorite arnicas from back home.

I gasped. "How did you know I loved daisies?"

"I didn't. When I went to the florist, they just called to me. I thought they looked simple, pretty, and sweet. Just like you."

I could feel my ears burning, and I slouched a bit before pulling my shoulders back and invited him in.

"Thank you. I love them. Let me find something to put them in. How was your day?"

"It was great. I just went to the library and studied. Now I'm here."

I poked around in the kitchen, pretending to find a vase. I knew I didn't have anything remotely like that, so I took out a tall drinking glass.

I placed the fresh flowers in the center of my coffee table. I didn't have a kitchen table. My studio only had a foldout couch which served as my bed, a coffee table, a lamp, a tiny kitchen, and a bathroom. It was small but all mine.

John scanned the walls and analyzed my sketches of Father, Aleksei, and Sasha. He turned back to me. "You look beautiful, Nina."

"Thank you. You, too." I could feel my face and ears burning again. Darn my fair skin. I turned away quickly and grabbed my sweater, hoping he didn't notice my blushing.

"Well, let's head out. I hope you like Italian?"

"I love it," I said. My voice was pitched

an octave higher than normal, and I felt another burn to my ears.

We walked to his shiny black car. It was an old Mustang. It looked new because it was in great shape, and he took good care of it. Hm. He takes good care of the animals at the shelter, his grooming, and his car. Those were good traits in a man. I really liked this guy. He opened the car door for me, and I slid into the seat just like Mother taught me when you wore a dress. Knees together while sitting and swing your legs in.

While we drove to the restaurant, I caught myself staring at him.

He noticed and just smiled.

When I looked away, from the corner of my eye, I'd catch him looking at my slender legs and my high heels. We both chuckled and struggled to find topics of conversation. It was obvious we were both nervous. He asked what kind of music I liked. I couldn't answer. I really wasn't into music. I couldn't afford to buy records or albums anyway. I deflected the question to him.

"I like jazz," he said.

He reached to his glove box and pulled out a tape. His fingers grazed my knee.

I pulled away.

"I'm sorry," he mumbled.

The tape had an unfamiliar name on it. He had several different tapes. While we listened, he took my hand and held it on the consol.

I looked over at him and smiled.

We reached the restaurant. He had impeccable manners. He told me to stay seated so he could open my door. He raced around the car and offered me his hand to exit. I obliged and he pulled me forward and closed the door. As we walked to the restaurant, he took my hand. He gave the hostess his name and she grabbed two menus and walked us to a private table in the corner.

The restaurant, decorated in red and gold, was beautiful. It was mainly lit by candles that gave a beautiful glow to his cheeks.

"Would you like some wine?" he asked.

"Yes, please."

"Red or white?"

"I think with Italian you're supposed to have red."

"Yes, but Nina, you can have anything you want. Step out of the box."

"I like both. You pick." I was lost in the ocean of his eyes.

When the waiter came over, John ordered a Merlot. We toasted to our first date.

I took a sip. It was scrumptious. It made my face flush and my whole body balmy. We looked over the menu.

"What would you like?" he asked.

"I'm not sure. Do you recommend anything special?"

"The waiter said the eggplant, lasagna, and pizza were good."

I remembered when I first moved to New York, my aunt had ordered pizza once a week. My cousins and I loved it. "Why don't we share a pizza?"

"Yes. What do you want on it?"

"Surprise me. I like everything."

"Even anchovies?" He laughed.

"Oh, I guess you're right. No anchovies for me." I giggled.

"Let's make it simple," he said. "How about pepperoni and mushrooms? Salad?"

"Perfect. That sounds wonderful."

We had a lovely evening. John did most of the talking. He spoke more of his family and where he grew up. I was shocked to learn he grew up in Michigan like Jennifer's boyfriend, in a small town near Ann Arbor. What a coincidence. I couldn't wait to tell her.

After we finished eating, John asked. "Well, are you ready for a movie?"

I gasped and placed my hand over my mouth. "I'm so sorry. I totally forgot that I was supposed to pick the movie." I could be so forgetful at times.

"That's okay, Nina." He winked at me and touched my hand on the table. "Why don't we stay here and have dessert? I'm enjoying just relaxing and talking."

We split a sugary dessert called Tiramisu. The evening was lovely. I truly enjoyed myself. John drove me home. He walked me to my door. A second panic seized me. Should I invite him in? Would that be appropriate for a first date? Was I ready for that? I decided not to. I thanked him at the door. "Thank you for a perfect evening. I had a wonderful time."

"Me, too." He touched my cheek and caressed it with his thumb. "May I kiss you goodnight, Nina?"

I looked at the ground and felt my face flush again. I slowly looked up. "Yes, I would really like that."

He gently leaned in and gave me a soft kiss.

I closed my eyes just for a few seconds. As I opened them slowly to look at him, I saw Pavlov. I pulled away and took a deep breath. What was that? A hallucination?

I shook my head, then thanked John and said goodnight. As he walked to his car, I opened my door, stepped in, closed and locked it behind me. I leaned up against it with my eyes closed, tapping the back of my head on the door asking myself. What did that mean? Pavlov. I hadn't thought of him in ages.

"Oh, my." I shook my head and went to bed.

Fifteen

Sunday morning, I didn't have to work. When I woke, I called Jennifer. Babbling for twenty minutes, I told her all about my date with John, ending with the kiss.

She was so happy for me. "He kissed you?" She squealed. "Like how? A peck on the cheek, a slobbery mess, or a heavenly perfect joining of lips?"

"That one," I said, my belly warming at the thought of it. What I didn't tell her was the vision of Pavlov. I didn't know what it meant. How could I explain it to her?

"How are things with you and Mark?"

"Mark and I are perfect. I want to hear more about John."

"Well, he's my new friend I mentioned to you who's in law school here at Columbia. Remember the picnic we had together a few weeks ago? Then he asked me out for dinner and a movie. He asked me to pick the movie, but of course, I forgot. We ended up staying at the restaurant just talking."

"And ... what else?"

"It turns out he grew up in Michigan close to where Mark grew up."

"You're kidding me."

"No, what a coincidence."

She sighed with happiness. "I'm so glad that you finally met someone. Are you going out again?"

"I think so."

"That's great. I'm so happy for you."

"Summer's almost here. When do you think you'll be coming home?" I asked.

"As soon as the semester ends."

"Will Mark come for a visit too?"

"Oh, yes. We're already making plans for the entire summer. I hope you and John will be a true couple by then so we can hang out and double date."

"One day at a time." I giggled.

"Okay Nina, got to go. Let's talk later."

"Good talking to you. Bye."

John and I saw each other almost daily after the semester ended. We were an official couple. I loved summer in New York. The trees and grass were a bright deep green. The flowers around our school campus and the city were bright and beautiful and the blazing yellow sun was warm. We always had a lot to do. Jennifer was coming home soon, and I couldn't wait to introduce her to John.

John took me out a lot, so I decided to invite him over and cook a nice meal. Perhaps my favorite meal, Beef Stroganoff. The next time we met at the shelter, I asked John to my apartment for dinner. He happily accepted.

Since it was a Friday night, neither of us worked. I gathered what I needed from the grocery store, returned home, and began to cook. As I was cooking, there was a gentle knock on the door. I opened the door and there was my tall, slender hunk of a man. Again, he brought me daisies. I kissed him on his cheek and thanked him.

The first thing he said when he walked in was, "Wow, it smells great in here."

"Thanks. I'm making my favorite meal, Beef Stroganoff. I hope you like it."

"I'm sure I will."

John looked around my apartment. "Nina, where are we eating? You don't have a kitchen or dining room table."

I chuckled "We're going to sit on the floor at my coffee table. I'll set it up now. Dinner's almost done."

"Okay. Can I help?"

"Not much to set up. I have it. Just sit on the couch and relax."

John sat and scanned the room with his glistening eyes. He then stood and walked to the walls of my tiny apartment. This time he asked, "Did you do these?"

"Yes," I replied softly.

"Wow, you have a hidden talent. I had no idea you liked to draw."

"Thanks. I love to sketch."

"Who are these people?"

I walked over and pointed to each one. "This is Father. This one is my brother, Aleksei. And this one is my dog, Sasha." Tears filled my eyes.

"Oh, Nina. I'm so sorry. Don't cry." He brushed a tear from my cheek. "I feel like I keep opening old wounds concerning your family. I wish you'd tell me a little bit about them. Sometimes just talking about things makes you feel better."

"Well, there's not much to say. I lost Father, Aleksei, and Sasha to different circumstances. I lost my dog when the Chernobyl plant exploded. We were nearby, and the explosion was so loud, it scared her. She ran off, and I never saw her again. While we were fleeing the area, my brother, Aleksei, was forced to stay. The Soviet military conscripted all unmarried males from fifteen to thirty years old to stay to deal with the devastation. He didn't survive. Then when we came to this country, Father got cancer and passed within a year."

"Wow, Chernobyl. I heard about it. That's a lot to carry around. I'm so sorry." He took my hand, raised it to his face, and gently kissed it.

I bit down on my lower lip, trying hard

to hold it together. I released myself from his grip and walked to the kitchen. I grabbed the spoon that was lying on the stove and gave my Stroganoff one last stir. Thank God, he didn't ask about Mother.

"Dinner's ready." I scooped the Stroganoff onto two plates and carried them to the coffee table.

"Can I help?"

"No, thanks. I've got it." As I placed the plates down, John grabbed my hand again and asked if I was okay.

"Yes, I just don't like to talk about it." I looked down and shrugged my shoulders.

"I understand."

We sat on the floor with some pillows and ate. We talked about school and work. I told him how excited I was for him to meet my best friend Jennifer and her boyfriend. He seemed interested too.

We finished cleaning the table and washed the dishes. It was getting late, but we sat on the couch. I really didn't want him to leave. I turned on the television for some background noise.

John pulled my face to his with a gentle touch and began to kiss me. My body grew warm, but it was a nice heat. We kissed softly for a few minutes. Then I felt his sweltering hand slowly crawling up the front of my shirt.

I panicked and pushed his hand down and backed from my seat. I looked down and nibbled my bottom lip. I squeezed my eyes closed for a few seconds, and there he was again. Pavlov.

"Nina, I'm so sorry."

"Don't be sorry. I guess I'm just not ready. I … I've never been with anyone before."

"Oh, I didn't realize that."

"Can we take it slow, please?"

He stood, adjusting his pants. "Of course. I should head out now, anyway."

I walked him to the door. "Again, I'm sorry."

"Don't be. You're worth the wait."

I was watching a romance movie a few days later when my phone rang. It was Jennifer.

"Hey, girl," she said. "How are you? I'm home. What's your schedule like?"

"Yay. I'm so happy. I'm working days at the hospital all week, so maybe we can do dinner tomorrow?"

"Perfect. I'll pick you up at six."

Jennifer picked me up, and we went to one of our favorite spots for dinner. She was the only one I could tell my inner most thoughts too. After we ordered, I asked her how school was and more about Mark.

"Well, we're in a lot of classes together so that's always fun. We eat lunch together every day too. I really like him."

"That's wonderful. When is he coming

in town?"

"In a few weeks," she said with a huge grin.

"Awesome. I can't wait to meet him, and I can't wait for you to meet John."

We chatted the rest of the evening about our boyfriends.

A few days later, Aunt Olga called and invited me for lunch on Saturday. We still got together every month. I loved her so much. I waited outside my apartment for her to pull up with her car. There she was. I slid in and reached over and gave her a big hug. "Hi, Aunt Olga. How are you?" I looked over at her as she sped away.

She didn't respond. Her eyes were glued to the road.

Something felt wrong. It was as if she didn't want to look at me. "Is everything okay?" I began entwining my hair with my right hand so she wouldn't catch me.

"Of course, dear. I just want to share something about your mother."

"Oh, is she okay?" I looked toward my window and rolled my eyes.

"Let's talk at lunch."

All I could do was ponder. What was going on? I would think if there were an emergency, I would have known about it sooner.

We arrived at a café and ordered sandwiches and drinks.

"All right," I said. "What's going on?"

"Well, your mother went to the doctor for her yearly visit, and they found a lump in her breast. She had a mammogram. It also showed a lump, and now she's scheduled for an ultrasound Monday."

"Oh. Well, I'm sorry to hear that. Please keep me posted." I looked down at my sandwich, and a tear slowly drifted down my face. Why was I crying? I didn't care what happened to my mother. She didn't care about me. But that wasn't true. I did care, even though I didn't want to. Why couldn't it be different? Why couldn't she be more like Aunt Olga? Why did Mother blame me for Father's death? I looked up at my aunt.

She gently placed her hand on my hand that was resting on the table. "I know, Nina. We've never spoken about your relationship with your mother, but I know and understand."

"Thank you, Aunt Olga. That's why I love you so much. You're my only family. I appreciate you always staying in touch and watching out for me."

"That's because I love you, dear."

"I love you, too."

My aunt called me the day after Mother's ultrasound. The lump was suspicious, and she now required a fine needle aspiration biopsy. Mother had this procedure the next day. The results concluded that it was benign. Mother would have to follow up in six months.

Sixteen

Jennifer and I spent a couple of weeks together alone, catching up on things before her boyfriend arrived. We knew once he came, the two of them would be inseparable.

Once Mark arrived, I left Jennifer alone for a few days. I didn't want to infringe on their time together. Then I couldn't stand it anymore. I had to reach out to her so we could all get together and meet. So, I called her. "Hey, Jen, how are you? Are you enjoying your time with Mark?"

"Yes, having fun taking him around the city."

"Where is he staying?"

"My parents are letting him stay in our guest house in the back."

"That's convenient." I giggled.

"Yes, it is." She laughed.

"When can we all get together?"

"How about this weekend?"

I glanced at the calendar on my wall, though I already knew it was empty. "I've been working a lot of days, so I'm usually free in the evenings. Let me check with John and get his schedule, and I'll get back with you."

The next day, after speaking with John, we set up a double date for Saturday night. What would Mark be like? Would he like me? Would Jennifer like John? What if we didn't all get along? How would that affect our friendship?

John suggested dinner and a jazz lawn concert at the University. Everyone agreed. We met at the restaurant at five. John and I arrived first and waited patiently in the reception area for Jennifer and Mark. I kept peering at the front door; each time it opened, I hoped it would be them. Finally, they arrived. Jennifer and I gave each other a hug, and then we introduced our beaus.

Mark, the cliché of tall, dark, and handsome, had an adorable dimple on the center of his chin. For some reason it made him look manlier. He and Jennifer looked like a perfect couple together. I had a good feeling about him.

The host seated us, and we chatted a bit before the waiter came over.

"So, John. I understand you grew up in Michigan," Mark said.

"Yes, in a small town named Dexter."

"Oh yes, that's just thirty minutes from Ann Arbor where I grew up."

"I love Ann Arbor," John said. "My friends and I often spend our weekends there. There's always so much to do, sports, museums, art shows, and neat café and restaurants. It's a unique, eclectic town."

After dinner, we drove to the University for the lawn concert. We found a great spot. John and I came prepared with a soft blanket, a basket, and a bottle of wine with some plastic wine glasses. We spread out the blanket and everyone picked a spot and sat down.

"Does anyone want some wine?" I asked.

Jennifer nodded to Mark.

"We'd love some," he said.

I poured for everyone.

"I hope everyone likes jazz," John said.

"We listen to it all the time," Mark said. "Who's your favorite?"

"I like Marcus Miller. He plays so many different instruments."

"Yes, I like him too. I also like Miles Davis."

"Sounds like we like the oldies." Everyone chuckled.

"Well, tonight we're listening to some New Age jazz. I hope you like it."

The concert started. The music was lovely. At one point, we got up and started to slow dance with our companions. The evening was perfect. We had a great meal, conversation, and music. I couldn't be happier that everyone got along.

For the rest of the summer, I worked at the hospital pretty much full time and continued to volunteer with John at the shelter. John went back home a few times to visit his family, but often stayed here in New York. He didn't want to lose his job at the hardware store, and he wanted to spend quality time with me before school started again.

Jennifer and Mark spent their summer flying back and forth to see each other's families. Whenever they were in town, we always double dated. We always had a great time together.

Jennifer was in town one last time before school started. I wanted some alone time with her. "Hey, how about some lunch and shopping."

"Sounds like a plan," she said. "I'll pick you up at ten."

We did a little shopping, and then picked a restaurant for lunch.

"Wow, I'm a little exhausted from shopping." Jennifer dropped her armload of packages on the chair beside her and then eyeballed my shopping bags. "You didn't get much."

"Money's always tight with me. You know that." I leaned in so I could speak barely above a whisper. "I wanted to talk to you about John. I really, really like him. However, I'm not ready to be one hundred percent with him."

Jennifer smirked. "Are we talking about

sex?"

I felt my face burn. "I'm just not comfortable yet. He tries and I back off. I can't believe how patient he is with me."

She bounced back against her chair and stifled a laugh with her mouth. "You mean you haven't been intimate yet?"

I looked around the room to see if anyone could overhear our conversation. "No, not all the way."

"Have you been with Mark?"

A cheesy grin spread across her face. "Yes, about a month after we started seeing each other. I take birth control pills for protection. What are you afraid of?"

"I don't know." I twisted my napkin in my lap. "Maybe getting hurt? Having my heart broken? What if he leaves me? What if I'm not good at it?"

"You watch too many romance movies," she winked and pressed the back of her hand to her forehead, Southern belle style. "He's stayed with you this long. Aren't you afraid he might give up and leave you?"

"Well, he hasn't left me yet. He tells me all the time that he'll wait until I'm ready. That's how special he is." A part of me wondered just how long would be too long. He was a red-blooded American male.

"Yes, he is special. Nina, get the courage one night. Have him over for dinner, set the tone, and take the plunge. It's a glorious feeling when you have that bond, that closeness. You will fit together like a puzzle." She looked out the window with a wistful smile on her face, almost as if she had a well-kept secret. Was that what sex with the right man felt like?

One day while volunteering at the shelter, I was approached by Pam, the director.

"Hi, Nina. How are you? I've got a favor to ask you. I know how much you like the cats as much as the dogs. Would you consider taking two kittens home and fostering them for a few weeks? Someone found them and dropped them off, and I can't find anyone to foster them. Would you be interested?"

"I've never owned a cat let alone a kitten. Is it hard? Can you give me more details on my responsibilities?"

"The hardest part will be making sure they get fed every three hours. Do you think you can commit to something like that?"

"I'm not sure. I have to work at the hospital. I might be able to sneak them in or get John to help me. How old are they?"

"We think two weeks. They're adorable. Do you want to come to the clinic and see them?"

"Sure." We walked to a dark cool room in the back. It smelled like the hospital where I worked. A silver table stood in the middle with instruments nearby. Small tables, counters, and crates lined the back wall. I hadn't even known this room existed. Was this an operating room? She went to the back, opened a crate, and slowly pulled out the babies. I gasped and cupped my hands over my mouth. I looked at her and then down at them. They were beautiful. Each had a soft white coat with black, caramel, and grey markings, like someone had taken a paintbrush and flicked the paint at their adorable faces and tails. Each had a dark freckle on its pink nose. How could I say no? I had to give it a try. "Do they need to be bottle fed?"

"Yes," said Pam. "I'll show you everything you need to do. Are you interested? I can set you up with a crate, blankets, food, anything you need. You must bring them back weekly for a checkup. We check their weight and make sure they are healthy. Can you handle that?"

"Yes." I cradled them in the palm of my hand, close to my face. Pam brought out a tiny carrier and I placed them in it on a soft towel. I quickly called John and asked him to pick me up after work. I couldn't walk all their gear home.

"What's up? Are you okay?"

"Sure, I'm fine. In fact, I'm great. I just have some stuff I can't carry home."

"I have an hour before I get off. See you soon."

I didn't tell him why. I wanted to surprise him. Pam had given me everything I needed. I brought it all to the front reception area and went outside and sat under a tree with the kittens waiting for John. They fell asleep on my lap.

I heard John's car pull up the driveway. I waved and slowly got up. The kittens began to wake up. John got out of his car and walked to me. As he got closer, his eyes grew bigger as he saw the kittens. He started to smile. "Whacha got there?"

"Just look at them. Aren't they adorable? They're only two weeks old. They're so tiny. Pam asked if I could foster for a few weeks. Just until they're old enough and heavy enough for adoption. What do you think?"

"I think you're a beautiful person for doing this." He reached for my face and gave me a soft kiss.

"Everything is in the reception area. Can you get it for me and put it all in the car?"

He packed the car and drove me home. He came in and helped me set up my apartment so they would be comfortable. Then he asked, "Do they have names?"

"No, Pam said I could name them if I wanted. What do you think?"

"Oh, I don't have a clue. They are adorable, though."

"I was thinking Patches and Paintbrush. Look at the markings on their faces. Don't they look like someone splattered paint on them?"

"Yes, I guess you're right. Those are cute names."

"She told me I have to bottle feed them every three hours."

"You're kidding me. Like human babies?" His eyes bulged, and he shook his head in disbelief.

"Yes, I hope I can do it. I'm a little scared. She said if I miss a feeding they can crash and possibly die."

"Wow. I didn't know that. What are you gonna do about work? You can't take them to the hospital with you."

"I was thinking of putting them in my lunch box and sneaking them in." I raised one eyebrow.

John laughed. "You think you're not gonna get caught?"

"All I can do is try. If it doesn't work out, can you help when I'm not home?"

"Sure, anything for you, my sweet."

I tucked the snuggly babies in their little crate and turned to face him. "Do you want to stay for pizza? I can make a salad, and I think I have some wine."

"Sounds good to me."

By the time we finished the pizza, John was sneezing, and his eyes were puffy and watery.

"Are you all right?"

"Yes, I may be coming down with a cold. I'm not sure. I think I'll head back to the dorm."

"Okay. Thanks for your help." I was a little relieved that he didn't stay. I wanted to make sure the fur babies would be good for their first night. He gave me a long soft kiss at the door.

Seventeen

I absolutely loved caring for the kittens. They were so soft and fun to play with. When I held them, they'd crawl up my shirt and snuggle themselves on my neck and in my long hair for warmth.

The day after I brought them home, I had to work. I put a soft towel in my lunch pail and placed them gently inside. My lunch pail had a zipper on the top. I didn't close it all the way to ensure they had enough air. I made sure to bring enough formula for them.

When I got to the hospital, I took the stairs instead of the elevator, just in case one meowed. We had lockers in the pharmacy, so I placed the lunch box on the bottom of my locker and kept it closed. I wasn't worried since the lockers had vents. I knew the kittens would get plenty of air. Every few hours I checked on them and took them to the bathroom for feeding. I hid in the stalls. My first day was complete without a hint of getting caught.

My plan worked beautifully for almost a week. The kittens were so young and tiny they mainly slept while I worked. John was surprised I didn't get caught until one day I did.

The head pharmacist called me in his office. "Nina, can you come in here?" he called.

Uh-oh. I knew it. Somebody ratted me out. I could feel my face flaming and began twirling my hair. I stomped to his office so hard I left gray marks from my heels on the white linoleum floor. I took a deep breath to calm myself. I stood tall and entered. "Hi, Dr. Jackson, what can I help you with?" I began to twirl my hair again. I quickly caught myself and placed my hands in the pockets of my white lab coat.

"Take a look at my computer screen, please."

He turned the screen to face me. I saw myself taking the kittens out of my locker and walking to the bathroom.

"There are cameras all over this hospital. I see you've been bringing some little friends to work with you."

My ears began to burn. "Yes, and I'm sorry. Are they bothering anyone?"

"No, however, the hospital has a no-pet policy."

"I know. But they're only about three weeks old. They must be fed every three hours, or they might die. I didn't know what else to do." I started to blush.

"Well, you can't bring them back here," he said firmly. He crossed his arms over his chest and stared directly in my eyes. "I admire your concern for animals, but this is not the place. I understand you volunteer at a shelter. Is that correct?"

I had to look away from his intense stare. "Yes, I do." My fingers itched to reach for my hair, but I left them securely hidden in my lab coat.

"That's commendable. However, you have to make other arrangements for your kittens."

"Okay, thanks. I understand." I walked out of his office relieved I hadn't gotten written up or fired. I took out a tissue from my pocket and wiped the sweat from the back of my neck.

Well, at least I'd gotten away with it for a week. The kittens were already growing. I took them back to the shelter on Saturday for their checkup and asked Pam if she thought they were ready for solid food. I was instructed on weening them off the bottle. It took two days for them to adjust to regular moist food. Now, I could go to the hospital and not worry about them. I made a little home for them in my bathtub on the days I worked. I included a hot water bottle wrapped in a towel to keep them warm, some tiny toys, a litter box, their food, and some water.

Perfect. If John was available on his day off next week, I'd ask him if he could check on the babies. I could check on them on my lunch or dinner breaks at work, too.

Jennifer's advice about being intimate with John kept needling at me. Maybe she was right. If I wanted to keep him, I couldn't play Mother Theresa forever. Even the most patient man would grow weary of waiting too long. He was still very much a man. I planned a scrumptious chicken marsala dinner with potatoes, a spinach salad with red ripe tomatoes, and a nice bottle of white wine. I placed two candles on the coffee table and left space for the fresh white daisies John always brought when I cooked. I loved that about him. It's the small little things he did for me that makes me feel special.

The bell rang. There was John. I quickly checked myself in the mirror. I combed my hair with my fingers and pushed my hair behind my shoulders. I opened the door to let him in. Again, behind his back were my flowers. We always played the same game. He liked me prancing around him until he gave up and handed them to me. I took a long whiff of the flowers. Then he softly kissed me with his moist lips.

After our kiss, I said, "Dinner is almost ready."

"It smells wonderful."

"Thanks. Do you want a glass of wine?"

"Yes, I'll pour."

John followed me to the kitchen and pulled two glasses from the cupboard and the wine from the fridge. He scanned the apartment. "Where are the kittens?"

"I made them a little home in the bathtub. They really like it."

He chuckled. "I'm gonna go see." He walked into the bathroom and peeked in the tub. They were napping. He came back out. "They're so cute."

"I know. I just love them. They're really growing, too. Do you think you can check on them when you're not working next week? When is your next day off?"

"I can check on them Tuesday."

"Thank you. Dinner's ready. Can you grab the salad? I'll get the plates."

I placed a piece of chicken and some potatoes on each of the plates and walked them to the coffee table.

"Nina, it looks and smells delicious." He held his glass up and gave me cheers.

In the middle of dinner, John's eyes started to tear up, and he sniffled.

"Are you okay?" I asked. "That's the second time you've seemed to be catching a cold."

"I'll be right back." He sneezed and headed for the bathroom.

"Nina?" John came out wiping his eyes. "I think it's the kittens. I may be allergic."

"What? You're kidding me? You don't have this reaction when you're at the shelter."

"Yes, but I just quickly pass the cats. Then I go straight to the dogs."

"Oh, that makes sense."

John backed to the door, his face already a puffy, blotchy mess. "I'm gonna have to leave."

"All right, I understand." So much for my special sexy night.

"Sorry, my sweet. How much longer will you have the kittens?"

"Probably two more weeks."

"Okay, we'll work around that." He gave me a delicate kiss on my cheek and left.

"Well, so much for my courage tonight and going all the way. I guess I'll stay a virgin another night," I said aloud.

I tossed the food in the trash, cleaned the kitchen, and went in the bathroom to clean up after the kittens. I picked them up and took them to the couch with me. "Well, you two certainly altered my plans. You ruined my special night." They looked up at me and mewed, the sweetest little noises. How could I be mad at those precious faces? I placed them on a pillow beside me. They liked to watch romance movies too.

I called Jennifer to see if she wanted to get together one last time before she went back to school. She picked me up after I worked.

"Where do you want to go?" Jennifer

asked. "A bar, grill, restaurant, or café?"

"I'm open to anywhere," I said with a sigh.

"What's the matter?" Her eyes scrutinized me. "How did your date go? Did you make dinner for John and finally do it?"

"Yes, I made dinner, but the rest of evening didn't go well." I crossed my arms in front of me and rolled my eyes.

"He started getting sick. We think he's allergic to the kittens. His eyes swelled up, and he started to sneeze. It's the second time it's happened. He left early. I was so disappointed. But what was I supposed to do?"

"I'd get rid of those fur balls. How much longer will you have them?"

"About two more weeks. I can't return them now. I made a promise and they're so stinking cute. I love them."

"Why don't you just get another dog? John's not allergic to dogs, right? I think you're ready."

"No, I work long hours at times and, remember, the start of school is around the corner. I can't leave a pet like a dog for long hours. It's not fair."

"Well, I'm sorry to hear about John." Jennifer patted my arm.

I placed my hand over hers. Friends were the best. "Another time. I'll plan it again when the fluff muffins are back at the shelter. Are you excited about going back to school?" I was rather anxious to change the subject.

"Yes, I can't wait to see Mark and start up my classes."

"Me too. I love school."

We finished our meal, and Jennifer drove me home. We walked to my door.

"I'll miss you." I wrapped her in a bear hug. "You're my best friend. It's hard for me when you're not here. Sometimes I just need a girl hug and an ear."

Jennifer gave me a big squeeze and released me. "You know I'm a phone call away."

I blinked, battling the tears that threatened to fall. "It's not the same."

We gave each other another long hug before I watched her head to her car, get in, and drive away. Tears let loose down my cheeks.

Eighteen

The kittens went back to the shelter and were adopted out. School started up again for John and me. Life was back to our normal routine with school, work, and volunteering. It was time to try again with John, so I invited him over for dinner.

One Saturday when we'd finished taking care of the pups, I asked, "What do you want to do tonight? How about dinner at my place?"

"Sounds good. Time?"

"How about six?"

"Any hidden kittens?" His eyes danced with laughter.

I giggled back. "Do you want anything special for dinner?"

"Just you," he said softly in my ear as he wrapped his arms around me and gave me a squeeze.

"Okay, I'll surprise you. See you tonight."

I didn't want the pressure of cooking, so I decided on takeout. John liked Chinese cuisine, so I ordered his favorite foods from a restaurant around the corner. I picked it up around 5:30, rushed home, and placed our dinner in the oven to keep it hot. I chilled my favorite bottle of Chardonnay. I was ready but my stomach was in knots. My mind started to race. What if I wasn't good at sex? I wondered how many partners he'd had. Would he know to bring protection?

The doorbell rang at exactly six. I quickly scanned my apartment. Everything looked perfect. I walked over to the door, glancing at myself in the mirror to make sure my hair and makeup were flawless. I opened the door holding the cool, metal doorknob. There he was, as handsome as ever. I wanted to run my fingers through his blond hair that was always expertly parted to the side with a dash of styling cream to keep every hair in place. He probably wouldn't like me messing it up. The tingling in my body had other plans. He wore jeans and a white t-shirt. Simple but beautiful. I grabbed his warm strong hands and pulled him to me, then I wrapped my arms around his neck and nuzzled my nose to his. I pulled my face back and stared at his beautiful blue eyes.

He leaned down to my face and gave me the softest, wettest kiss I'd ever had. It felt like it lasted hours.

My mouth wasn't the only body part that was wet and warm. I gently closed the door. We didn't play the flower game. He just handed them to me. The electricity in the room could light up Times Square. His face was serious. He had to feel it, too. He must have known tonight would be the night.

I reluctantly pulled away and walked to the kitchen to tend to the flowers. "I picked up Chinese for us." Was he watching my ass as I walked away? I almost tripped on the throw rug by the sink.

"I can smell it. It smells great," he said with a slight stutter.

I giggled to myself. He must be a little nervous. "Are you ready to eat, or do you want some wine first?"

"Actually, I'm famished."

"Me, too. Let's eat."

We made small talk and quickly ate our supper. The subjects were lame and neither one of us cared about who was playing football or what was happening on the political arena. The tension kept mounting. We both knew what was gonna happen next. I realized I was twirling my hair again and forced myself to stop. Grabbing the dishes, I rushed them to the sink and then turned my radio to some soft jazz.

John sat on the couch, watching my every move.

I excused myself to the bathroom. I looked in the mirror. Oh, my god. Oh, my God.

I was really doing this. I quickly brushed my teeth and sprayed a little perfume behind my ears and on my decolletage.

When I came out, John was standing waiting for me near the couch.

I stood at the bathroom door for just a moment, staring at his beautiful, chiseled face and ocean blue eyes. Then I crossed the room in a few big strides, and he met me in the center of the room. I raised my arms behind his neck. He picked me up off the floor, squeezing me close to his strong body, and we began to press our lips together. Our tongues danced and twined. I didn't know if it was minutes or hours. I didn't care. I was lost in my reality. My body was flushed and overheated like a car with steam coming from the hood. I began to moan and sank my fingers in his soft hair. Oh god, did I really moan? I opened my eyes and pulled away.

He gently placed me back on the floor.

My legs felt like jelly. Would they even hold me up?

He stared at me for a few seconds while holding my face between his warm, strong hands. "Nina, are you sure you want to do this? Are you ready?"

"Oh, yes, John. I want you." My words came out in pants.

We moved the coffee table without verbal direction. Then we removed the pillows and cushions from the couch. I placed them gently on the floor on the side of the couch. My heart was pounding loudly in my ears. I tried to maintain my composure.

John pulled up the bar of the sofa bed to open it, and it screeched loudly. I didn't think he heard. He looked determined. I watched his strong arms assemble the couch into a bed. We sat on the foot of the bed and started kissing again. With shaking hands, I scooted higher on the bed and placed my head on the pillow.

John flipped his shoes off and got on his knees and crawled over to me. His face was two inches from mine. We gazed at each other for several seconds. I caressed his bottom lip with my thumb. He rose and swiftly pulled his shirt over his head and threw it to the floor. His bare chest was creamy white and had a sprinkling of blond curls, damp with sweat. His abs were rippled like steel. My mouth went dry. I began to pant, and my chest heaved. He was so beautiful.

He came back to me and began kissing me softly. He lay on one side so his hand could be free to touch my flushed face and run his hands through my hair. Our tongues couldn't stop swirling together. I wrapped my arms around his back and dug my nails into him. I couldn't help myself. I was consumed by passion. It was so hot.

His warm heated fingers brushed my skin as he reached under my shirt and touched my bra. With one hand, he reached behind my back and unhooked it. I pulled the straps through the arm holes of my shirt and tossed it to the floor. His hand moved to the front and stroked my breasts, gently, calmly. I opened my eyes to see if he was watching me. He wasn't. He too was absorbed in the moment.

I placed my hand on his face and pushed him back gently. I needed to breathe. I couldn't stop panting. I sat up enough to pull my shirt off. He assisted me pulling it over my head. I laid down again, bare breasted, letting him look at me in the soft candlelight. My body ached for more.

"Nina. You're so beautiful. I'm so happy you're mine. All mine."

He unbuttoned my slacks, pausing to look for my approval.

I didn't stop him. I smiled and helped pulling them down.

He finished by tugging them at my ankles until they were free from my body.

I was breathing hard, but it was my turn. He was back on his side close to my face. I reached below his tight abs and unzipped his jeans. Parting the opened zipper, I slipped my fingers in his pants and through the opening of his boxers. My fingers felt cool against his hot flesh. I pulled back, got on my knees, and slipped his pants off.

All that remained was my bikini under-wear. I shivered with nervous anticipation. I bit my lower lip. This time I didn't care. I couldn't stop. My body was quivering from excitement.

John pulled the sheet up to my neck.

Did he think I was cold? No. I was heated and ready to go. I felt him pull my underwear down with one hand slowly, sensually. That too went to the floor.

His hand came to my breasts, and he kissed my neck. Then his hand traveled to my stomach where it stayed, caressing me for several minutes. I was shaking with excitement. Butterflies danced in my stomach. I could feel my body change. Suddenly on fire, I pushed the sheets down to our ankles with my foot. Then his fingers were inside me, swirling, while he kissed my breasts. His soft, wet tongue licked all around them, making my nipples stand erect. It felt glorious. I felt lost and couldn't think straight. I was overwhelmed with pleasure.

He slowly came back up to my face with his fingers still inside me. "Do you like that?"

I groaned, "Oh, John, you have no idea. You make me feel so special. It's beautiful."

"You're beautiful, Nina."

It was my turn. I slowly caressed him all the way down his body. I touched his manhood and wrapped my fingers around it, stroking it.

He stopped touching me and lay on his back, embracing the moment.

I nibbled on his neck and stroked him, slowly at first, then faster and faster as his breath quickened. I peeked at him. His face said he was enjoying my strokes.

He picked up my head, holding my chin. "Are you sure you want to do this? We don't have to if you don't want to."

I couldn't stop now if I wanted to. "I want you. I want all of you."

Suddenly, he got up and picked up his jeans. What the hell? Was he leaving? It was like a cold shower, having the heat of his body suddenly taken away. He opened his wallet and pulled out a condom. Oh. Good idea. My panic subsided.

He sat on the edge of the bed. I could hear him tear it open. It crinkled like a peppermint candy wrapper. I could tell he was rolling it on his flesh. The world stood still. He turned around and crawled onto me. Our eyes met, and he began to kiss me softly. I closed my eyes. I wanted him to do the work. I waited. There it was. He slowly placed himself inside me. He asked if I was okay. I nodded. He was so gentle. My body resisted a bit for him to get all the way inside me.

I breathed deep. It only hurt a little. I remembered Jennifer told me it would. I pretended to enjoy it. My hands caressed his back. His heavy body consumed all of me. I loved his weight pressing on me. He was so strong. For the first time, I finally felt safe.

I could tell he came. He gave me one last hard thrust and suddenly stopped. He started panting and rolled off me.

My insides began to sting, and I felt like I

was on fire. I got up and went to the bathroom. There was a spot of blood on the toilet paper. I flushed it and looked at myself in the mirror. I was no longer a virgin. I felt like a woman for the first time.

Nineteen

Weeks went by and John and I were acting like bunnies. He spent many steamy nights with me. My stomach swirled with butterflies when I was with him. It felt like I was in one of those romance movies that I liked to watch. I loved it when he picked me up and twirled me around my apartment and our moist lips met. When I wasn't with him, I would have sexy thoughts of our time together.

One evening when I was alone sketching, Aunt Olga called.

"Hi, Aunt Olga. How are you?"

"I'm fine dear. How are you?"

"I'm fantastic. I have so much to tell you." I wanted to tell her about John.

"Are you working tomorrow? Can I take you to lunch?" she asked.

"I'm off work. That sounds good."

"Wonderful, dear. I'll pick you up at 11:30."

"Looking forward to it."

My aunt picked me up. Her faced looked different when I got to the car. I slid inside, reached over, and gave her a hug. Her hug was weak, and her face looked gaunt.

"Is everything all right?" I asked.

She looked over at me and placed her warm soft hand on my knee while she steered the car with her left hand but did not answer. She drove to our favorite café around the corner. Neither of us spoke. I knew something was horribly wrong.

We reached the café and got a quiet table in the corner near a window. I waited for her to talk first. I wasn't bringing up John now.

She stared at the menu, but she wasn't really reading it.

What was going on? I waited.

Finally, her eyes rose from the menu and met mine. "Nina. there is no way to say this without shocking you. So, I'll just say it. Do you remember several months ago when your mother had a lump on her breast and, after tests, it was benign?"

My breath caught, and I think my heart skipped a beat. I stared at her. I knew what she going to say next.

"Your mother went back for her appointment earlier than expected, and they found more lumps in both breasts and now enlarged lymph nodes. More tests were administered, and it turns out she has stage three breast cancer."

My vison blurred. A tear trickled down my face like dew falling from a leaf. Mother and I had been estranged for so long; I hadn't expected this reaction from my body. It was in direct opposition to my head. I couldn't forget what a bitch she'd been to me since Father died. But in my heart, I missed the mother I had before: before Aleksei died, before Father got sick, before the Chernobyl explosion. I tasted metal and realized I'd bitten my lip. I pressed my napkin on it.

Aunt Olga stared blankly out the window. This was her sister. Of course, she was upset.

When I lost my Sasha, I was sad. When I lost my brother, I was devastated. When Father got sick and lost him, my heart was torn in two. This was different. My heart and head were in conflict. A part of me felt badly for her; I didn't like to hear about her suffering. However, some of my thoughts were cold and not very nice. I assumed I would get blamed for this cancer, too. "How is she?" I asked.

"She's in shock. I am too."

The waiter came over and asked for our order.

I didn't look at the menu. I wanted to order anything so he would go away. My head was spinning, and I couldn't concentrate. "I'll just have a cup of chicken soup."

Aunt Olga ordered the same.

I sat back in my chair and let out a deep sigh. I crossed my arms and gripped my elbows.

I tried to control my quivering body.

My aunt placed one elbow on the table while she rested her head on her hand. I saw the love and sorrow she had for her sister.

My heart was in control, and my mind flashed back to the happy times we'd had in Chernobyl like when we made cookies together in the old cast-iron oven or when she taught me how to make Stroganoff, my favorite dish from back home.

"I'll need your help, Nina," Aunt Olga said. "I can't take care of her alone. I can't lose my job in the city. She'll need a double mastectomy and chemotherapy just like your father. Remember, how sick he got?"

I nodded.

She reached over and broke my crossed arms to hold one of my hands. "I know how you feel about your mother. I don't judge either of you. But do you think you can bring yourself to help?"

"Yes," I said softly. "When is her surgery and the treatments?"

"Her surgery is next week, and after she heals, her treatments will start."

"Does she know that you are telling me?"

"Yes, I told her yesterday that we were meeting for lunch."

The waiter came over with our soup. It was steaming hot. It fogged up the window. I unwrapped a saltine cracker and popped it in my mouth while I waited for my soup to cool.

My lip exploded in pain. Salt. I forgot that I'd broken the flesh of my lip biting it. I didn't care. I still ate it. I licked the salt from my lip and swallowed the cracker whole.

"How can I help?" I asked. "This is going to be difficult because I don't have my driver's license."

"Yes, I know. I was hoping we could take turns taking her for her chemotherapy and staying with her the nights she'll get very sick. As you know, Mandy and Margo are away at college."

I blew on my soup. "Well, I'll work on getting my driver's license." This was something I should have done a long time ago anyway. "I can use her car to take her for her appointments. I'll give you my school and work schedules. My work schedule changes often."

"We can iron it all out weekly."

We both stared into our soups. We grew silent. I couldn't eat. I'd lost my appetite. I stirred the soup with my spoon. What would these next few weeks bring? Would Mother even accept my help? Could I forgive her for the way she'd treated me enough to help her?

That evening, John came over for dinner. I told him about Mother.

His skin grew ashen. "What are you going to do? You have such a strained relationship with your mother."

"I have to help my aunt. You should have

seen her. She looked drained. When we came to this country, it was one problem after another for her from us. Yet, she remained kind to us." How could I explain to him that I was also feeling something new for Mother? Empathy, perhaps? Compassion? Feelings I didn't understand myself yet.

He walked to the kitchen with our glasses and grabbed another bottle of wine. He poured us another glass and leaned against the kitchen counter. His forehead puckered. "How are you going to help? You don't even know how to drive or have a car."

I rose, grabbed the dishes, and took them to the kitchen. "Will you teach me? Then I can take Mother's car and drive her to her appointments when I can or stay with her when I need to."

"Of course, but you also have to go to driving school."

"I'll do that, too."

"How are you going to work, school, volunteer, and take care of her?"

I shrugged, feeling the weight of it all. "I don't know. I'll figure it out. I'll probably have to back off the volunteering for a while."

He picked me up and gave me a big squeeze and a peck on my cheek. He held me all night with his warm, strong body.

The next weekend before Mother's surgery, I stopped by the house. I took the bus and walked a couple of blocks to get there. I knocked first, no one answered, so I used my key to enter, calling out as I walked in. Mother was lying on the couch with her head propped on a pillow. A garment rested on her lap along with a spool of thread and a thin, shiny needle, but her eyes were closed. She must have been sewing, but the task had been too much for her.

I placed my purse down on the side of the matching armchair. "Hello, Mother. I'm sorry to hear about your illness."

She opened her eyes but wouldn't look at me. She stared straight ahead at a bare, blank wall. Her eyes became glassy. She didn't blink.

"Aunt Olga and I talked about making a schedule to get you back and forth to appointments. Did she tell you we spoke?" Still nothing.

I went to the kitchen and got her a glass of water. I gazed out the kitchen window while the cool water raced into the glass. I shook my head. Why did I come? She would never stop blaming me. I had to muster the courage to commit to this and be the better person. I was doing this for Aunt Olga. And maybe for the woman my mother used to be.

"Here you go, Mother. Drink this. It looks like you need it." I placed the cool glass on the coffee table and sat down.

She pushed herself up and swiveled her legs to the floor in a sitting position.

We sat in silence for several minutes. I watched her. She didn't look sick yet. Aunt Olga looked more drained than she did. But this was pre-chemo. I knew how quickly things would change. "Can I fix you something for lunch? Are you hungry?"

"No, Nina." She turned and finally looked at me. Her eyes crawled up and down me from head- to-toe. What was she seeing? Her daughter? A stranger? Someone responsible for her husband's and son's deaths?

I swallowed. I could do this. I had to do this. "When do you start your treatments?"

"A couple of weeks after my surgery. Olga will take me for the surgery."

"Okay, I start driving school next week. When I finish and pass the tests, I'll be helping Aunt Olga take you to your chemotherapy appointments, driving you in your car."

"That's fine, Nina." Her voice sounded flat and resigned. She finally picked up the glass of water and took a sip.

I bent and lifted my purse and placed it on my lap. I fiddled with the strap. My feet itched to get out of there, and I fought the urge to twirl my hair. "I'll speak to Aunt Olga next week, and we'll get a plan going."

"That's fine."

We sat in silence for another three minutes. It felt like a lifetime.

I couldn't take it anymore. Was this how it was going to be? Two strangers filling the silence with sighs and blank stares. "Well, I'll head out now. I'll give you a call next week to see how you're doing." I got up and walked out the front door.

As I walked slowly to the bus stop, I saw the Orthodox Church Mother and I frequented with the passing of Aleksei. I had time to go in. I crossed the street and opened the heavy wooden door. I walked in, my heels making the only sound on the marble floors echoing off the ornate walls. I stood and raised my head to the ceiling. I remembered how beautiful this church was. Light filtered through the colorful stain glass windows and reflected off the crystal chandeliers hanging from the domed center of the church. I lowered my eyes to the front where a big bright shiny golden cross hung on the wall in the center. The walls were adorned with angels and saints. A tear ran down my cheek. I wiped it with the back of my hand.

I stood for several minutes. "God, give me strength to do this. Help me to forgive Mother and help her to forgive me. Take this anger away." I sighed and turned back into the bright sunshine. Looking back, I scanned the beautiful church again. All I could think of was Father and Aleksei. Would Mother be next?

Twenty

Mother had surgery the following week. I often took the bus to visit and cared for her the best I could. She still rarely spoke except for one-word answers: yes, no, thank you. Was her silence the bitterness toward me? Or was she in pain? Some days, I wanted to scream at her, "Just let it go. This silence is negative energy, and you won't get better by being bitter." But I said none of that. I held my tongue. Instead of being bitter myself, I made meals for her, helped her shower, and changed her bandages from the double mastectomy which mutilated her once perfect body.

Every evening I was drained. The conflict spinning in my mind because of Mother's continued silent rejection pained my heart. I felt like a mouse racing in a maze. When would I get to the cheese?

Aunt Olga and I worked out a schedule to take Mother for her treatments and if she needed someone to spend the night with her. Mother and I took the bus the first couple of weeks for my shifts. She wasn't happy about it, but she had no choice. I made sure she wore a mask since her immune system was compromised from the chemo. She seemed to be handling the chemo all right. I didn't have to spend any nights with her.

In the meantime, I signed up for driver's education. John helped by showing me how to drive using his car. He said I had a natural knack for driving and he trusted me completely with his car. I enjoyed the freedom of driving, and it made me feel independent.

I finally got my driver's license and was able to use Mother's car to take her to her appointments. This went on for weeks. Exhaustion settled in. I missed my time with John. I also couldn't work extra hours at the hospital.

John came over for dinner one evening. He brought me my beautiful daisies. They put a smile on my face. "Nina. You look so tired."

"I am. I'm so sorry for not spending as much time with you as we used to."

"How's your mother?"

"Well, she still doesn't talk to me much. I'm just numb over everything right now. I'm depleted."

John picked me up and held me. "I can't believe how much you do for her. She's so unappreciative of you."

I wrapped my arms around his neck and legs around his waist. We kissed on the lips for several minutes.

"I miss this," said John.

"Me too. Again, I'm so sorry, but I have to do what I have to do. Do you understand?"

John stared at me with his beautiful blue eyes. "Not really. But I'll support you as much as I can."

"What do you mean as much as you can?"

"Nothing, I just miss you."

"Well, I'm here now. Let's make the best of our time together."

We cooked a simple meal and went to bed early. Our love making was short but as always, sexy, and beautiful.

The poison from Mother's chemotherapy took a lot out of her. I watched her get weaker and weaker. Her body was shriveling away, and clumps of her hair stuck to the hairbrush when I groomed her. I'd pull the hair from the brush behind her and stuff it in my pockets so she wouldn't see. I didn't want to upset her.

Aunt Olga and I met for lunch one day to discuss what we'd have to do next for Mother.

"How are you dear?" my aunt asked.

"This is so hard, Aunt Olga. I am so tired. I am doing my best for Mother."

"I'm sorry. This has been tiresome for

me too."

"I know. I'm trying not to complain, but it's affecting my relationship with someone very special to me. I can just feel it. He's growing distant, and he doesn't really understand."

She leaned in. "Oh? Who are you talking about?"

"Well, I was going to tell you about him the day you told me about Mother's illness, but it hardly seemed appropriate under the circumstances. His name is John. He's a great guy who's going into law. He attends Columbia, too. We met at the animal shelter. I really like him. He reminds me a lot of Father. He's good to me."

"That's wonderful, dear," she said absently, clearly with something different on her mind. She quickly redirected me to Mother's care.

"We need to work out a new plan for your mother. She's so weak I'm afraid she'll fall. She can't be left alone at night anymore. We'll have to rotate. Are you okay with that?"

I shrugged. What choice did I have? "I'll do my best. At least I have her car which helps with time. I'm not sure John is going to be happy about it."

"Does he love you?"

I nodded.

"Then he'll understand."

Mother's chemotherapy went on for months. One week on, one week off. The weeks

off didn't improve her health. The toxins res-
onated in her body, and she always felt nau-
seous and weak. Her slender body had turned
skeletal, fragile bones poking through thin,
transparent skin. She reminded me of a prisoner
in a concentration camp. She couldn't stand up
straight anymore. We rented a wheelchair to
move her from room to room. Besides having
no appetite, sores in her mouth limited her to
soft foods with little to no appeal.

John wasn't happy that I was never available anymore, and my studies were slipping. I
had always been a perfect straight A student,
and now I was barely passing my classes. It
was tempting to give up on everything, but I
forced myself to continue. Thankfully, everyone
at work understood what I was going through,
and my coworkers always had my back.

The holidays were once again around the
corner. Aunt Olga wanted to have Thanksgiving
at Mother's. I decided to work. I needed the
money. They had a small turkey with the fix-
ings, just the two of them. Mandy and Margo
stayed at school, John flew home to be with
his family, and Jennifer stayed in Michigan to
spend the holiday with her boyfriend. I wasn't
in the holiday spirit.

Sadly, John and I grew distant as the
weeks went on. I missed him so much, but I had
to help Mother and Aunt Olga.

Mother wasn't getting any better. Her beautiful long locks were gone, so I helped her wrap silk scarves around her head. I could tell from the glistening in her eyes when she looked at herself in the mirror that they made her feel better.

At Mother's bi-weekly checkup, I spoke privately with her doctor. His news was not hopeful. He told me he could try radiation, but the prognosis wasn't good. Her cancer had moved to stage four, despite all the chemo that was supposed to kill the cancer cells. Her time was limited.

I met with Aunt Olga that evening for dinner and relayed the doctor's prognosis. The fatigue and stress showed on both our faces. These were the hardest months of our lives.

"What do you think about the radiation idea?" I asked.

"I don't know." She shook her head. "I don't think she can take much more."

"Me, neither." I picked at the food on my plate, with the same enthusiasm Mother showed for the soft food presented to her.

Aunt Olga attempted a smile, but it didn't make it to her eyes. "How's John doing?"

"Not good. He's starting to resent the time I spend between Mother, work, and school. He doesn't understand that, despite how she treats me, I need to do this. Maybe's he's losing respect for me not standing up for myself. We're getting together on Saturday night. I'll make him something special for dinner and spend some much-needed quality time with him."

"That's sounds like a good idea, dear. Should we pass on the radiation?"

"This shouldn't be our decision. It should be Mother's. Perhaps you can discuss it with her. I can't. She still doesn't speak much to me. We just coexist," I said, hanging my head down and feeling sad.

"That's a shame. You've done so much for her. You're a beautiful young lady, Nina."

"Thank you. I love you." A tear ran down my cheek. "I keep thinking of John. I don't want to lose him over this."

Twenty-One

I planned to cook for John Saturday night, but he wanted to take me out to dinner. This was new. He usually preferred to have me all to himself, not out in a crowded restaurant. He knocked on the door, and when I opened it, there were no daisies. That surprised me and sent a small red flag to my brain. What was going on here? We drove in silence. None of the usual chatter about things at school or funny office water-cooler stories. We went to our favorite Italian restaurant, the one where we had our first date. I breathed a little easier. We'd just been away from each other for too long. He probably wanted to remind me of our first official date and how much fun we had.

We sat down and ordered wine and dinner. John and I barely spoke. This wasn't like John. He was usually the talkative one. I couldn't eat. The food was stuck to my throat. Whatever he needed to say, for God's sake, he should just say it.

He looked at me with his soft blue eyes. "Do you know how much I love you?"

Did I? I wasn't sure anymore, but I answered, "Yes, and I love you too. Is everything okay."

He shrugged his shoulders. "Not really." He looked down on his plate, placing his elbows on the table and crossing his arms.

I slumped down in my chair. "You're breaking up with me, aren't you?"

He continued to look down on his plate. "Nina?" He reached across the table, took my hand, and finally looked up at me. "I really do love you, but I don't think I can continue like this. I barely see you. I'm sad and lonely without you."

"I miss you, too. You said you'd stand by me and support me throughout this." My body grew cold and limp. I bit my lower lip, fighting back the tears that threatened to fall. I looked up, and his eyes were glistening too. We stared at each other for several minutes. It was over. I swallowed hard, stood, and put my coat on. I bent and gave him a kiss on his cheek. My tears were flowing freely now, and I didn't care who saw. Our faces touched, and one of my tears ran down his face. He didn't say another word. I turned my back on him and walked to the exit. Other customers and the servers stopped and stared as I swished past as quickly as I could. I stepped outside and took a few deep breaths.

I tried to gather my composure as I waited for the bus. Thankfully, I was the only one at the stop that time of night. Once on board, I wrapped my coat tighter against the cold as I gazed out the window and took more deep breaths trying to collect myself. My breath landed on the window and fogged the glass. I took my freezing finger and drew a heart on the window. It eventually disappeared, just like my love. I twirled my hair. How could this have happened? He'd said he loved me; had said he'd support me on this. What happened to that? I shook my head over and over. I was getting angry. How could this have happened? I felt guilty. I'd sacrificed my boyfriend for a mother who didn't appreciate me. John and I were supposed to have a future together.

I couldn't believe I was even thinking that way. I was starting to turn into her, a cold heartless bitch. No, thank you. I was a better person than that. I convinced myself that maybe this was for the best. I was juggling too much at the same time.

When I arrived home, I put on my pajamas and crawled into my sofa bed. I put a movie on the television just for the noise and lay in bed staring at the ceiling where one of my sketches of Sasha was taped. I cried until I fell asleep.

Christmas was around the corner. My aunt and I knew it would be the last one for Mother. Not only did Mother decide not to do the radiation but she also discontinued the chemo. We understood. She was so frail and weak.

A few days before Christmas, I picked up a tree for Mother. She always loved the smell of our Christmas trees, always a traditional Douglas fir. When I hauled it in, she was on the couch, wrapped in a soft blanket. Was that a slight smile when the scent started to fill the room? She watched as I decorated it. We were both silent. Was she, like me, thinking of Father and Aleksei?

Normally, I'd be making sketches for everyone for Christmas. But my heart wasn't in it. I couldn't get Mother and John off my mind. I couldn't concentrate, so I decided to buy bracelets for everyone at the Dollar Store. That was the best I could do.

Mother was so sick that we cooked Christmas dinner at her house. Margo and Mandy were home from school, so they joined us. They finally gave up their meanness. They were actually polite. Had they finally matured? Perhaps when they saw Mother, they were shocked into thinking about everyone's immortality and decided it wasn't worth holding childhood grudges against me.

This year, for Mother, we decided to have a traditional Christmas dinner. We cooked all of Mother's favorites. Aunt Olga taught us how to make Olivier's Salad, meat dumplings, dried mushroom soup, and deviled eggs.

Dinner was ready. Mother could barely walk. Mandy and Margo struggled to get her into the wheelchair by holding on to her skinny elbows with both hands. I moved a chair aside so they could wheel her right to the dining room table. They looked up at me with a warm smile. Mandy actually gave me a wink; I winked back.

While eating, Mother's face paled to a pasty white before our eyes. Her body began to sway, and her eyes rolled so only the whites showed. She collapsed on to the table, right into her plate.

Aunt Olga yelled to Margo, "Call an ambulance."

I rushed to the living room to grab the soft blanket. I picked up her head, and Mandy helped me lower her from the wheelchair to the floor and wrap her tightly. Placing my fingers to her neck, I checked for a pulse. It was there but weak. Aunt Olga, with her hand over her mouth, knelt beside Mother and stared at her. I heard the roaring sirens as they grew closer to the house.

Mandy let them in.

The emergency technicians took Mother's blood pressure and pulse while I gave them her history. She was gently placed on the stretcher and whisked away to the hospital.

We all stood for a few minutes in shock, staring at the door. Was this the end for Mother? Aunt Olga began to cry. I held her as tightly as I could.

She choked out instructions. "Mandy and Margo, stay here and clean up. Nina and I are going to the hospital. I don't know when we'll be back."

They looked frozen.

Aunt Olga was more shaken up than I was, so I drove. On the way, I looked over at her several times. Tears flowed down her face like a thundering river. She was shivering. I reached over with my hand to touch hers. She picked up my hand, held it to her face, kissed it several times, and placed my hand on her lap.

The emergency room was a buzz of activity. A woman with a dishtowel wrapped around her bloody hand. A child vomiting into a wastebasket with a distraught mother holding her hair back. An old man in a turban moaned and clutched his stomach.

We approached the front desk with a tired-looking nurse checking the computer in front of her.

"We're here to see Natalia Kravets," I said.

"I don't see that name."

"No," my voice raised an octave, and I clutched at Aunt Olga's arm. "She has to be here. The EMTs brought her by ambulance a few minutes ago. Please check again."

The nurse nodded. "Ah, it just popped up on my screen. They must have just checked her in. She's in A3."

"Can we see her now?" Aunt Olga asked.

She shook her head. "The doctors are working on her now. Have a seat. We'll call you when you can go back."

We waited fifteen minutes before a doctor finally came out and said, "Family of Natalia Kravets?"

We rushed to him.

He took my elbow and moved us around the corner for more privacy. "I'm sorry. She doesn't have much time."

"Can you give us a time frame?" I asked.

"It could be hours or a couple of days. I know you were anticipating this, but it's never easy. You may go back and be with her. I'm so sorry."

Aunt Olga wailed. I tried to calm her by caressing her back, but it wasn't working. Due to all the commotion, I pinched my bottom lip trying not to make it bleed. My head was spinning, but I had to take the lead. My aunt had had enough.

"Will you keep her here or do you recommend hospice?" I asked the doctor.

"It's up to you," he said. "But I'm not sure she could handle another transfer."

"I'd like to keep her here."

"Okay, I'll have the nurses find her a room. We'll make her as comfortable as we can. Again, I'm very sorry." He turned and headed back through the double doors as the woman who was bleeding was ushered in.

A nurse put us in a small private room

while she arranged for Mother to be moved. We heard a gentle knock on the door, and someone walked in. She introduced herself as Mrs. Baker, a social worker. She brought a box of Kleenex and placed it on the table for Aunt Olga. She asked if we needed anything.

"I can't think of anything at the moment," I replied.

"May I ask what your religion is?"

"We're Christians, Russian Orthodox."

"Would you like to see a priest? I can send one to you if you'd like."

I turned to Aunt Olga. "Aunt Olga, what do you think?"

She couldn't stop sobbing. She couldn't speak.

"Thank you, not right now."

She handed me her card and left the room. "Please let me know if you need anything."

Mother was placed in a private room. When we entered, she had an oxygen mask over her gray face. She was sleeping.

Aunt Olga pulled up a chair close to Mother's bed and held her hand. Then Aunt Olga placed her head on the bed and continued to sob.

I stared out the window. "Please, God, give me strength. Please don't let Mother suffer anymore. She's had enough." We stayed for several hours. A nurse came in and told us that visiting hours were over. We had the option of staying, but I was worried about my aunt.

"I think we should go, Aunt Olga. We can come back first thing tomorrow morning." My aunt stood, leaned down, and kissed Mother on the forehead.

I held Olga's hand all the way to the car.

The drive home was silent except for Aunt Olga's weeping. I was sad for her. Mother was her only sibling, just like Aleksei had been mine. We had so much in common. Maybe that's why Aunt Olga understood me and always had a special fondness of me.

Twenty-Two

The next day, Aunt Olga and I watched Mother slowly dwindle. Her breathing grew shallower. She could barely open her eyes, much less speak.

My strong aunt was no longer strong; she was falling apart and all I could do was hold her.

The doctor said it was almost time. I called Mandy and Margo and told them if they wanted to say goodbye that they needed to come soon. They were there within the hour.

After they said their goodbyes, they took Aunt Olga down to the hospital cafeteria for coffee. She needed a break. They hugged me when they left. For the first time since we met, I felt close to them. Why did tragedy bring spirits closer? So much time wasted. What a shame. I could have been best friends with them for years.

I needed some air, so I went outside

for a short walk, even though it was freezing but stayed close to the hospital. I kept my coat open to cool my warm body. The snow crunched under my boots. It took me back to my childhood when Pavlov and I walked to school together in the snow. So many happy memories rushed through my mind of Mother teaching me to cook and the beautiful clothes she adored making me. I caught myself smiling. And then, my cell phone rang. I dug it out of my coat pocket.

"Nina, this is your mother's nurse. Can you come back here? We feel your mother is going. You'll probably want to be with her."

"Yes, I'm in the parking lot. I'll be right in." Should I get Aunt Olga and my cousins? No, I decided to go upstairs alone. My aunt wasn't strong enough. I opened Mother's door and slowly walked toward her bed. My heart pounded out of my chest. Her eyes were partially open. She stared out the window. "Hello, Mother."

She turned her head to me. The pretty scarf around her head was askew, so I gently rewrapped it around her head. She wouldn't want to die looking disarranged. I stood and waited to see if she would reach her hand out to me. She didn't. Dying and still bitter? Wow.

I walked over to the chair and pulled it close to her bed. I took her hand and held it. She didn't shove it away but gave it a little squeeze. Finally, something. Did that mean she still loved me? "Mother?" I couldn't let her go like this. I had to tell her that I loved her, regardless of how she felt about me. I didn't hate her. Why did it take so long for me to understand that?

Suddenly she gasped, then I heard a whoosh as life left her. She was gone. I'd missed the opportunity. I sobbed as I rubbed her limp hand on my cheek. Tears poured down my face onto the sheet. I stood and looked down at her. She looked relaxed, peaceful. There was the mother I knew before the Chernobyl explosion, back when we were a family.

My eyes wandered down her delicate, thin body, and I pulled the sheet up under her neck. I made sure it was perfect without a single wrinkle. As I looked at her beautiful face, I leaned down and kissed the top of her forehead and whispered, "Goodbye, Mother. I love you." The squeak of the door broke my catatonic state.

The nurse walked in.

I just looked at her.

"I'm sorry," she said.

"Thank you," I said and quietly left the room. I cried harder. I couldn't catch my breath. I clutched my hand near my heart and took slow deep breaths trying to calm myself. I grabbed my hair and fisted it, wrapping it around my hand. I took the elevator down to the cafeteria to tell Aunt Olga and my cousins the news.

As I approached, they knew. They could see my face was red and my makeup had been washed off by my tears.

Aunt Olga screamed at the table. "No. Not my sister."

Mandy and Margo stood her up and held her tight. Mandy waved me over into a group hug, weeping.

I felt numb as I drove home. I was sad for Mother. Not only because of her illness and the pain she endured but because of the grudge she'd held against me all these years. So much pointless bleakness, I prayed she was finally at peace with the demons that had tormented her all these years.

As I lay in bed that night looking at the sketch of Sasha, I was reminded of all my losses. I looked back at my past and realized I was alone. I could hear Father and Aleksei whispering to me from the grave, "It's all right, Antoniya, she is with us now." Even though I lost Mother's love with the passing of Aleksei and Father, she was still my mother. *I will always be my mother's daughter.*

The next morning, I drove to Aunt Olga's. I sat beside her on the sofa. "Do you prefer the funeral in a church or the funeral parlor?"

"What do you prefer, dear? I think it is really your decision."

"Well, I believe the reason we didn't have Father's funeral at the church was because Mother frequented it after Aleksei's passing. It was too haunting for her. We should do the same as we did for Father. I vote for the funeral parlor."

"Okay," she said still weeping. "Nina." She touched my face. "You will always have me. You will always be my family, and I don't ever want you to feel alone."

"I love you, Aunt Olga."

I called the funeral parlor, and they picked up Mother's body from the hospital. I went to her house and went through her closet to find something special for her to wear. I puttered through her garments and stopped at a fancy dress she wore only for special occasions; a soft pink, like her skin before she became ill with shiny gold buttons down the front. I reached down and grabbed the matching pink shoes. Picking up her treasured barrette, I held it up to my hair and looked in the mirror for a minute. Oh, I looked just like her. Adding the barrette to her favorite pink blush and lipstick, I placed everything in a bag and took them to the funeral parlor.

The funeral two days later was lovely. Mother looked beautiful and peaceful. I knew she was with Father, Aleksei, and Sasha in heaven. I whispered back to them that I understood.

So unlike Father's funeral, there were few people in attendance since Mother worked out of her home and didn't socialize.

While I sat in the front row, I felt a hand

touch the top of my shoulder. I turned. It was Jennifer and Mark. She whispered in my ear, "I'm here for you."

I was elated to see her. I gripped her hand tightly and held it for a few moments.

Aunt Olga, Mandy, Margo, and I drove together to the cemetery. We didn't take the courtesy limo.

The priest made a few last comments and asked if I wanted to say something.

I shook my head. I was too upset and feared the words would stick to my throat. Aunt Olga was inconsolable. Mandy and Margo comforted her. Jennifer stepped forward and clutched my hand. We all looked down on Mother's casket which slowly lowered into the cold ground.

When it was over, I turned to walk away and there he was. John.

Jennifer noticed him, too. "Want me to stay?"

"No."

She squeezed my hands, "Let me know when we can get together."

I nodded.

She and Mark said hello to John and then walked away.

I looked up at John and gazed into his beautiful eyes. He removed his glove and placed his warm hand on my cheek. I touched the back of his hand.

"How are you, Nina?" he asked.

"How do you think I am?" I replied angrily glaring in his sad eyes. "At least it's finally over." My head was spinning at the irony that I'd lost them both. I started to walk away.

He grabbed my arm. "Can we talk... please?"

I glared down at his hand then looked up. "About what?"

"Us."

"There is no us, remember?"

"I miss you so much. I dream of you every night. I want you back." His voice was soft, and his eyes glistened from tears.

I brushed his arm away, the spot suddenly cold where the warmth of his hand had been. "Right now, I'm so exhausted I can't even think straight. Tomorrow, I need to clean out my mother's house. I have to give the keys back to the property owner. I need to get my schedule back to normal at work, plus school is starting back in a few days. It's all just too much."

"Would you like me to help you tomorrow?"

"Not really, John," I said with a stern voice. "Quite frankly, I'm not sure why you're even here. You left me when I needed you the most." Tears spilled from my eyes, and I wiped them away with the back of my hand.

He dropped his chin to his chest. "I don't know what I was thinking. I'm so sorry. Please forgive me."

"I can't."

My aunt stood near the car watching us and started walking to me. I motioned for her to stop. "I'll be right there." She got in the car.

I returned my attention to John. "I have to go now. You made your choice weeks ago. As hard as it was, I've moved on and can't possibly trust you again. Best to you." I walked away briskly and got in the car. From the car window, I watched him standing there with his head looking at the cold wintry ground. As handsome as he was, I could not forgive him.

Mandy, Margo, Aunt Olga, and I met at Mother's house. Aunt Olga brought a box of garbage bags. We thought we'd donate Mother's clothes to Goodwill. I ran my hand across her beaded jewelry box, opened it, and picked out another of her barrettes, a silver one with shiny pearl beads. One of my favorites. I walked over to the bedroom mirror and pulled the top of my long wavy mane to the back and closed the barrette in my hair.

My aunt looked up and gave me a warm smile. "I'm glad you chose something of your mother's to keep."

I nodded. That was all I wanted. I reached back into the box and handed my aunt a beautiful gold barrette.

She softly smiled at it.

While I continued to go through her jewelry box, I noticed Father's antique yellow gold pocket watch. I gasped, picked it up, and held it tightly to my chest. With glassy eyes, I looked over at my aunt. She nodded her approval as I tucked the watch into my jeans pocket. My aunt gathered a few items that held special memories for her. She kept some and gave one to each of her daughters. The rest was donated.

The next day, I picked Jennifer up in Mother's car, and we went to lunch. My aunt thought it was a good idea for me to keep the car.

"How are you?" Jennifer asked as I drove to our favorite café.

I couldn't speak. Still numb from the funeral and packing Mother belongings, I drove in silence all the way. It felt like forever, but we finally arrived.

"May we please have a private table in the back?" Jennifer asked.

The hostess walked us to a private booth.

I sat down and shook my head and raised my hands to my face. "How did you know about Mother?"

"John contacted us. I didn't realize you two had broken up. He was devastated about it and called Mark. He said he learned about your mother from friends at school."

I slumped lower in the booth. "I'm confused. He's the one who broke up with me, and he's devastated?" I shook my head. "I'm sorry

I didn't contact you about Mother or John; I've been too busy taking care of her. I thought I'd wait for you to come in for Christmas break. I didn't want to bother you, and there was nothing you could do."

Jennifer offered a sad half-smile. "That's okay. I understand. Anyway, John looked so lost after you left the cemetery, so Mark and I met with him for coffee. He's truly fond of you. I think he still loves you. Can't you forgive him?"

I stared down at my hands folded on the table. "No. He left me when I needed him the most. Caring for Mother was one of the hardest things I've ever had to do; she was ungrateful to the end."

Jennifer leaned closer to the table, forcing me to make eye contact. "I know you've been through a lot, but you shouldn't be so hard on people. People make mistakes. You have a shell around you, protecting you from everyone, but not everyone's planning to hurt you; if they do, it's not intentional."

I sipped on my hot cocoa and looked out the window at nothing. "Did he ask you to speak to me?"

"No. but I think you should give him a second chance."

I turned back to look her in the eyes. "Well, that's not happening. Thanks for caring." I forced a smile. "Catch me up on you and Mark," I said as I sighed from being mentally exhausted.

"Things are great. We're talking about getting married when we graduate in a couple of years. We're living together now in a small apartment off campus."

"That's wonderful. I'm so happy for you."

"Please, Nina. Find peace with all of this and let the demons go. Sadly, your mother's death is a fresh start for you. Think about it that way if you can."

School started back up. I kept myself busy at work and at the shelter. I never saw John again, not even at the shelter. He must have stopped going. I continued to sketch fond memories of the family that I lost, even Mother.

Jennifer phoned frequently to check up on me. Aunt Olga and I still went out for lunch every month. I found myself comforting her more than ever. Mother's death had been hard on her. Mandy and Margo were away at school, so she spent evenings alone and was probably a little lonely.

Twenty-Three

The next several years flew by. I finished my classwork and began an internship at a local elementary school not far from the hospital. My boss accommodated my school schedule by giving me the graveyard shift at the hospital. Sleep was at a minimum, but I loved the kids and enjoyed the training at the school with my new mentor, Mrs. Brown. She reminded me of Ms. Babin, back in the Soviet Union, before Ukraine gained its independence.

I was always tired, but I only had to maintain the pace for one semester. I felt I could do it. I enjoyed working with the little kids; they were so sweet. They were worth the long night shifts.

One day while on my lunch break at school, I went outside to enjoy the cool fall air. I slumped under a big maple tree watching the vibrant colored leaves cascade to the soft grass.

I leaned against the tree and closed my heavy eyes and fell asleep.

I was awakened by the school principal, Mr. Clark, who tapped me on my shoulder. "Miss Kravets, please come to my office."

I stood and looked at him. With the sun behind him, all I could see was his large silhouette. I could tell by his stern voice that he wasn't happy. I wiped my eyes, but it didn't help. I still couldn't see.

I looked at my watch, it was 3:30. My heart pounded in my ears, and my hands began to sweat. Feeling ten years old again, I pinched my bottom lip and followed him to his office. My mentor, Mrs. Brown, was sitting in one of the chairs in front of his large shiny cherry wood desk.

"Hello, Nina. We were worried about you," she said in a stern voice. Her arms were crossed over her chest, and she tapped the linoleum floor with one foot. "I had such high hopes for you. I really thought this would work out, but I'm afraid that's not the case."

My heart pounded louder, and I could feel my face getting hot.

The principal sat in his large swivel chair and said, "I understand you're working long hours at a hospital, volunteering, and trying to do your practicum with us. It's too much. You were missing for hours today. Even though Mrs. Brown says you are a fine student teacher, I'm afraid we cannot have you back. What you did today is called 'classroom abandonment.' I called your intern professor, and we have all agreed that you are to leave immediately. She shared with me about your mother's passing, and for that I'm truly sorry. But I can't allow you to continue your internship here."

Tears raced down my face. Oh my God. This couldn't be happening. I stood with my hands over my face. I grabbed a tissue from his desk, wiping my tears and smearing my makeup. "Please give me another chance. I'll do better. I promise. I've just been so tired—"

Mr. Clark raised a hand to stop me mid-sentence. "Your professor would like you in her office tomorrow morning."

I continued to sob as I stood, my shoulders slouched, and I removed myself from his office. I went back to her classroom and collected my few belongings. Shame morphed into anger. I hurried out of school by passing children who called to me. All my hard work down the drain. I made it to my car before I released a scream at the top of my lungs. I needed that release, and I cried all the way home.

At home, I threw my things on the floor and reached for the closest bottle of wine. I poured myself a glass in hopes of calming my frayed nerves. I took a few gulps; it wasn't working. I paced and twirled my hair. What am I supposed to do now? Did I just ruin my chances of becoming a teacher? I sat on my couch, wrapped my arms around my body, and rocked. I slumped and stared at the black screen of my television.

The morning sun blinded me from my rumpled place on the couch. I looked down at yesterday's clothing and an empty bottle of wine at my feet. Ugh. I had to meet with my professor. Could this day possibly be any worse than yesterday? I hadn't had a hangover yesterday morning; so yes, it could. I undressed and jumped in the shower. If I was late for my appointment, things would go downhill faster than an Indie 500 car. I arrived at school with two minutes to spare and walked briskly to her office. I rapped lightly on the door.

"Come in."

I took a deep breath and slowly opened the door.

"Hello, Nina. I've been expecting you. Have a seat." She got up and closed the door and sat back down at her desk.

"Hello, Professor Morse." My eyes filled with tears. Damn those tears. Why couldn't I control them?

She handed me a tissue. "I heard what happened to you yesterday. You were so close to finishing."

I reached for a lock of hair, then forced my hand down, and clasped them together in my lap. "What's going to happen to me now?"

"I spoke to the Dean of the College of Education, and we've decided to allow you to repeat your internship in the winter semester. Right now, I want you to get some rest."

"What am I gonna do for two months?" I shredded the tissue in my hand. "I was supposed to graduate in December." I sobbed harder.

"You're lucky we're giving you another chance. I believe in you. He would have expelled you from this university if I hadn't sung your praises, insisting you'll be a great teacher someday. I'll find another placement for you next semester. Hopefully you'll graduate in the spring."

This was a nightmare. I watched her turn to her computer and begin to type. I guessed I was excused. This was her way of saying you can leave now. I rose from the chair, opened the door, and left. I drove to the shelter to care for the animals. Maybe I could find some peace there.

"Hi, Nina," the director said. "How are you doing? Your eyes are swollen. Have you been crying?" She looked at her watch. "I thought you were student teaching."

"I was, but it didn't work out for me this term." I wiped a tear from my cheek with the back of my hand as I looked down.

"Oh, I'm so sorry. Does that mean we'll be seeing you more here?," she asked with a soft smile. "We can always use your help."

"Yes, I'll be here more at least until the new year. I love caring for the animals." Thank

God, somebody wanted me.

"We loved it when you and John came. I don't see him anymore. Are you still together?"

I shook my head.

"Sorry about that. You were such a beautiful couple." She paused as if hoping I'd tell her what happened to us.

I stood in silence.

"Well, I'm glad you're here. The animals will be happy to see you more."

"Thank you." I went to the back to walk a few dogs and clean out their kennels. It helped me get my mind off my devastation from school. A cute little dog was so excited to see me, she jumped into my arms, wagging her tail and licking the salty, dried tears from my face.

I phoned Aunt Olga and we met for lunch the next day. I told her what had happened.

"Nina, I'm so sorry. We've all been through so much. You don't deserve any of this."

"I'm okay. Just devastated. I could have graduated in a couple of months. Now I have to wait." I glared out the window. "How are you doing? How are Mandy and Margo?"

"They're wonderful. They both finally got good jobs. As you know, they're back living with me, which is nice. I enjoy the company. They're thinking about renting an apartment together."

"That's great."

Teardrops filled her eyes. This time I comforted her. I placed my hand over hers that was resting on the table. "You miss Mother, don't you?"

"Yes, very much." Tears slid down her cheeks. I could see the anguish in her face. The lines on her forehead were more prominent. Her fresh pink flesh was pasty white now. Mother's death had aged my aunt.

The next couple of months went by quickly, and Christmas was upon us. I worked more hours at the hospital which allowed me to purchase gifts for my aunt and cousins. Mandy and Margo had rented their own apartment in the city close to mine.

My cousins were hosting Christmas this year. That was great for Aunt Olga. She needed to rest and be pampered.

I phoned my aunt Christmas morning.

"Hi, Aunt Olga. How are you doing? Merry Christmas. I'd like to drive you to Mandy and Margo's. Is that all right with you?"

"Merry Christmas to you too, dear. And yes, that would be lovely."

"I'll pick you up at noon."

I dressed and wrapped my last gift. I put the gifts in a big colorful Christmas bag. I got in the car and started to drive. Shoot. I forgot the cranberry sauce. Sometimes I thought my memory was slipping. The sauce was homemade. I loved to put a vanilla bean in the cranberries while I watched them pop on the stove. The smell was sweet and glorious. Cranberry sauce was my favorite. I turned around and dashed back to the house for them. Where was my mind?

When I picked her up, Aunt Olga didn't look well. Too gray and thin. I didn't want to bring it up due to the holiday, but I made a mental note to talk to her about her health another time.

When we arrived at my cousin's apartment, they greeted us at the door with hugs.

"Nina, how are you?" Margo asked. I handed her presents and asked if she could place them under the tree. Mandy helped Aunt Olga with her coat.

"I'm fine," I said. "Work is pretty good and I'm still volunteering at the shelter. I brought you some cranberry sauce."

"Mm. It smells wonderful, thank you," said Mandy.

"How are you both doing? Your apartment is lovely," I said as I scanned their living room.

Mandy noticed me looking around. "Well, this is the best we could afford right now. You know how expensive rent is in the city."

"Yes, I've been in my studio for a little over four years now. I'm grateful my landlord hasn't raised my rent. However, he's turned off my electricity several times when I didn't pay on time. Dinner smells wonderful, can I help?"

"No, we're pretty much set. We're just waiting on the turkey. Have a seat," Margo said. "Make yourself at home."

I walked in further. Their home was decorated in a contemporary fashion. Fluffy red accent pillows complimented the white couch. The furniture had clean straight lines. The rectangular coffee table was glass with a shiny brass stand. Two matching end tables flanked either side of the couch. A large television hung on the wall along with pictures of red poppies. It was nice. Their apartment was a little bit bigger than mine, and each had her own bedroom. The dining room table which aligned with the living room was white-washed oak with matching chairs. There was a beautiful bright red poinsettia on it for a center piece. The table was already set with white plates and shiny silverware on top of a beautiful red tablecloth with matching napkins.

I walked toward their Christmas tree. A beautiful Douglas fir, just like the ones we had in my old home in Chernobyl before Father passed. I brought my face close to smell it and inhaled a big whiff. The piney odor was fresh, sweet, and refreshing. It brought back fond memories of when I was a little girl. Mother and Father had decorated our tree with our hand-made ornaments and a bright red skirt lined in gold trim coiled around the stem. Mother had made it. I heard my father whisper what a wonderful artist I was. I looked around to see if anyone else heard, then realized they hadn't heard a thing.

The presents I brought to Mandy and Margo's had been placed nicely under their tree. I looked a little closer and could see a few presents with my name on it. Wow. How times had changed between all of us. In a good way. I was happy to have them as family.

We gathered at the table and enjoyed our delicious dinner. We made small talk about school, jobs, and the weather. After dinner, I offered to help with the dishes. I walked through the swinging door and was blinded by the crisp white cabinets and countertop. They were shiny and clean. Margo was in deep conversation with her mother in the other room, so Mandy and I were alone washing and drying the dishes.

"Mandy, I'm a little worried about Aunt Olga," I whispered.

"We are too. She hasn't been the same since Aunt Natalia's passing. Can you do us a favor and check on her more? We're doing the same."

"Of course," I said. "Do you think she is sick or just depressed?"

"We've been encouraging her to go to the doctor, but she says she's fine and can't take the time off of work."

"Okay, I'll take her to dinner in the next

few weeks and push our concerns."

"Thank you for being a part of our family." She gave me a big hug.

While we embraced, I looked over her shoulder. "What's this, Mandy? You made my favorite Christmas desert? Are you getting soft on me?" We both chuckled. It was my favorite Chocolate Salami.

Twenty-Four

The next day my phone rang. It was Jennifer. "Hey, Nina, I'm back in town. Lunch today?"

"Yes, I have so much to tell you."

"Me, too," she said, her voice monotone.

"You okay?" I asked.

"Yeah, we'll talk when I see you. Shall we meet at our favorite café?"

"Hey, there's a new café across the street called the Blue Moon. Let's try something new."

"I could use a fresh change. Sounds good."

"What? I don't think I heard you correctly."

"Nothing. I'll see you at noon."

I walked in the café and spotted Jennifer sitting in the back staring at her coffee. She looked dazed and unsettled.

She saw me coming and got up to hug me. Her beautiful green eyes weren't glistening the way they used to.

"Hey," I said while I sat down. "How was your holiday?"

"Okay. How was yours? I thought about you a lot yesterday without your mother, father, and brother. How'd it go?"

"Good. Mandy and Margo are still being nice to me. They cooked dinner at their new apartment. Their place is adorable."

"How's your aunt."

"Not so good. We're all a little worried about her. She hasn't been the same since Mother's passing. I think she's depressed."

"Sorry to hear that. She was always so strong."

"I know. It makes me sad. How are you doing? You look a little sad to me. How's Mark?"

Her face quickly looked stone cold. She twisted her napkin over and over.

"Oh, no. Problems?"

She slouched in the booth. "A little. He's been drifting apart from me for some time now."

"What? Why?"

"I'm not sure."

"Ugh. Do you think he's cheating on you?"

"I'm not sure. He didn't come home with me. He wanted to stay in Michigan the whole break."

"Well, that's unusual, isn't it?"

"Yes, he always splits his time on breaks between Michigan and New York. This time, no."

"Have you spoken to him about your concerns?"

"A little; he doesn't say much. I think he's bored with me. I'm scared he's going to leave me."

"Well, maybe this break will be good for both of you. Maybe he'll miss you. You never know."

"Enough about me. How are you doing?" Jennifer said.

"Better. I have a new internship at a different school. I'll be doing my student teaching in second grade. Then I'll graduate in the spring."

"That's good. I was a little worried about what happened to you with your first practicum. We'll graduate at the same time."

"Yeah. I can't wait. I keep on forgetting that your program is longer than mine."

"Shopping tomorrow?"

"I have to work. I'm doing a double shift, too. How about the next day?"

"Sure."

We finished our salads and soup and left the café. We gave each other a hug by our cars.

"Listen, Jennifer. What's meant to be is meant to be. Look what happened to John and me. If I can survive, so can you. Mark may not be your serendipity."

My student teaching started, and I had to go back on the graveyard shift at the hospital. I stopped volunteering at the shelter. I couldn't take the chance of falling asleep on the job again.

My new teacher-mentor was great to me. She encouraged me to think outside the box. I created many lessons for the children that we both enjoyed.

"You're a natural," said Ms. Garner. "The students are really taking a liking to you. They're so excited about learning. In my entire teaching career, I've never seen so many hands raised when you ask questions. If you keep this up, I'm recommending you for a position here next year. We'll have a few openings."

"Really? What grade levels?"

"Kindergarten, first grade, and fifth grade. Do you think you might be interested?"

"Yes, I thought I wanted kindergarten, but I like second grade. So, a compromise could be first grade. I'll think more about it when I finish this practicum."

I promised my cousins I'd check on Aunt Olga more. I called a few weeks after the holiday and picked her up on a Saturday evening and took her to dinner. She stumbled as she walked to the car, and I clutched her arm to keep her from falling. My fingers felt like they touched bone with a thin layer of skin under her long sleeve sweater. No muscle, No firmness.

"Are you all right, Aunt Olga?"

She looked up at me, her face was drawn

and pallid, her skin hung loose on her jowls like melting ice cream.

"Yes," she replied, irritation ringing in her voice. "I'm fine. The girls said the same thing last week. Why's everyone so worried?"

I looked down at her hands. Her veins were sunken, and they appeared to be scaly like a fish. We arrived at the restaurant and ordered. I probed further. "You don't look healthy. Will you please go to the doctor? Humor me. I'll take a day off from student teaching and take you."

Aunt Olga shook her head. "No, thank you, Nina. I appreciate your concern, but I'm fine. I'm just a little tired."

I noticed when she picked up her fork that her hand shook, like a tremor. Her posture was off, and she was stooped. We didn't speak much. She stared at her plate, motionless. My thoughts raced trying to diagnose her. Except for the hand shaking, she had signs of depression. I'll talk to one of the pharmacists tomorrow at work about her symptoms.

When I dropped her off at home, she sat in the car going through her purse.

"Can't you find your keys?" I asked.

She shook her head and started to panic. Saliva crawled down a crease in the corner of her mouth on the left side. A drop landed on her coat. She took a deep breath.

I tapped her shoulder and asked for her purse. "Let me see if I can find your keys." I reached inside and pulled at the pockets. They weren't there. Did I see her lock the door when she left? I offered a reassuring smile. "Let's see if your door is unlocked. Maybe you just forgot to lock it, and the keys are in the house." Holding her elbow, I helped her from the car and up to the front door. It was unlocked. I motioned her to enter first and followed behind. I'd closed the door and started to walk to the living room when I stepped on something hard. I looked down, and there they were. The keys.

"See, here they are. It's okay now," I said lightly, pretending I wasn't gravely concerned. There were too many signs that something was wrong. I didn't remember seeing that many symptoms that something was wrong at Christmas. "Are you all right?"

"Yes, dear." She walked to me and held my face with her warm, fragile hands. She gave me a weak hug and walked me to the door.

"I'll give you a ring tomorrow to see how you're doing. Lock up behind me, please."

My head was spinning all the way home. I called Mandy and Margo and told them about my visit with Aunt Olga. "I was a little concerned at Christmas. We spoke about that. Remember, Mandy?"

"Yes, I do. We just saw her last week and noticed her getting worse."

"I'm working at the hospital tomorrow. I'll speak to one of the pharmacists about her symptoms."

"That would be great. Thank you, Nina."

"I'll call you on my break."

I spoke to Dr. Davis, the head pharmacist, about my aunt's symptoms. He didn't hesitate to say it sounded like Parkinson's disease. I wasn't familiar with that disease, though I'd heard of it.

"It's a disorder of the central nervous system that affects movement, like her posture, her slow walking, and her tremors. Nerve cell damage in the brain leads to this disease."

"Is there a cure?" I asked.

"No."

"Is there medication to control the disease?"

"Yes, she should be seen right away by a physician. If she does have Parkinson's, there are different stages. The sooner it's diagnosed, the sooner she can be treated."

"What kind of doctor should she see?"

"A neurologist."

"Can you recommend one, please?"

He did. During my break, I called my cousins and explained the conversation I'd had with Dr. Davis.

"I knew it was serious," said Margo.

"Well, we won't know for sure until you get her to a neurologist." I gave them the information. "Let me know if you need my help taking her."

Twenty-Five

My cousins finally were able to get Aunt Olga to the doctors. Sadly, Dr. Davis had been correct. It was Parkinson's disease. Fortunately, she was in the early stages. Mandy and Margo tried to convince her to move in with them and get a bigger apartment, but she refused. We decided to each take turns visiting her every couple of days and phoning her daily. This felt like a repeat of Mother's illness.

My student teaching was almost finished. I had one more week and would graduate. What a wonderful experience I'd had with Ms. Garner and her students.

One day when I arrived at school, the students had a wonderful surprise for me. They'd each made me a beautiful goodbye card, and we had ice cream sundaes to celebrate my graduation. They stood in the front of the room and read their handwritten notes. My eyes filled joyful tears. I would miss them.

The principal stuck his head through the doorway. "A little birdie told me you might be interested in teaching with us next year."

I looked at Ms. Garner. She gave me a wink and a smile.

I started to shake from the excitement. Was this for real? I couldn't believe it. I sobbed happy tears. I ran over to her and gave her a huge hug. "Thank you so much. This never would be happening without you." I blew kisses at the students and thanked them for being so good. I walked over to the principal and shook his hand. "And thank you sir. Yes, I'd like that very much."

"What grade level would you like to teach?" he asked.

"What's available?"

"We have an opening in first grade. Mrs. Cohen is retiring."

"Oh, my, yes. I'd love that."

"It's yours. Congratulations."

The students started screaming and cheering.

I swiped my tears with the back of my hand. Finally, something good for me. I couldn't wait to call Jennifer, my cousins, and my aunt. I said my goodbyes, packed my things, and gleamed all the way home.

Mandy and Margo insisted on taking me out with Aunt Olga for a celebration.

I could see Aunt Olga's disease had progressed. She was no longer lucid. It was painful to watch her eat. Due to her shaky hands, she continually missed her mouth, and her food plopped down, falling from her fork to her. Mandy tried to help, but Aunt Olga wouldn't allow it. She pushed Mandy's hand away. All her daughter could do is scoop up the droppings with her napkin.

While Margo took Aunt Olga to the ladies' room to clean her up, Mandy and I spoke of what to do.

"Clearly she can't be alone anymore," I said softy, knowing how sensitive an issue this was. "At this point, she needs to be in a nursing facility so she can be watched and cared for twenty-four hours a day. What do you think?"

Mandy teared up.

I placed my hand on her shaking hand. "I know it's difficult. I've always thought of Aunt Olga as a second mother. She's always been so good to me. You know how tarnished my relationship with Mother was by our personal events. But your mother continually looked after me. Did you know we met once a month for a bite to eat?"

"No, she never shared that."

"Well, it was our little thing. I don't think Mother knew either. That's how special your mother is to me. She liked to check on me, and

I enjoyed seeing her. I never felt alone because I knew I had her." I changed the subject. "We can go look at some living facilities together if you'd like."

"That would be nice. Thank you."

Margo and Aunt Olga came out of the ladies' room all freshened up.

It was difficult finding a nursing home for Aunt Olga in the city so she could be close to us. She only had a small retirement from the department store where she worked and Social Security — which didn't amount to much. The places we visited in her price range were awful. The rooms were small, and they stunk like moth balls.

We finally found Aunt Olga a nursing facility in Brooklyn close to her home. It was a little far for us but was the best we could do. When we approached her about moving, it was difficult. She didn't want to leave her precious home of over twenty years to move into a single room in a nursing home. We had no choice. She couldn't be left alone anymore.

We agreed to meet one Saturday. The day we packed her things, she tried to fight us but didn't have the strength. She only managed to frown at us a few times which broke our hearts. The crinkles in her pale face increased as she tried to speak. Margo wept the entire move, so Mandy and I took over.

"Just comfort your mother," I said.

"We've got this."

We collected her favorite things like her best garments and photos. Mandy fetched the sketches I made all those years from the walls in the living room and her bedroom. "She loved your sketches so much, she had them framed."

With eyes full of tears, I looked at her and nodded.

We packed our cars, and it was time to get Aunt Olga into a vehicle. Mandy and Margo took her by her elbows and walked her to the car. Aunt Olga put up one last fight. We couldn't believe it. She kicked, screamed, and even tried to bite Mandy. It was an awful scene from the front door to the car. They finally managed to get her in their car, and we followed each other to the facility.

By the time we got there, she had no fight left. As we walked her in, we boasted about how beautiful it was and how she would meet other residents and get involved in fun activities.

She just glared forward, ignoring us.

After she had been checked in with the director, we arrived at her room. It was small but had a window which faced the courtyard so she could see all the seasons as they came and went. She'd like that. Mandy and Margo laid her on the bed so she could rest. The morning had been rough on her. They unpacked her things while I hung the sketches on the walls around her bed so she would never forget her beautiful family.

"Goodbye for now, Aunt Olga. I love you and will visit you soon." I blew her a kiss from her bedroom door. I looked at Mandy and Margo as they lay on either side of their mother and blew them a kiss. "We'll touch base next week."

They blew me a kiss back.

I wanted to be the first to leave. It was best to let my cousins say goodbye in private.

I drove home very sad. Life was hard. So much sadness. People like Father, Mother, and Aunt Olga worked hard only to become ill, crumble apart, and die an early death.

At home, I poured myself a glass a wine and watched a romance movie trying to get my mind off Aunt Olga. However, I was grateful she was in a safe place.

Graduation Day. I'm finally crossing the stage and getting my college diploma.

Jennifer had graduated from her school a week prior to mine so she was home and attended. It was glorious to see Mandy and Margo. Ms. Garner also came. Sadly, Aunt Olga wasn't well enough to attend. Mandy and Margo promised her they'd take lots of pictures.

As I crossed the stage listening to my friends and cousins cheer me on, I bit my bottom lip. I looked out in the audience pretending Mother, Father, and Aleksei were out in the crowd. I felt my face turn red as I fought the tears wanting to roll down my face.

"I knew you could do it," I heard a whisper in Aleksei's voice. I turned, but of course, he wasn't there. I caught Jennifer's eye as I almost cleared the stage. Her face was red, too, and gave me a wink.

We all went out to celebrate my success that night. Mandy and Margo treated everyone to a couple bottles of champagne. "Congratulations!" everyone said in unison.

The bubbles from the champagne tickled the tip of my nose and made me cough. Everyone chuckled and wished me well.

I began my summer working normal hours at the hospital and the animal shelter while I waited for fall to come so school will start. Jennifer and I hung out in the evenings barhopping and shopping. She and Mark were permanently broken up. She didn't speak much about it, and I didn't push the issue. I could tell she was disappointed, but I admired her positive attitude of moving on. She waited to apply for a job because she wanted to have a couple of months relaxing, reflecting, and partying.

Once a week I checked on Aunt Olga. I brought her fresh flowers whenever I visited. She still remembered me. Her speech was slurred, so she didn't speak much. She was incontinent but refused to wear adult diapers. The nurses continually had to change her bed. They shared with me they didn't mind; she was adored by the staff.

One day while working at the hospital, I met a new pharmacist intern. He introduced himself as Jim Tucker. He turned out to be a nice guy and super kind to me. We ate lunch a lot with the gang from the pharmacy, but he began looking for tables for two for us to have more privacy. He reminded me a bit of John. Not bad on the eyes. Tall and slender, fair skinned, with sparkling light brown eyes and wispy ringlets of blond hair. He was quite a gentleman and had a bright future as a pharmacist. Everyone liked him. I liked him, too, but wasn't sure I was ready to date again.

I just wanted to hang with Jennifer for the summer. She liked frequenting the bars in the evening. It wasn't my cup-of-tea, but I went out with her. She loved to dance and liked to drink a lot; therefore, I was usually the designated driver.

"Come on out here on the floor," she shouted to me while surrounded by a few guys that she was dancing with.

I wasn't confident enough to dance. Then I saw a tall handsome blond walk through the crowded dance floor straight toward me. Jim.

"Hi, may I sit with you?" His caramel-colored eyes lit up the room.

"Sure." I scooted over to make room at the small table.

"Hello, Nina. How are you tonight?"

"I'm good, Jim. Do you come here often?"

"Not really. As you know I'm not from here." He did air quotes with his fingers. "I'm just doing my internship in the Big Apple."

"Oh, that's right. I forgot. You grew up and went to school in North Carolina. Sorry about that."

"Do you come here often?"

"Not really." I turned to Jennifer. "See the pretty blonde dancing with everybody out there?"

He turned to look at the dance floor and glanced at her. "Oh, yes, I see her." His eyes quickly came back at me.

"That's Jennifer. She's my best friend. She just graduated from University of Michigan. She had a bad break up, and I think she's letting loose." I chuckled.

"Yep, it looks like it. At least she's having fun. Why aren't you out on the dance floor?"

I felt the heat creep up my neck and light my face on fire. I hoped it was dark enough he couldn't tell. "I don't know. I'm not comfortable dancing."

"I bet you're a great dancer. Do you know how pretty you are?"

I bit my bottom lip. "Thank you." I looked away.

"You're kidding, right? Everyone thinks you're beautiful."

"No, they don't." I reached for my hair but quickly stopped myself.

"I'd ask you to dance, but I'm guessing you'd turn me down. How about a drink instead?" He pointed his chin toward the bar. A very nice chin indeed.

"No, I can't. I'm the designated driver."

"Not even one glass of wine?"

"Okay, I guess." I pressed my hand against my thigh to still it. "I'll have a glass of Chardonnay, please."

"I'll be right back."

He walked over to the bar.

I quickly pulled out my mirror to check my makeup and hair.

He came back with my wine.

I sipped it slowly. I was grateful the bar was dim. Could he tell how nervous I was? We turned to the dance floor and watched everyone dance.

"Nina," he said turning back to me. "May I take you out some time?"

I looked down and bit my lip, then I quickly stopped, hoping he didn't see. I looked up at his soft brown eyes. "I don't think so. We work together, and if something should happen it would be uncomfortable seeing you all the time."

"Wow, do you always think about relationships as failures?"

"No, no, I don't mean it that way. I just… well, I'm not sure. Can I think about it? You kind of caught me off guard."

He leaned over and whispered in my ear.

"Sure, I can wait. I'm a patient man."

I leaned back, sucked in a deep breath, and had a sip of wine. I had to get out of there before I made a big mistake. "I think I'm gonna grab my friend and head out now. Thank you for the wine."

He grinned, revealing that perfect smile—too perfect. "You're welcome. I'll see you Monday at work."

I nodded, grabbed Jennifer's purse, went to the dance floor, and pried her out of the nightclub. I walked her to my car, holding her up with her arm over my shoulder.

She stumbled and giggled all the way to the car.

I opened the car door and helped her in.

As I was driving her home, she attempted a conversation. "Who was that cutie you were talking to?" she asked, slurring her words,

"Someone I work with."

"He was hot for you?"

"Let's not talk about it." I wasn't having a conversation with a drunk while concentrating on my driving.

"Why not?" she said with a grin, her head resting on the car's head rest.

"No point. You'll never remember the conversation. Breakfast tomorrow? I'll call you in the morning as a reminder in case you forget."

By the time I got her home, she was one hair short of comatose. I wrapped her limp arm around my neck and half-dragged her into the house. With the lights off, I could barely see. I crashed my knee into a table but made it to her room. Dropping her on the bed, I took her shoes off and gently swung her legs around, so she lay straight. I placed a quilt over her.

Even though it was dark, the moon from outside the window glowed on her pretty face. She looked relaxed, but I knew her well enough to know she was troubled about something. Probably Mark. I'd thought she was okay about the breakup, but maybe not. I'll find out in the morning. I quietly let myself out.

Twenty-Six

The next morning, I phoned Jennifer before picking her up and taking her to our favorite café. She looked a little ragged. She ordered coffee, and I ordered iced tea and an egg sandwich.

"Do you remember last night?" I asked.

"Not really. Did I make an ass out of myself? I feel awful."

"You look awful. And no, you didn't make an ass out of yourself, but you were clearly drunk and dancing with every single man in the bar."

She gasped and placed her perfectly manicured fingertips on her forehead and shook her head.

"What's all this drinking about? Is it Mark? You never told me why you broke up. I didn't want to pry, but now I'd like to know."

She began to sniffle and wiped her eyes on a napkin. "He found someone else. I think he was getting bored with me." She stared into her coffee mug.

"Oh, Jen, sorry, I'm surprised. I thought he was perfect for you."

"Me, too. I'm still in shock."

"Clearly, but you need to move on just as I did with John. I still think of him but..." I shrugged.

A slight smirk twisted up one corner of her mouth. "Did I see you with a handsome blond last night? Or did I image it? My head's still a little fuzzy."

I snickered. "That was Jim from work. He's a pharmacist intern. We hang out for lunch at the hospital."

"Really. Do you think he likes you?"

"Well, he asked me out last night and bought me a drink."

"I told him I would think about it. But probably not. I want to focus on my new teaching job in the fall, and I enjoy spending time at the shelter. I'm so glad you had me fill out the application."

"You still go there?"

"Yes, I adore it there. I guess I'm an animal lover at heart. They can't break your heart." I changed the subject, "Jen, you need to find a hobby, something positive to do so you won't keep thinking about Mark. Don't turn your sadness into drinking." My mind flashed to Pavlov's father beating on him after he got drunk. Just then I heard Father whispering,

"You've got to stop her from drinking." I shook my head. I couldn't believe what I'd heard. Did Father know Pavlov's father was a drunk?

"What were you just thinking about?"

"Nothing worth repeating," I said. "Maybe you should start finding a physical therapist job. You need to stay busy."

"I want a few more weeks before I get a job. I'm still mourning."

"I understand. I'm bringing home an application from the hospital. They're always hiring physical therapists. I think you'd be a good fit there."

"Okay, but I'm still taking a few weeks not being employed. Maybe I'll bury myself in a few novels first."

"Perfect idea."

Jennifer and I still went to bars on the weekends, and I remained the designated driver. I was worried about her, but thought it was best to simply look out for her. I hoped, when she got a job, it would take her mind off Mark.

Sometimes when we were out, we'd bump into Jim. He was persistent in asking me out, but I wouldn't give in. My life was full enough. I was getting ready to quit my hospital job. School was starting soon, and I wanted to prepare my classroom. I didn't need any distractions.

Jennifer finally got a job at the hospital. I was so happy for her. We went out the following weekend to celebrate. We both glammed up and went to her favorite bar.

When we walked in, I spotted Jim sitting with a friend at the bar. Jennifer and I walked up to him and his friend.

"Hi, Jim. How are you?" Everyone introduced themselves.

Jennifer looked a little smitten with his friend.

Finally. I was glad to see her interested in someone else.

"Would you like to join us?" Jim asked.

I looked at Jennifer. She nodded.

Jim moved one seat over so Jennifer and I could sit next to each other. "I heard you were leaving the hospital," he said with a grin.

"Yes, next Friday is my last day."

"Maybe you should let me take you out to celebrate." He came close to my face and whispered, "No excuses this time."

Our eyes were locked. I felt heat warm my ears. I cleared my throat and took a special interest in the scratches in the gleaming wooden bar. I wrapped my hair around one finger.

He lifted my chin with his gentle warm hand and gave me a long, fixed stare.

I was paralyzed. How could I say no to all that attraction? I let out a deep breath. "Yes, okay. You win. I'll go out with you." I looked over at Jennifer, but she already had a drink and was occupied with Jim's friend. "May I have a glass of wine?" My mouth was suddenly dry. I swirled my tongue around my lips trying to get some saliva so I could swallow.

"Bartender," he said loudly.

One looked at him.

"Can I have a glass of Chardonnay for this pretty young lady?"

As I looked at the bartender, my eyes caught a familiar face on the other side of the U-shaped bar. But I couldn't place it. He was handsome with dark features, poker straight dark hair, and very dark eyes. When he smiled at someone he was talking to, dimples popped out on each cheek.

"Nina? Nina?" Jim's voice echoed in my ear. "Where were you right now? I was speaking to you. Did you see someone you know?" He glanced in the direction I'd been looking.

"No, I'm sorry. I didn't mean to be rude. I was just thinking."

"About what?"

I shrugged and quickly changed the subject. "When will you finish your internship?"

"The end of the year."

"And then what? Will you go back to North Carolina to practice near your family?"

"I'm not sure yet. I'm taking it one day at a time."

I looked back at Jennifer. She was gone. I scanned the bar, and there she was, on the dance floor with Jim's friend.

"Do you want to dance, too?"

"Oh, no, thank you."

"You don't like to dance?"

"Not really." I took another sip of wine hoping it would calm my nerves. Why was I always a mess with men? We made small talk for a couple of hours, and I began to relax. He was kind and gentle.

The evening finished with me taking Jennifer home again—drunk.

My last day of work was Friday, and Jim took me out that night to celebrate. "I hope you like Italian."

"I love it." I couldn't believe it. We went to the same restaurant that John and I went too on our first date. Coincidence? I started to open the car door, but he took my arm.

"Let me get it for you."

I watched as he briskly walked in front of the car and then to the door on my side. He opened it and put out his strong hand to assist me.

"Thank you."

He had great manners. He opened the front door of the restaurant, and we strolled in. We were seated right away. Thank goodness it wasn't the same table as my first date with John. I needed to clear my head.

"May I have a glass of wine?"

"Of course," he said as he motioned for the server. "This pretty lady will have a glass of Chardonnay, and I'll have a scotch neat."

Then he turned his attention to me. "Do you like working at the hospital?"

"Yes, the hospital job has helped me pay my bills and put a roof over my head. I'll be forever grateful. Jennifer has a job there now as a physical therapist."

"She appears to be the opposite of you. She's a little wild." He chuckled.

"Nah, she's just going through a rough patch. Her boyfriend broke up with her. I think she thought they were getting married. I feel bad."

"Nina," he said softly. "Enough about her. Tell me more about yourself. You never talk about your family. All I really know is that you're from the Soviet Union."

I stared into his buttery soft eyes for several seconds. I decided not to hold back. I told him everything but kept it short, all the way through Mother's death and Aunt Olga's illness.

He listened intently without interrupting. "Wow, that's quite a story. I'm so sorry."

"I'm fine, thanks. I'm looking forward to teaching now. With every chapter that closes, another one opens. Right?" I lifted my glass.

He raised his, too. "To a beautiful woman who knows the meaning of perseverance."

Our glasses clinked, and we sipped. Dinner was lovely, and Jim drove me home. He helped me again out the door and walked me to my door.

"Thank you for a lovely evening."

"I hope we can go out again," he said.

"I'd really like that." He took my hands and gently pulled my arms behind me, pulling me closer to his tall physique. Our bodies touched. I looked up at him. Then he placed his right hand on the back of my neck with his fingers. His thumb caressed my warm, flushed cheek and then my moist lips. He didn't ask. He leaned in and planted a warm, soft kiss on my heated lips.

I closed my eyes and embraced the moment. I pulled my hands free and wrapped them around his waist. He parted my lips with his warm, juicy tongue and swirled it with mine. I got lost in all the sexiness of it. After a couple of minutes, I pulled back and wiped my bottom lip with the back of my hand.

"Would you like me to come in?" he asked.

Oh God, I've got to get away before I give in. "Way too soon for me. Sorry."

He inclined close to my face and pulled my hair behind my ears and whispered in my ear, "You're worth the wait. Goodnight, Nina."

Twenty-Seven

School started again, and I was elated to meet my new students. I peered through the glass window in the door while they waited outside, perfectly organized into a straight line. I opened the door. They were adorable. I pretended that I didn't notice them scanning me up and down by pointing my finger while I counted each one.

One student whispered to a friend loud enough for me to hear, "I wonder if she is our teacher."

I chuckled and let them in. "Good morning, class. I'm your new teacher. Please place your backpacks on the hooks along the wall and go to your desks, which have your names on them."

They did. They were very quiet. Probably a little nervous like myself. They each sat down and looked straight at the board.

"Now, my name is Miss Kravets. Can you all say, 'Good morning, Miss Kravets?'"

"Good morning, Miss Kravets." Their piping voices were music to my ears. I'd made it. I was officially a teacher.

"Let's start off getting to know one another. I'm going to start with this row to the left going down. I would like each of you to stand up and tell us your name and what you did for the summer."

They did, and it was glorious to learn about each one of my students.

"It was lovely getting to know a little bit about each of you. Along this wall is our daily schedule that includes lunch and recess." As I pointed to a chart on another wall. "These are our classroom rules which you will follow, or you will be making a trip to the principal's office. Let me read them to you as you follow along." I read them slowly and looked back at them to make they weren't confused. I didn't see any frowning faces.

"Does everyone think they can obey these rules?"

"Yes, Miss Kravets," they said in harmony.

We had a perfect day. I was lucky to have such a nice class.

That evening Jim called to see how my day went. I told him it was perfect.

"Do you want to go for quick bite to eat? I'm so proud of you. I know it's a weeknight, and you're probably tired from your day, but you probably don't want to cook dinner for yourself."

"Actually, I can't. I'm visiting my aunt in the nursing home."

"Oh, how's she doing?"

"The same. She still can't talk much, and her memory is compromised along with her bladder. It's so sad."

"Okay, will I see you this weekend?"

"Looking forward to it."

I raced to my car and visited my aunt. I arrived at her room, gave a gentle knock, and walked in. She was staring at the television, which was turned off. "Hi, Aunt Olga. It's Nina. How are you?"

She glanced at me.

I wasn't sure she even recognized me. As I walked to her, an acrid smell made me pinch my fingers over my nose. I looked down, and there was a yellow puddle under the chair.

"How long have you been sitting like this?"

She just stared at me. She looked like she wanted to talk but couldn't. Her eyes overflowed with tears.

I bent down and gave her a soft kiss on her pasty cheek and wiped away the tears with a Kleenex. "It's okay," I said. "I've got this. Let me get you up." I pried her from her chair. Her nightgown was stuck to the chair with the dried urine. It was so disappointing to see her in such bad shape. The lack of care was killing me.

She had a walker, so I placed it in front of her and assisted her to the bathroom so she could shower. I removed her clothes and walked her to the shower chair. I sat her in the chair and turned on the water. I waited for the water to turn lukewarm. When it was at skin temperature, I rinsed her, cleaned her with a washcloth, and rinsed her again.

I reached for the shampoo and asked her to lean back. Her long, stringy hair was coarse, and gray. It was hard for me to see her like this. She had been a woman of class but was now helpless. I kept smiling at her, despite the anger building in me. This was inexcusable. While I massaged the shampoo in her scalp, I told her about my first day teaching. I could see a little glisten in her eyes. I think she understood and was proud of me.

After drying her off and brushing her hair out, I put a fresh nightgown on her. I placed her in bed, then cleaned the chair and the floor.

"Would you like the television on?" Her eyes widened. "All right, I'm going to scroll through the channels slowly, and you wink when you want me to stop."

She did. It was an old romance movie, An Affair to Remember. I was so much like her. We were both hopeless romantics.

"I'll be right back." I marched out of her room and headed straight for the nurses' station.

"Can I help you?" asked one of the nurses.

"Yes, I would like to speak with whom-ever is in charge tonight," I said sternly.

"Is there a problem?"

"Absolutely."

"Maybe I can help."

"No, thank you. Who's in charge?"

"She's at dinner and will be back in half an hour."

"Call her now, please. I'll wait right here." I could feel my heart racing and face heating up. A few moments went by.

A large ugly beast appeared and intro-duced herself. "How can I help you?"

"For starters, you can take proper care of my aunt who I found sitting in a puddle of urine and staring at a blank television. I had to clean her. I'm so disappointed in this place that I'm going to speak with my cousins. Perhaps we can find a better home for her." I couldn't believe how curt I was.

"Well, we've been short staffed for sev-eral weeks."

"I don't give a hoot," I said abruptly and stormed off. I knew my blood pressure was going through the roof, but I had to calm myself back down before going back into my aunt's room. I took a few deep breaths. It would do no good for her to see me upset.

I sat back down with Aunt Olga and made small talk for about an hour. It was getting late, so I assisted her to the bathroom, helped her brush her teeth, and have one last potty visit. I helped her get in bed and tucked her in. "Don't worry; I'll speak to Mandy and Margo about this."

She lifted her shaky hand up to my cheek and touched it.

I phoned Mandy on my drive home from my cell. Margo was home too so they put me on speaker.

I told them how I found her. "We've got to get her out of there."

"The last time I was there, it appeared she wasn't getting good care. Her food was untouched, and she smelled as if she hadn't showered in days," said Mandy.

"Okay, back to square one. Let's do some research and get together this weekend and make some visits elsewhere," said Mandy. "Thank you, Nina. You've been such a good friend to us. My mother loves you, and we are so happy you are part of our family."

"Your mother was always so good to me."

After doing research, we narrowed it down to three nursing homes. We took a drive Saturday morning to explore each one. Then we went to lunch to discuss it. We all agreed on one, which was close to me. It was the cheapest and Medicare covered some of it. That was fine. She'd watched over me all these years, and it made me feel good to return the love.

Our plan was to move her the following

weekend. We were lucky a room was available on such short notice.

Jim and I went out for a bite to eat and then a movie. I was exhausted both physically and mentally from teaching and taking care of Aunt Olga's issues. However, I went anyway.

And once again as a perfect gentleman, he walked me to my door. "Nina, can I come in for a night cap?"

"I suppose, but you better be good," I said with a childish giggle.

"I'll be good," he said with a sly grin.

Inside, I poured us wine. His fingers lingered over mine when I handed him the glass. We both took a sip. It warmed me, or was his presence doing that? I turned on some music, my favorite Marvin Gay, and we placed our wine on the coffee table. He tugged me close to his strong body, he clinched my hand between our bodies and placed my other hand behind his back. We slow-danced for a few minutes to the soft music.

Then he caressed my face gently with his hands. He looked in my eyes. "Close those baby blues for me," he whispered.

I felt him giving me warm kisses on my eye lids. I took a deep breath. He sat down on the couch and pulled me toward him, so I straddled his strong thighs, facing his beautiful face.

We started unbuttoning each other's shirts staring into each other's eyes. His hands raced down my shirt. When he finished, he opened my shirt and gazed at my bosom. I was wearing a sheer black lace bra and matching panties. He pulled my shirt off one shoulder at a time, kissing the tops of each. My shirt fell to the floor.

Now it was my turn. I ran my hands through his soft curly hair and kissed his forehead. I gently pushed him all the way back, so his head rested on the back of the couch. I fisted his shirt and pulled it off his shoulders. He quickly removed his arms for me. I leaned down as I swirled my tongue around one large, hard nipple while my hand caressed the other. I peeked up at him. His eyes were closed, and his breathing was hard and loud. His hands rested on my waist as his thumbs caressed me. It tickled a little.

I moved up to his neck, nibbling his ear. We kissed. His lips were warm and soft, and our tongues stroked each other. My body was on fire. I rested my hands on his strong shoulders while his hands roamed down my spine. I couldn't stop moaning; I arched and leaned.

He reached for my breasts and began caressing me. My eyes were closed when he moved one hand to my back and undid my bra. I gasped. He flung it to the floor. He pulled me closer so he could kiss my breast. My fingers were running through his curly locks.

I leaned down to kiss the top of his head.

His hands raced to my black bikini. He

moved the crotch so he could put his fingers inside me.

I watched and rhythmically moved up and down. My hand ran down his pecs. Between my legs, I could feel his hardness. I unsnapped and unzipped his pants and slid my fingers over his throbbing penis. We played for a few more minutes, studying each other's faces. I couldn't take the teasing anymore. I took a deep breath and let the ecstasy flow like a river. I couldn't catch my breath. It felt so good.

He quickly leaned toward the coffee table to fetch a condom from his wallet. He pushed his underwear down slightly with one hand so he could slip it on. Then he maneuvered around so he could slide his cock in. I moaned. He placed his hands on my hips and pushed me up and down.

I leaned back with my arms crossed behind his neck. My long hair was touching his thighs. He loved it. Suddenly he gasped. It sounded like an explosion. The rhythm slowed down. We were both breathing loudly.

I rested my head on his shoulder.

"That was wonderful, Nina."

I slid off him and sat beside him on the couch. I reached for my wine.

He took my hand and kissed it. "You're so beautiful."

Twenty-Eight

Weeks had gone by. My teaching was going smoothly, and my relationship with Jim was heating up. We spent many evenings cooking and making love at my studio. Aunt Olga was in a good nursing home, and I kept in touch with my cousins. Jennifer was not so good. I was seriously worried about her drinking and partying. Now that she was making good money, she went out almost every night.

One Saturday morning, I phoned her.

"Hello?" she mumbled.

"Get out of bed. I'm taking you out for breakfast. I'll be there in an hour."

She hung up on me.

I drove over to find she was still in bed. "Get up." I found some jeans and a t-shirt and threw them at her while she still lay in bed.

She only rolled over and groaned.

"I'm not leaving so you better get up."

She was sleeping in her bra and underwear and her clothes she had on the night before were laying on the floor next to her bed. Her face had remnants of make-up. After much prodding, she finally got up and got dressed and I hauled her to my car.

She said nothing on the way to the restaurant.

I looked over at her. Her face was colorless, and she looked like she'd lost a lot of weight. I watched her slap a hand over her mouth. She was going to hurl. I quickly pulled over, ran to the other side of my car, and opened the door. She leaned over and vomited on the cement road. I held her head with my hands, pressing hard on her forehead to alleviate the nausea. That's what Mother did to Father when he spewed over the toilet. Jennifer spit out the last of her puke.

I knelt and pushed her hair back. "Feel better?"

She nodded.

"What am I gonna do with you?" I kissed the top of her head and then drove to the café. She only wanted coffee, but I ordered her some eggs and toast. I hoped the smell didn't set off another bout of nausea.

"Let's talk," I said.

"I don't want to." She slumped in the booth, a pout on her face.

"Well, when I was feeling down about my family issues you were there for me. Now it's my turn to be there for you. Are your partying habits about you missing Mark?"

"Yes."

"Well, have you heard from him at all?"

"No, nothing," she said as she stirred her coffee.

"Have you thought about phoning him and telling him how much you miss him?"

"No."

"Can I be honest with you? You look terrible. I'm worried. You need to find some positive tools to get over him. Drinking is not a tool. It's a crutch."

"Easier said than done." She sipped her coffee.

"How about some motivational CDs you could listen to in your car? You also need to eat more. You're too thin."

"I can't. I don't have an appetite."

"Try." I gestured at her food. "Eat some toast or these eggs, please. Aren't your parents worried?"

The look on her face said that was a no. "They work a lot, and we all work at different times, so I rarely see them."

"Maybe you should start dating, and I mean date. Not these one-nighters. What about the hospital? Is there anyone there you may be interested in? That's where I met Jim."

"No, I'm too busy to socialize there."

She shook her head, and some confetti fell from her hair.

Where the heck had she been last night?

"Remember when you had me fill out an application from the shelter? It was the best thing I ever did. Find your passion and go for it. Hey, I know you like to read. Get some books you can get lost in, go out and read in a coffee shop. Can you do that for me?"

"I'll try." Her blood shot eyes filled with tears and rushed down her pale face.

I dropped her off at home after she promised to find something besides alcohol to occupy her mind. I wasn't letting this go.

Thanksgiving was approaching, and I adored my students. My class was perfect. I enjoyed making holiday projects with them. Jim and I were going strong.

Jennifer, on the other hand, was a bona fide alcoholic. She lost her job, and her parents finally put her in rehab. Hopefully she could get the help she needed there. I felt like I had failed as a friend. The facility was far, I could only visit on weekends.

Mandy and Margo enjoyed hosting Thanksgiving and Christmas. They had boyfriends just like me, so they invited Jim and me over for Thanksgiving.

Jim and I picked up Aunt Olga and drove to their apartment. It was difficult. Jim had to carry her. Everyone introduced themselves. The men hung out in the living room watching football while the women were in the kitchen cooking a traditional Thanksgiving feast. Aunt

Olga could only sit, but we made sure to include her in our conversations.

Dinner was great, and everyone got along beautifully. Sadly, my cousins had to take turns feeding their mother. She could no longer feed herself. She only stared forward with glassy eyes. No one made a big deal of it. We knew how much pride she had.

Due to the long weekend, I drove up state to visit Jennifer. This was my second visit to her. I waited in the freshly painted visitors room which had couches, chairs, tables, and fresh flowers. She came around the corner as perky as ever. She looked great. She looked healthy, her hair was shiny again, her face had some color, and she'd put on some weight. She had life in her again. She rushed up to me and gave me a huge hug.

"Hi," she said in a squeak. "I'm so glad you came. Let's sit over there." She pointed to a small table by the window.

"You look beautiful," I said. "How are you doing?"

"Much better. This was the best thing my parents ever did for me. I'm doing a lot of activities and am learning skills to control my addiction."

"What kind of activities are you doing?"

"Yoga, meditation, going for long walks. I made some friends in here, so it's nice in the evenings when we have free time to sit around and talk, or I'll go to their little library and read."

"That's wonderful." I clutched her hand. "I'm sorry I failed you. I tried to get you interested in something other than alcohol and partying."

"You didn't fail me. You've always been here for me. I wasn't ready to listen. How are you doing? How's Jim?"

"He's good. We went to Mandy and Margo's for Thanksgiving. We picked up Aunt Olga."

Her face showed her concern. "Oh, how's she doing?"

"Not good. Her disease is eating her up. It's sad and painful to watch her slowly diminish. When are you getting discharged? Hopefully soon?"

"Yes, the week before Christmas. I'm so excited to start over again. I'm gonna get a job, save some money, and get my own apartment. Those are my goals."

"I'm happy for you. That sounds wonderful."

"How are your students?"

Her question put a smile on my face. "Wonderful. I have a great class, and I love them all." We talked for hours. It was great seeing her.

Christmas break came quickly. I hugged each of my student's goodbye and wished them happy holidays. Jim had one last week of his internship and Jennifer was discharged from her rehabilitation center.

On the last day of Jim's practicum, I took him out for dinner to celebrate. He'd been offered a pharmacist position at the hospital, so this was a double celebration. However, I'd sensed something different all week. Maybe the feeling was due to all the excitement.

While sitting down at dinner, I asked. "Is everything all right? You seem to have a lot on your mind, or are you just excited about graduating?"

"Nina, I have to tell you something." He then took a big gulp of his scotch. "I accepted a job back home in North Carolina."

"What?" I gasped. What the hell? He was bailing on me? Stay calm, Nina. I sucked in a big gulp of air. "What are you talking about? You already accepted a position here." Heat rushed through my whole body. I pinched my bottom lip; I didn't care if he saw. "You waited until now to tell me this? How long have you known?"

"I found out last week."

"Does the hospital know?"

"Yes, I told them today. I'm sorry. I didn't know how to tell you."

"Did you interview over the phone?" My lip trembled, and I bit down harder on it to keep my tears at bay. "What about us?"

The silence filled the space between us.

He concentrated on his glass, spinning it slowly around in his fingers. I wanted to grab it and throw it across the room.

His silence was his answer.

"Oh, I see. That's interesting because I thought we were fully committed."

"I don't know. We can try a long-distance relationship if you want, but that kind of relationship rarely works."

I couldn't bring myself to weep. I felt anger building. I felt like he'd just punched me in the stomach. "What am I supposed to do about my ticket to North Carolina? I was supposed to come home with you for Christmas, remember?"

He kept swirling that damn glass.

I pressed my hands together under the table so I wouldn't hurl his scotch across the room.

"You can still come if you want," he said.

Was he afraid I'd make a scene?

"For what?" I shouted.

Other patrons turned and looked.

I didn't care. I stood, grabbed my purse and coat, and stormed out of the restaurant. I hailed a cab and cried all the way home. There, I sat on the couch with a glass of wine and sobbed all night.

I'd lost so much. Father, Mother, Aleksei, Sasha, and Pavlov. And almost lost Jennifer to her alcoholism. Now Jim.

Christmas was sad for me without Jim. Our relationship had ended so abruptly I was still in shock. My heart was broken again. Maybe I wasn't meant to be in a relationship.

I spent Christmas with my aunt and cousins as usual. At least I had them. However, Aunt Olga really didn't recognize us anymore. It was a very sad Christmas. I could see it in my cousins' faces. With the realization that her mind was completely gone, reality set in for us that she was only existing.

The rest of my time off from break, I spent at the shelter. Caring for animals always made me feel tranquil.

Jennifer was home, and I spent some time with her too. I talked her into volunteering with me.

Twenty-Nine

The next few years I taught and volunteered at the shelter. I wasn't interested in getting in a relationship.

The animals at the shelter were my closest friends. If only people could be as reliable as them. Even the children at school, as darling as they were, did not offer me the same unbridled affection that I received from the dogs and cats at the shelter.

While on spring break, Dr. Best, one of the veterinarians approached me. "Nina, I can't help but notice your dedication here. You have a natural talent with the animals, especially the dogs."

It was rare for anyone to shower praise on me, and I wasn't sure how to respond. I nodded as I placed a pair of identical collie pups back into their newly cleaned cage. "Thank you."

"I have a situation that you might find interesting," she continued. "Would you consider traveling out of the country to help other dogs and cats?"

Out of the country? My mind immediately rushed back to Ukraine. Did she know that I wasn't a native American? "Ugh, I don't know. Where and what would I be doing?"

"Ukraine," she said. "Chernobyl, to be exact."

My heart stopped. A lump formed in the back of my throat. I gave a slight nod.

"You've heard about the explosion in Chernobyl in the 80s, haven't you? Well, animals were left behind — people's pets."

She was still talking, but the buzz in my head blocked out everything she said. The animals? Of course, I knew. My little Sasha had been one of them. And the ones Aleksei had had to shoot. Were there still some left?

"Nina?"

My name brought me back to the present.

"Are you okay?" Dr. Best said. "You seemed to have drifted away."

"Oh, yes, ma'am. I'm sorry. You were saying?"

"Two men with backgrounds in nuclear energy and emergency response started this program in the Exclusion Zone in Ukraine. They were there for the plant, but when they saw these sad animals, the descendants of the dogs and cats that were left behind from the explosion, they wanted to help. They developed a program to assist the animals. They enlisted some veterinarians to help start the program. It's a non-profit organization called, Clean Futures Fund."

I widened my eyes and took a deep breath. All I could think of was Sasha.

Dr. Best continued, "It's a five-year program. This summer will be the second year. I'm on the team and would like to recruit you if you're interested. You'd be a catcher and assist with some surgeries. Do you think you might want to join the team?"

Could I do that? Go back to my home? What would it look like? Would it bring back too many sad memories of losing Sasha, Aleksei, and later Father, and then even Mother?

I gave a hesitant nod. "I ... I think so. Yes, of course. I would love it. Did you know that I'm from Chernobyl?"

She shook her head. "I'm so sorry. I knew you were from the Ukraine because I reviewed your application when you first started volunteering. But I didn't realize you were from Chernobyl. Maybe it would be too hard for you?"

I stooped down and rubbed the ears of a little beagle pup that stared up at me with big brown eyes.

"I was there when the plant exploded. My family fled to New York." I knew my voice sounded off, scratchy in the back of my throat.

"Oh, my God. I'm glad you got out. Maybe this is a bad idea for you. I can find someone else." She seemed to be dismissing the invitation.

I had to speak up. "I think I can handle it, might even be a little cathartic. I was only a child and had to leave my precious dog, Sasha, behind. I still think of her often."

She looked at me skeptically. "The dogs and cats that were left behind have been breeding for years, and now there are approximately five hundred roaming around the plant. Wild wolfs have started interbreeding with the dogs. The previous plant workers go back every few days to feed them. When we learned of this, some of the veterinarians here wanted to join the program. We go twice a year to spay, neuter, and vaccinate them and figure out a way to consistently get them food and water."

The more I heard, the more I felt called to do this. What did I have keeping me here? This could be good for me, maybe even patch a few internal wounds. Suddenly, I was excited. I nodded. "I'm on board and thank you for thinking of me. When will you need me?"

"This summer. You'll have to commit for the month of June."

School would be out. The timing couldn't be more perfect. "I can definitely do it."

"If you're sure you can handle it, we'd love to have you. We'll start a social media page for you to get funding to pay for your flight, hotel, and meals."

As I drove home, I wondered, Would I find a descendent of Sasha? Then I could bring it home. The excitement was building in me, and I couldn't wait to learn about this program. I'd be a part of this life-saving team.

School ended, and I was looking forward to my trip to help the animals. I hugged each student goodbye and wished them well for the summer. I was glad all I had to do was concentrate on my trip.

I phoned Mandy and Margo and told them I'd be leaving in a few days.

They were thrilled for me.

"I'll phone you as often as I can." I wanted to see Aunt Olga before I left even though she no longer knew who I was. Her Parkinson's disease was only getting worse.

I stopped by the day before I left. I walked in. She was propped up on a chair next to her bed. I leaned over and gave her a kiss on her cheek. "Hi, Aunt Olga. How are you today?"

She only looked up at me.

I sat on the edge of her bed and began babbling about my trip. I could tell she did her best to understand me. She would gaze into my eyes, and the creases on her forehead would appear stronger. I walked over to her dresser where her hair bush was and brushed her long coarse white hair. I could tell she liked it, her wrinkles would soften, her face beam, and she'd close her eyes.

It was such a nice day that I took her outside in her wheelchair. I found a bench near a beautiful maple tree, so we could sit and enjoy the smells of summer and relish the warm glowing sun on our faces.

When it was time for her dinner, I took her back in the dining area where she sat with other residents. An assistant came over, sat next to her, and began to feed her.

I leaned down, gave her a kiss on top of her head, and said my goodbyes. I whispered in her ear, "I'll see you in a month. I love you."

While packing, I couldn't stop thinking about Sasha. Would I find her descendents? I couldn't believe this was happening. I was going back to my childhood town. I couldn't wait to see what it looked like. The Exclusion Zone, too. It'd been many, many years since I'd seen my homeland. Packing for the trip, I was only allowed two suitcases, so I did my best with what clothes to bring, deciding to bring mostly jeans and t-shirts. I packed a dress just in case I made some friends, and we went out someplace nice for a dinner.

I scanned my tiny apartment and walked over to my wall with the sketches of Father, Mother, Aleksei, and Sasha. I gently peeled off the tape that attached them to the wall, placed them in a stiff folder, and packed them, along with new paper and pencils. I might have time to draw some memories of Chernobyl.

I went to bed early so I could catch my 6:00 a.m. flight out of John F. Kennedy Airport. I couldn't sleep; my stomach was in knots. I was excited yet nervous. I lay in bed twisting my hair and gazing at the ceiling. I tried to get the visions out of my mind: how Aleksei had killed himself and, of course, Sasha wandering the streets trying to find me. I hoped she made some furry friends. I hoped she had a peaceful passing.

Before I knew it, my alarm went off. I hadn't had any sleep. I quickly showered, grabbed my bags and passport, and took the bus to the airport. I caught up with Dr. Best and some of the other volunteers. We introduced ourselves and boarded the plane. It was impossible for us to get seats together, so we were scattered around the aircraft. I didn't care. I just wanted to get there. I sat in the back of the plane and peered out the window.

My anxiety was taking over, and my excitement was turning to fear. I thought of my life events, lessons, and the passing of my family. Was I doing the right thing by going back to where it all began? Would it give me closure so I could heal from my internal pain?

Thirty

I'm wakened from sleep on the airplane by a light tap on my shoulder from the flight attendant.

"Wake up, dear. We're getting ready to land. You slept the entire flight, so I saved you a bagel. Eat it quickly before we land." She winks as she hands it to me.

I'm famished and gulp it down. I stand and look at the backs of some of the team members sitting several seats ahead of me.

As we disembark, Dr. Best takes a head count at the luggage pickup area downstairs.

I look around the airport; nothing seems familiar. But why should it? I was so young.

We pile into a van and head to our hotel in Kiev, a town south of Chernobyl and an adjacent to a small town called, Pripyat, where many workers of the nuclear power plant, had lived before the explosion.

We finally arrive. I gaze out the window of the van at the hotel. It's pink with white shutters and a glass front door. It looks adorable and quaint. When we enter the lobby, the floor tiles and walls are chipped and need a total remodel. Ugh. What did I get myself into? I don't know why I was expecting the Ritz.

While in the lobby, Dr. Best shouts out who we'll be rooming with. I'm happy to get Alice, a short, slightly overweight, giggly girl. She always has a smile on her pudgy, bright-pink face. I can't wait to get to know her better.

We get our keys and walk up a few flights of stairs as the hotel doesn't have working elevators. I manage to pull my heavy suitcases going up backwards, one step at a time. Alice and I open the door to our room and walk in. It has two single beds with light blue bedspreads and matching sheets. The tiny bathroom has black and white cracked tiles on the walls and floor and a single stained, wall-mounted sink. Not very impressive but doable. We collapse on our beds.

"I can't believe I'm still tired," I say. "I slept the entire flight here."

Alice giggles. "I'm excited about tomorrow."

"I'm a little anxious; I'm not sure what to expect." I reach for my hair but quickly pull my hand down. "I can't wait to meet the rest of the team. Let's unpack and head downstairs for dinner. I wonder what the other vets and team members are like."

After unpacking our clothes in a six-drawer dresser and a small closet with only four hangers, Alice notices the sketches I hung on the wall near my bed. "What are those drawings? They're beautiful."

"Those are mine. They're sketches of my family," I say as I lay on the bed and gaze at them.

"Wow, you're really talented."

Alice asks who they are, and I tell her a little bit about my family. Not the personal details, though. I don't know her well enough to disclose that information. "Let's head to the lobby now and see what's going on."

There are more team members, and everyone introduces themselves. We decide to walk to a restaurant a few blocks away and chat to get to know each other. A few team members haven't arrived yet, and we're told we'll meet them in the morning. I hope the restaurant has my favorite meal. I look through the menu. Yeah, they do. I'm so excited to taste the Stroganoff here.

Dr. Best stands to make a toast. "Thank you all so much for coming all the way to Ukraine to help the feral descents of Chernobyl. You're all beautiful people. It's going to be a great month. We'll have our first briefing with the head of this program tomorrow morning. His name is Dr. Paul Bonder. Have a restful night."

I'm not paying attention. I'm scanning the menu for my favorite chocolate dessert. Nope. No such luck on desert. We finish eating and walk back to our rooms.

The next morning, Alice and I get ready and go downstairs for our continental breakfast. From what I can tell, there are about twenty of us. Two vans pull up, and we quickly finish eating and pile into the vehicles.

As we get closer to Chernobyl, some volunteers are pointing and commenting on some of the animals they see, mainly dogs and cats. I press my nose up to the window as we drive on. My heart races. Stray dogs are barking at our van and running behind us. I look back and clutch my chest. It's sad to see the strays, but I know I'm there doing something good for them. I hope to find a dog that looks like Sasha, some sign that she survived.

We arrive at our destination and meet in a premade clinic in a small old, grungy-looking building in Pripyat. It looks very Third World. I walk in a circle and see a few tables with intravenous solution bags already hanging. There are blankets with an indescribable stink, perhaps mold on the floor along a wall that's chipped and peeling. I wondered if perhaps it was the best they could do.

Dr. Best gathers us in one area of the clinic and asks us to sit on the blankets.

I hesitate before I choose one that looks

less grungy and sit.

"Hello, everyone," she says. "First of all, thank you again for coming. You'll be performing lifesaving efforts on the dogs and cats of Chernobyl. Most of us know each other from yesterday, but we do have some newcomers. Let me introduce to you two of our veterinarians that arrived late last night. This is Dr. Walsh and Dr. Bonder."

A man with a deep voice speaks up. "You can call me Dr. Paul or just Paul."

"Dr. Paul is lead for this program," Dr. Best continues. "He's worked closely for two years with the founders of Clean Futures Fund."

At first, I'm not paying attention. I'm still scanning the room, trying to figure how this will work. When I look up, I catch my breath. Heat warms my face, and my ears begin to tingle. Did she say Dr. Paul? I shake my head and squint my eyes. He looks so familiar. I feel like I've met him before. But where? He has the most beautiful, shiny, dark eyes I've ever seen. They're almost jet black. He brushes a slender hand through his dark brown hair and smiles. Dimples. Oh my. My body starts to get warm. I lift my hand to grab my hair, but instead I place my knuckle in my mouth and bite down.

Dr. Paul stands and scans all the faces in the room. For a second, his gaze settles on me. "Hello, thank you all for coming and donating your time. We appreciate you being here. Let me explain what's happening over the next few weeks. Every morning we'll have a briefing. You'll be assigned to a team. If you're not comfortable on that team, please come to me, and I'll place you somewhere else. We'll stop for lunch, have another briefing, and then continue our day. We'll finish every day at 4:30. Make sure you clean your area and meet at the vans by 5:00. Today we'll set up and get everyone trained for their positions. Dr. Best will split us into three teams. We'll have a catch team, a surgical team, and a postoperative team. Our goal is to catch the feral dogs and cats and spay or neuter them. Then we'll set them free. This is so they will pass naturally. We're hoping our five-year plan will stop the breeding."

"Thank you, Dr. Paul," says Dr. Best. "When you hear your name, please go to the area I direct you to."

I finally hear my name and am placed on the catch team.

Dr. Best comes over and explains what we'll be doing. She assigns someone who came out last year as the lead.

He directs us outside.

We go stand by the vans.

Our new leader speaks, "My name is Josh, and we must all stay together. Before we drive to the Exclusion Zone, I'll explain the rules you must follow to stay safe. Please do not wander off. Wild wolves roam with the feral dogs and cats. They're mainly afraid of us, so we shouldn't have any problems, but we must be very careful. We'll each grab a bag of food and put it in the back of the van. The food is how we lure the animals to come to us. You'll place a small amount in your hand or on the ground near you, bend down, and allow them to come up to you. They're hungry, so it shouldn't take much to catch them. Most of them are friendly because the ex-workers of the plant come back every few days to feed them and care for them. You'll be given a lead to drape gently around their necks. We have crates for them in the back of the vans where we'll house them to take back to the clinic. That's it. Any questions?"

I look around. No one has any questions. I have plenty, mainly what am I doing here? I decided to lay low and watch the others to get an understanding of their techniques.

As we get closer to the plant, I feel sweaty and a little dizzy. I grab my stomach and look out the window, hoping no one can see how I must look. I take deep breaths and bite on my lip to calm myself and reduce my anxiety.

We're entering the Exclusion Zone or the dangerous zone. Dogs and cats are all around us. How many are there? There must be dozens. It's so surreal. The dogs are barking at the vans. Some have their ears curled back and their tails between their legs, running the other way. Some are unsure of us. Others are jumping up and down and barking as if they're excited to see us.

Before getting out of the van, I look out the side window at the plant. A scene of that horrific night, the night that changed my life forever, flashes before me. A huge ball of fire appears as the plant erupts in huge, ugly explosion. Me, screaming for Sasha who never comes back.

Alice touches my shoulder. "Nina, are you all right? We're waiting for you outside."

I get up and rush outside, leaning against the side of one of the vans for support. My knees feel weak. I'm not sure they'll hold me up. One of the dogs comes right up to me and places his front paws on my thighs. I bend over to pet him. He licks the side of my face. It's like manna from heaven. I feel my strength coming back.

Josh walks over to me and wipes my cheek with a bacterial wipe. "Nina, try not to let them lick you. They're full of radiation, remember?"

I nod. I must remember that.

"Put your gloves on," he says.

We walk ten to fifteen feet apart from each other, almost like a chain. We grab the easy ones first. Even some of the cats are starved for attention. When the van is full of the furry ferals, two of our team members drive them back to the clinic while the rest of us catch more.

As we start to get closer to the plant, I see broken homes afar. I see pieces of people's lives: broken pots, a wire bed frame, a family photo hanging on a wall. Everyone was not as lucky as I was to escape. They either didn't have the financial means, or their family members were already stricken with illness, and they couldn't bring themselves to leave their loved ones.

I bite my lip. What was I thinking coming here? This might be too much for me. I have four weeks of this? I keep taking deep breaths while catching each precious pup and some kittens. As I work, I try to find a dog that looks like Sasha. Nothing so far.

The animals are so needy, yet so beautiful. Even as mangy and unkept as they are, some are happy to see us. Their tails don't stop wagging. A few actually show us their teeth, not in anger, but as if they're smiling.

I think of Aleksei and what he endured when shooting these fur babies. It's sad that there are so many here, but that means many escaped the bloody cruelty of the guns of the Soviet military. At least I can be positive about that.

When we finish our day, the van takes us back to the clinic. We caught over twenty fur babies. The clinic looks completely different. It's no longer a pale, boring, little room. It now looks like a surgical suite, albeit primitive, of warm, kind people loving each animal. Some volunteers are on the floor, petting the animals to gently wake them from the anesthesia or holding the smallest animals cradled in their arms like babies. Some fur babies weep and howl. Others look dazed and confused.

The vets are still performing surgeries on

the last batch of animals while the rest of the volunteers are cleaning up for the day. What a great experience. However, I'm still conflicted about spending the many days I committed to this project. My stomach aches with worry.

When we're ready to leave, we make sure all the pups and cats were safe in crates for the night, and we drive back to our hotel. While dressing for dinner, Alice asks if I'm okay. "How are you doing, Nina? You seemed a little quiet today. I know it's our first day, but I found it exhilarating."

"Me, too. It just brought back a lot of memories."

"Like what?"

I hesitate and try to slow my pounding heart. If I'm rooming with her, I guess she should know my circumstances. "Well, I wasn't going to say anything to anyone. Dr. Best knows, because she brought me here and I volunteer at a shelter in New York where she works. That's how I know her. I grew up in Soviet Union. Right here in Chernobyl. We left the day of the explosion to go to New York to live with my aunt. We had to start over. I lost my dog and my brother here over the crisis, and then later my father and mother due to cancer."

Alice sucks in a deep breath, places her hand over her mouth, and sits on her bed. "No wonder. This must be so hard for you. Why did you come?"

"Many reasons. To face the guilt of leaving my dog, Sasha, that's haunted me my entire life. For the experience. I thought it might provide some healing for me. Most of all, I hope to find a descendant of my beautiful Sasha to take home."

"Wow, that's a lot." She sits down next to me, squeezes my hand. "Let me know if I can help you get through this."

I appreciate her concern. "Please don't say anything to anyone. I don't want anyone to think I can't handle it here." My fingers instinctively fly to my hair. "I just need some time to sort this out." Even if I'm not sure I can.

"No worries." She stands and wraps me in a big bear hug. "Let's head downstairs to meet the group and go out to dinner."

"Okay." I take one last look in the mirror from the bathroom, finger-comb my hair back, and place the barrette from Mother's jewelry box in my hair.

We meet everyone in the lobby and get in the two vans.

I sit next to Josh. "You did a good job today, Nina. Did you enjoy your first day?"

"I did, thank you. I know this will be a great experience, and I feel fantastic about helping the animals of Chernobyl. What a wonderful program." I bite my lip and look out the window. Taking a deep breath, I turn back to him. We chat all the way to the restaurant.

Dinner is fun. Everyone is laughing and talking about their first day, telling inventive stories of how they lured the animals out of hiding spots. It's nice to hear tales from the people who work in the clinic. Perhaps I can assist there one day. For now, I'm happy to stay outside and look for a piece of my Sasha.

I look over the long rectangular dining table and catch Dr. Paul looking at me. He has this quizzical look on his face like he's trying to place me. I quickly look down and glance at my plate which has a few bites left on it. When I look back up, I meet his gaze.

He lifts his beer and gives me a nod.

I nod back, feeling my face flush and my ears getting warm. I haven't felt this way in a long time. I assume he's with Dr. Walsh. They arrived at the same time, and I've caught her gazing at him a couple of times today. Why not? They're both single. But then, why is he giving me the eye? I must be imagining it.

I still can't figure out why he looks so familiar to me.

Thirty-One

The next morning, we head out again. My stomach is in knots, but I stick close to Alice seeing that she knows what's going on in my mind. While looking at the plant, I try to remember where the bridge that Pavlov and I frequented was located. I remember the front of the plant faced the bridge. I position myself at the front gate and turn around and scan the horizon. No bridge. The dead trees are much taller. Perhaps if I walk in a path directly away from the plant, I can find it. There it is. As I get closer, a cool breeze washes through my body. It's bone chilling. I look ahead and see a faint silhouette of Palov and me sitting under the broken bridge looking up at the stars. I see tiny Sasha playing with her toys on my lap.

As I move closer to the now barely recognizable crumbled bridge, a tear runs down my face. This is where I last saw Sasha. I look down to see if I could find one of her toys. Nothing.

Alice walks up behind. "You okay?"

I shrug, trying to shake off the memories. "Yes, it's just very eerie to be here. This is where I played with my best friend on cool summer nights and where I last saw my little Sasha."

Alice wraps me in a bear hug, and we walk away from the broken bridge. She's good at hugs. "Let's get some more animals," she says, then chuckles. Two dogs, who are clearly related by their size and markings, run up to us. I bend and give them some food from my hand and wrap my lead around one of their necks. The other, wiggling with glee, jumps into Alice's arms. They seemed starved for attention and food.

"Remember, no kissing them," I say.

Alice holds her dog tightly and laughs all the way back to the van. We had another great day catching the dogs and cats.

A week goes by, and I am feeling stronger and stronger. I still can't stop perseverating about Aleksei and Sasha, but I hold my head high. I enjoy catching the animals and knowing how much we're helping them.

Every couple of days some of the ex-workers of the plant, those that couldn't evacuate due to personal circumstances beyond their control, come by with food. They stay a bit and talk to us, telling stories of how the explosion destroyed this town and events that happened afterward. Events like shooting the dogs. I can't listen. I walk away.

One day, I get separated from the team while trying to catch this adorable little brown doggy with white spots. He keeps running from me as if he's playing. He waits until I get within reach of him, then he takes off like a bat-out-of-hell, only to turn and sit, looking at me with a catch-me-if-you can grin on his face. I'm not paying attention to how far away I am from the others. I give up, thinking if I turn back, he'll follow me. I start to turn when I hear something behind me. A soft growl. When I turn completely, I'm confronted by a gray wolf, his ears flat against his head and his sharp white teeth barred.

My body begins to shake uncontrollably. Don't make eye contact. I try to remember the instruction Dr. Best gave for these situations. My mind is completely blank.

He takes three steps closer.

I stand frozen. I can't move to even grab my hair.

He paces around me in a circle several times, getting closer.

I stand motionless and hold my breath. Without moving my head, I scan the area. No one's around. My mind screams at me. Do something. I look at the dusty ground and see a large stick three feet to my side. Three feet? It might as well be three miles.

He circles closer.

I slowly move toward the stick.

The wolf moves nearer. He smells like burned rubber. He takes a stand in front of me, inching his way closer, one slow step at a time. He's practically on top of me.

I forget about the stick. I back up, very slowly, still not making eye contact.

It's as if he's pushing me into the woods so he could show me off to his friends. Then, they'd have a slice of me for dinner.

Shaking, I try to see how far away I am from the team. Would it do any good to scream? I must be completely out of earshot. Would a scream only make him attack? I slowly walk backwards for about thirty minutes — which felt like hours — as he follows me closely. I don't know where I am, where I'm going, or what's behind me that I might bump into or trip over. Not good. Tears run down my face. My mind spins. I nip at my lip and taste the blood and the sting from my salty tears landing on my lip. I don't have a good plan. Hell, I don't have any plan. How am I going to get out of this mess?

I turn slightly and see something familiar. A Ferris wheel. Why does it look so familiar? I remember now. Pavlov and I were gonna go to the amusement park there. It was supposed to open the day after the explosion. New plan. Ha! A plan. I'm gonna head toward the rides. Can I make it? Can I hide in one of them until I'm found? The metal of the cars would protect me.

Who am I kidding? I can't outrun a wolf. He'll attack at my first sprint. I can almost feel those fangs piercing into my neck, the weight of his body as he tackles me to the ground.

Suddenly, I hear a van. Someone's honking the horn like a fast drummer pounding on a drum. Thank God. As it gets closer, the wolf turns and runs off. The van quickly speeds up to me, and someone leans over and shoves the door open from the inside. I jump in and wipe my tears off with the sleeve of my shirt. I look over. It's Dr. Paul.

"Nina, are you all right?" he says, worry clearly on his face. "Josh radioed me and told me you were missing."

At first, I can't even speak. I lean over and clutch the front of his shirt with my head pressed on his chest. I feel his hand caressing my back. As my heart rate subsides, I realize what I'm doing and quickly pull away. "I'm fine now that you're here. I was so scared. I was trying to catch a little dog, but it kept running from me. Before I knew it, I was confronted by that wolf who was trying to force me into the woods. Thank you so much for finding me."

His dark eyebrows furrow. "Always remember to stay with your team."

"Look!" I shout and point to where the rides are, a rusty Ferris wheel car sits on its side. "It's that little pup. Do you see it?"

Dr. Paul follows my eyes. "Yes, let's try to get it." He speeds the van forward to get as close as we can.

I shout out the window. "Come here, little baby."

It crawls from its hiding spot under one of the go-karts.

I open the door and tap my lap.

He comes running. He jumps right up on my lap with his tail wagging a mile a minute. He keeps running back and forth between Dr. Paul and me, going from lap to lap. We can't stop laughing. He finally settles on my lap.

I watch as Dr. Paul stares, almost like a trance, at the debris from the carnival that never happened.

"Are you okay?" I ask.

"Yes," he said as he points to the rides. "That's the famous amusement park of Pripyat that never opened due to the plant explosion."

I look down, petting the dog and saying nothing about my upbringing in Ukraine. We drive back to the team, and Alice comes running.

I jump out, and she picks me up and twirls me around.

"You're shaking," she says. "I'm never letting you out of my sight again. Are you all right?"

"Yes, I was being followed by a wolf. It was awful."

She pulls me back and stares at me. "Oh, my God. What happened?"

I explain the entire horrid ordeal while

trying not to lose it all over again.

"So glad you're back and you're safe," she says with tears filling her eyes. She gives me one last squeeze.

We pile into the vans and head back to the clinic for lunch. The same yummy sandwiches and cool beverages don't go down as easily as usual as Alice tells everyone my wolf story.

Dr. Paul keeps looking over at me.

I pretend not to notice.

When lunch is over, Dr. Best motions for me to meet her outside. Am I in trouble? I throw my scraps out and walk outside. She says, "Dr. Paul and I feel it's best you stay in the clinic for the next few days. I understand you were pretty shaken up out there. We think you'd feel safer here. I can put you on the post-op team. I think you'll really enjoy it. Are you okay with that?"

"Yes," I say as I twist my hair. It doesn't matter. I'm still quivering. It's probably a good idea.

The team leader, Marcy, trains me on what to do. "It's simple," she explains. "When the dogs and cats are finished with their surgeries, they're placed with us on towels or blankets to slowly wake them. Then we keep them calm by petting them or rocking the smaller ones in our arms."

I loved it. I usually sit in the corner with the smaller ones and watch the three doctors perform the surgeries. I find it very interesting.

Occasionally, I catch Dr. Paul looking over at me. He always wears a cap and mask which are adorned with pictures of dogs and cats, so I can only see his beautiful dark eyes, like bitter-sweet dark chocolate.

One day, he catches me looking at him and gives me a wink.

I feel my face warm. I'm sure it's bright red. I can't control it. I hear a chuckle from him across the room. Now my face is on fire. I shake my head thinking it will go away.

That evening we do our usual and go out to dinner.

This time Dr. Paul sits next to me. "Hi, Nina. How was your day? You seem to enjoy being on the post op team."

My stomach is slowly growing butter-flies. Oh my. Do I have a crush on him? "Yes, I really like it." It's hard for me to sit up straight and look at him and his gorgeous dark eyes. I know I'm obsessing over him. My shoulders turn in a bit. I want to grab my hair but don't.

"Tell me about yourself," he asks.

I look around to see if anyone is listening. Everyone is having idle conversations with each other. "I'm from New York," I say. It's almost the truth. "I grew up there as a young girl and went to Columbia to pursue a teaching degree. I teach first grade near the University." I don't want to go into the drama of living here in Chernobyl as a child.

"Wow, I grew up in New York, too. I went to vet school at Cornell. I was fortunate to get scholarships. It's a great school."

Had I met him somewhere in New York and don't remember it? Possibly. We both went to school in New York. I stare into his eyes. My mind begins to race at our potential interactions in New York but come up with nothing. Maybe I just walked by him one day and thought he was attractive. Who knows?

As the days and nights go by, I'm feeling a lot better about being in Chernobyl. I'm healing from the scars and the guilt Mother bestowed on me. They're vanishing. And the whispering has stopped. I feel like Dr. Paul and I are developing a strong connection. We always sit next to each other for our group dinners.

One evening, while all of us are walking to dinner, Dr. Paul and I lag behind the group. We babble a bit, and then suddenly he grabs my hand and rushes me in a nearby alley.

"Nina, I have a surprise for you," he says as he holds my hands.

My stomach starts to churn. Here comes those butterflies.

"I hope you don't mind, but I made a private reservation for us in a quaint little café around the corner. Are you interested? It's not far."

I'm shocked but try to regain some semblance of composure. "Okay, I'd love to."

A gleam appears in his peaceful eyes.

My heart pounds a little harder.

We walk through the alley holding hands. By the time we reach the other side, I feel like I'm in a dream. The street is lit up with thousands of white twinkle lights draped from each streetlight in scallops. I stop and take it in the area with its small cafés, restaurants, and a few stores.

"Where did you find this? It's beautiful."

"Sometimes I go for walks alone at night, and I stumbled on it." He pointed to the café where we're going to eat. "I made reservations outside. Is that all right?"

"Yes, it's a beautiful night." We sit outside the café in black metal bistro chairs at a small round table with a shimmery white tablecloth and matching napkins. The napkins are shaped like flowers and tucked in the wine glasses. I smell fresh bread baking every time waitstaff or patrons open the café door.

A waiter comes over and Paul orders us a bottle of wine. "I hope you like European food."

I look up and nod. I scan the menu and decide on gnocchi with fresh vegetables.

Paul orders the beef ribs and vegetables. He picks up his wine glass, and I pick up mine. "To a beautiful young lady that I get to share an evening alone with, and to saving the animals of Chernobyl." Our glasses touch, and we both take a sip.

After a little wine, I'm getting woozy. Is it from the wine? Or from my attraction to him? Probably both. He's so handsome; his dimples are so adorable.

"So, I've been thinking these last few days that you look a little familiar to me. We both grew up in New York, so we must have met there. I can't place you, though. Do I look familiar to you?" he asks.

I nod. "Yes, from the first moment I saw you, I felt I knew you from somewhere."

"What part of New York are you from?"

"Sheepshead Bay. It's in Brooklyn."

"Oh, my gosh," he says as his eyes grow big. "So am I. What high school did you graduate from?"

"James Madison."

A grin crosses his face, and dimples pop on each cheek. "Me too. I can't believe this, Nina. What a small world. We went to the same high school and were in the same grade? I don't remember you in any of my classes."

"Me, neither. Were you in any sports?"

"Yes, I was on the football team."

"I was in the band as a pom-pom girl. Wow, I still can't believe it."

We babble on the rest of the night about our high school and people we knew. We walk back to the hotel and up to my room. We pause at my door. I wish I could invite him in, but I know Alice is probably back from dinner and either waiting up to hear what happened to me or sleeping.

Still holding my hand, he looks down at me. "Would you like to learn how to assist in some surgeries tomorrow? I can put you on my team."

"Yes, I'd love it. Thank you for tonight." I turn to unlock the door then twist to gaze once more into his dreamy eyes. I want to kiss him so badly, but I need to collect my thoughts. Can I allow someone in my life again? Is the old saying 'the third time is a charm true'? "Thank you, again."

He smiles and waits for me to go in and close the door.

Alice is already in bed sleeping.

I tiptoe around the room and get ready for bed. As I lie in bed, I can't stop thinking of him. My stomach swirls with butterflies, and my heart feels like it will explode right out of my chest. Then I get it. This is the Paul that Jennifer wanted me to meet. Oh, my gosh. This is the Paul I used to catch looking at me. I remember now, the pizza joint, the mall, and the carnival. I can't wait to tell Jennifer when I get back. She's gonna die.

Thirty-Two

I wake the next morning to Alice giggling, lying on her side, her elbow pressed in the pillow, and her hand holding her head up. She stares at me.

"Good morning, Nina. How was your night?" she asks in a sing-song voice, then chuckles.

I roll on my back with a huge grin on my face and peer at the chips in the painted ceiling. "It was divine." I raise the back of my wrist to my forehead.

"Everyone wondered where you two went."

"Oh, Paul took me to a charming café not far from the hotel."

She raised one eyebrow. "Oh, so it's Paul now. What happened to Dr. Paul?"

I laugh and throw my pillow at her. "Time for a new day."

"You didn't answer me," Alice says. She

sits there on the bed with a Cheshire cat grin on her face as if she has something on me, a look that's clearly not going away.

"I'll meet you downstairs," I say, avoiding the question. "I need to place a call back in the States." I need to check on how Aunt Olga is doing. The reception is bad and getting through to my cousins and aunt is impossible, so I give up.

At breakfast, I decide to sit at a different table than Paul. Rumors are already starting, and I'm not sure where our possible relationship is going. I catch him glancing at me several times, a warm smile on his face. I smile back and study his adorable dimples. Butterflies continue to whirl in my stomach to the point where it almost aches.

When we arrive at the clinic, Paul reassigns me to his surgical team. There are three tables so three surgeries can go on simultaneously. Training is easy for me because I had many days on the post-surgical team while I watched surgeries. Paul says I'm a natural. He shows me how to insert needles for IV's and about all the instruments I'll need to hand him. After the surgeries, I help re-sterilize them. We make a great team. Dr. Best keeps looking over at me asking how I'm doing. My first day goes over without a hitch.

That evening, Paul wants to take me out to dinner again. I accept. We walk down the same beautifully lit-up street and find another quaint restaurant. Just after we're seated, a surprise appears. It's Dr. Walsh.

"Hello, you two. May I join you tonight?" She sits before Paul can even respond.

I lean back in my chair. She must have followed us. Wow. That takes balls. I knew something was up with her. Does she have a thing for him? Paul doesn't look happy with her at all. A few wrinkles appear on his forehead, and he isn't smiling. What could we do?

"So, I hear you're just a first-grade teacher," she says with her nose in the air, and she flicks her long, blonde hair back.

I catch the just. It's a dig.

Dr. Walsh is pretty. She looks a bit like Jennifer except she has brown eyes and her long, shiny hair is thin and straight. She's short and slender like me.

What can we do? We don't want to be rude. We let her stay and watch her babble most of the evening about herself, about how wonderful she thinks she is. When dinner is over, we walk back to the hotel together. I say my goodbyes to them in the lobby and head to my room. Alice isn't back yet.

I get ready for bed and crawl in. I can't wait to talk to her.

Thirty minutes later, Alice arrives. "You're back early."

"No choice. Guess who joined us?"

"I don't know. Some of us split up and went to different restaurants."

"Dr. Walsh. She must have followed us. We were not happy. She pretty much took over the evening. She doesn't like me. I caught her giving me snarling looks, and she positively glared at Paul. She monopolized the conversation. She pretty much made an ass of herself all night. Poor Paul kept looking over at me with a blank stare. I lightly kicked him under the table a few times."

"What a bitch. How bold is that? I did see her giving you a funny look in the van coming back today. Do you think she's upset that you're on the surgical team now?"

"Probably. She must have the hots for Paul."

"Be careful. Women can get ugly."

Something hits our window. I get up and look outside. It's Paul. My whole-body tingles, and my knees go weak. I try to lift the window, but it's stuck.

Alice asks, "What is it?"

"It's Paul. I can't get the window open."

"Do you want me to try?"

"No, he motioned for me to come downstairs." I raise my index finger toward him and mouth, one minute. I quickly throw on a pair of jeans and a t-shirt, run my fingers through my hair, and apply some shiny lip gloss and pink blush to my cheeks. I rush down the stairs and outside.

There he is, waiting for me on the side of the building, as handsome as ever in a pair of indigo jeans and a light blue t-shirt. "I can't believe she did that."

"I know. What's up with that? She must really like you."

"She's a vet I hired six months ago at my clinic. I guess I didn't realize she had feelings for me. Do you want to go for a short walk? The stars are out tonight."

"Sure."

He takes my hand, and we walk down the beautiful street with the glistening lights. "When I was a little boy, I had a friend, and we'd walk to our special place and watch the stars. It was my escape." He looks down at me, and I look up at his dark eyes. He raises my hand and kisses the back of it with his warm lips.

My knees almost buckle from under me. I feel my cheeks flaming. My stomach aches with happiness. Why am I falling for him so quickly?

When we finish with our late-night stroll, he walks me back to my room. I lean against the wall in the hallway, and he moves forward, his arm resting above my head. We gaze at each other for a moment, and then he tilts forward and gives me a kiss. He's such a gentleman. He doesn't use his tongue for our first kiss. Just his hot, slippery, perfect lips.

"Catch you tomorrow," he whispers in

my ear.

I feel his warm breath on my neck as he pulls away. He waits while I try to open the door. I'm so nervous I drop the key. He bends down, picks up the key, unlocks the door, and opens it a little. I take the key from his warm hand and walk in.

I turn back before I close the door. "Thank you, goodnight."

Alice is staring at me, pretending to be reading a book in bed. "OMG, I watched you walk away from the window. You're so adorable together."

I belly-flop onto the bed, flip over, and let out a huge sigh.

"Your face is glowing."

I'm grinning so widely my cheeks hurt. "I can't help it. He's wonderful. He makes my stomach spin."

"That's love, for sure."

I roll over, prop up on my elbows, and look at Alice. "I found out he hired Dr. Walsh six months ago to work in his veterinary clinic. He didn't realize she had a thing for him. Men are so oblivious to things right in front of their faces."

"Well, that explains a lot. You better be careful of her. I don't have a good feeling about her."

Thirty-Three

The next few days are perfect. I work closely with Paul and Dr. Best. She wants me to assist her too. Every time I'm with her, Paul looks over and gives me a wink and a smile. I can't really see the smile behind his mask, but his eyes dance, and I know the smile is there.

I really like helping the animals. However, my thoughts are still on Sasha. None of the animals coming through here resemble her at all. It's been almost three weeks now. We only have one more week.

One morning, Alice wakes up vomiting. I can hear her hurl from the bathroom. "Are you okay?" I ask, pressing my forehead against the door.

She comes out of the bathroom looking white as a ghost and crawls into bed. "No, I think I have the flu or maybe food poisoning. Can you tell Josh I'm sick?"

"I'm gonna get dressed, go downstairs, and get you some toast before I leave," I say. Down in the lobby, some of our team members aren't looking so good either.

I see Josh and walk over to him. "What's up?"

"It appears some of our group got food poisoning last night. We're gonna be very short staffed today."

"Alice is sick, too."

"All right, I'm gonna do a head count, and we'll have a briefing and come up with a new plan when we get to the clinic."

We only need to take one van. Half our crew is sick, even Dr. Best. While we wait for our placements for the day, Paul, Dr. Walsh, and Josh are in the corner pointing to each of us. Dr. Walsh is giving me dirty looks with sinister eyes. I'm assuming that means I'll be staying here continuing to assist Paul with the surgeries. The clinic has two vets and two assistants for the day. Darci is the other assistant. Post-op only has two also. Everyone else is on the catch team.

As they're bringing back the ferals, Paul and I work beautifully together.

I guess I'm flinging instruments and swabs around in a rushed manner because, in a kind whisper, he says, "It's important not to rush."

Suddenly, Darci doubles over and spews on her scrub booties. She steps outside and pulls them off. She comes back and crawls on the cool cement floor and rolls on her back.

Now it's just Paul, Dr. Walsh, and me. The other two in post-op aren't trained to assist and are needed to stay with the animals waking up.

Paul leans over and asks if I can check on Dr. Walsh.

I remove my gloves, put on a fresh pair, and walk over to her. "Can I help you with anything?"

"I don't want your help," she says in a snarly tone as her eyes get all hard and squinty. She straightens from a stooped position, leans back, and faces Paul. "Paul, can we get ahold of Josh and have him bring us some help?" Her words drip with venom.

"Nina, grab the walky-talky and reach out to him," Paul says.

Stepping outside, I explain what happened to Darci and ask for help.

"Of course, I'll bring two catchers back to the clinic for you."

While Paul and I work together, we hear Dr. Walsh barking orders at the two untrained catchers. One looks like she's about to cry. She looks over at me as her eyes tear up.

I pull my mask down and mouth silently, "Take a deep breath."

Paul and I exchange glances each time we hear Dr. Walsh's rudeness.

For obvious reasons, we end the day a

little early. While we're caring for the animals and cleaning up, Paul asks to speak to Dr. Walsh outside. When they come back a few minutes later, her face is beet red, and she doesn't look at anyone. We pretend not to notice. The drive back is excruciating. Dr. Walsh ends up sitting right behind Paul and me. I swear I could feel her beady little eyes on me. The tension in the air is thick with her animosity.

When we're almost back at the hotel, Paul whispers to me, "Dinner tonight?"

"Can I shoot you a text later? I want to check on Alice first and see if she needs me to stay with her."

"No worries. I understand. Catch you later," he says with a wink from his dark twinkly eyes. They almost put me in a trance.

I rush upstairs, then slow my steps. Catch you later. Where have I heard that phrase before? Catch you later. It's so familiar. Someone whispered that to me once upon a time. Who?

I open the door. Alice is sleeping. I pull the blanket up under her neck and head back downstairs to get her some soup and crackers from a café around the corner. While I wait for her to wake, I take a shower and throw on a pair of jeans and a pink t-shirt. I try calling my cousins again. Nothing. No reception.

Alice finally wakes.

"Hey there, how are you feeling?"

"Like crap."

"I brought you some soup and crackers."

"Thank you. I haven't eaten all day. How'd it go today?"

"Well, half the team is sick. You all ate at the same restaurant. It must be food poisoning."

"Wow, did you survive today?"

I drop onto my bed. "Yes, it was hard but a bit joyful. Paul had to speak to Dr. Walsh for being rude to some of the volunteers. She's such a bitch. Dr. Best was sick, too, so she stayed here."

"So, Dr. Bitch got into trouble. Good." She slowly sits up and takes a slurp of her soup. "Thank you for the soup. It's delicious. I'm feeling a little better already." She slowly lays back down.

I check her temperature with the back of my hand. "Good. Do you mind if I go out with Paul tonight? I won't be too long."

She shakes her head but doesn't lift it from the pillow. "Of course not. Go have fun."

"Well, I don't want to leave you alone. You've been alone enough today. Besides, I'm extra tired tonight."

"Don't be silly," she says. "I'll be fine. I'm only going back to sleep anyway. Go, seriously, go."

I give in. What kind of friend am I leaving my friend to be with a guy? I should be ashamed of myself. But, unable to resist temptation, I text Paul and we meet downstairs.

While we sit at our favorite café, we don't speak much. We sip our wine, take small bites of our food, and beam at each other. The moon bounces off his masculine face, and his dimples twinkle like shining stars. He pushes my hair back with both hands and cements a kiss on my lips. It takes my breath away. I gasp for air. My whole body is heating up.

We walk leisurely back to the hotel, holding hands, saying little.

"Nina, I find you so adorable. I love to watch you take care of the animals. You have such a big heart."

"I admire you too." I want to say, *you are so beautiful,* out loud but refrain. It's almost like being in a fairy-tale, this adventure with such a handsome and special man.

He walks me upstairs, and we say our goodnights. He whispers, "Catch you later."

My head spins again from that phrase.

Thirty-Four

We have one more week to do our best to catch the last of the ferals. I'm falling hard for Paul. My stomach tickles and my body warms every time I'm near him. The rest of the crew are on to us, but we don't care about being discrete anymore.

One evening, Paul asks if he can take me somewhere special for dinner. I'm glad I packed one of my favorite dresses. It's a dusty blue, which makes my eyes pop. It fits my slender body perfectly. Its narrow waist widens to a full hem which swishes back and forth when I walk. It matches my crème stilettos. As I finish putting on my makeup, I take a step back and stare at myself in the mirror for a minute. I look like Mother. It takes me by surprise to see her face in mine. A few tears slip down my cheeks. I fix my face and head downstairs to the lobby.

Paul comes down the stairs right after

me. He's wearing a soft yellow shirt tucked in his khakis. He smiles and plants a light kiss on my cheek.

I return the smile.

Taking my hand, he walks outside to one of the vans. He opens the door for me, I step up with one foot, and slip in.

"Where are we going tonight?"

"I found a nice club out of town. It's deep in the Ukraine, too far to walk. I thought it might be nice to savor some other native cuisines while we're here and perhaps go dancing."

"Sounds good to me."

He takes my hand and kisses the back of it. His lips are always so moist and warm. We enjoy idle chat on the way. It's interesting to see some life beyond the area where we've been staying. I see some live trees. They're growing back. I marvel at the resiliency of nature. And there are children playing. They remind me of elementary school in Chernobyl.

When we arrive at the restaurant, Paul parks and opens my door for me. I swing around and look up at him. I wrap my hands around his neck for support while he takes my waist and picks me up to help me out. It's quite steep. I could have handled it, but I let him be chivalrous. He brings my body close to his and slowly lets me down. I let out a gasp.

He has made reservations so we are seated right away at an intimate table in the back.

"Wine?" he asks.

"Yes, please." He orders us water and a bottle of white wine. We look at the menu while peeking at each other over the tops.

"Nina, may I order for you?"

I nod.

The waiter comes back to take our order.

"We'll have the house salad, then the chicken Kyiv, the nalesniki, and some varenyky." He looks up at me. "Those are like pierogis."

"It all sounds wonderful." I smile.

While we sip our wine, I realize we've never talked about where we live or where his clinic is in New York.

"Paul, where do you live now?"

"I live in Park Slope in a brownstone in Brooklyn. My clinic is just around the corner from there. I really like the neighborhood. There are parks, museums, and cool cafés within walking distance. You?"

"Just the other side of the Brooklyn Bridge near Columbia."

"Nina, that's so close. I can't believe it."

I was so happy. My cheeks hurt from smiling.

"Do you think you might want to continue what we have going when we get back to New York?"

I can only nod and stare into his dreamy, dark-chocolate eyes that glisten when he smiles.

I'm a little in shock. My body stiffens. Can Paul be my true love? We continue our conversation about Brooklyn.

"Isn't it expensive in Columbia?" he asks.

"Yes, that's why I'm contemplating moving, even though my apartment is rent-controlled. My landlord isn't the kindest when it comes to his tenants paying late. When I get back, I'm thinking, now that I'm teaching and making a salary, of looking for a more spacious apartment. I just ended up there to be close to the university and the hospital where I used to work.

"It's cheaper on the other side of the bridge," he says. "I'll help you find a new place."

Our salads arrive first, then dinner. The food is delicious. When we finish, we go for a short walk to explore the area and ended up at a dance club. We have a blast. This is the first time I'm not shy about dancing. Paul has complete control of me. I really like it. We finish drinking and dancing, and then hold hands as we stroll through the streets. There's so much life here compared to the ghost town of Chernobyl.

We head back to the van and then the hotel. He walks me back to my room.

"I can't believe we only have a couple of days left here," I say.

"I can't believe how close you are to me back in New York. I was starting to get a little sad thinking I might never see you again."

"Me, too."

"You make me happy, Nina." He leans down and gives me a gentle kiss on my lips. He takes my key and unlocks the door for me and taps me on the nose with his finger. "Catch you later."

Alice is once again waiting up for me.

I start babbling right away. "You won't believe it. He lives in New York, close to me. We're just on opposite ends of the Brooklyn Bridge."

"Don't you get it? It's serendipity. Everything about you and Paul meeting has been fate. So, I guess this means you'll see each other back home?"

"Yes, we've already spoken about it. Oh, Alice, I'm so happy. It's been a long time since someone's made me feel good about myself. He has such kind words and gentle touches. He's amazing."

We have two days left. Today is our last day for surgeries, and tomorrow will be free for exploring and one last check on the fur babies. Paul and I work together one last time. We have two more female pups to spay.

When we finish, I pick up the last pup from the operating table to give her to the post-op crew. Her ear flips over. Inside is a tiny heart birthmark. I turn and place her back on the table. Slowly shaking my head, I look up at

Paul. I feel sweat flowing down my back. My knees start to buckle. I hold on to the table for support.

"What's the matter, Nina? You look like you just saw a ghost."

"Do you see this tiny birthmark that looks like a heart? I had a puppy with the same birth mark, except it was on her chest. Can this dog be a descendent of my dog?" My voice comes out weird, choppy and strained, like someone else is talking. She looks so much like my Sasha that my eyes tear up.

"What are you talking about? We're in Ukraine, not New York."

"Yes." I nod. Time to tell the whole story. I swallow my tears and stroke the little pup's ear. "But I originally grew up right here in Chernobyl. When I was a little girl, I was given a puppy for my birthday. I named her Sasha. I still have a stuffed animal I named after her, a gift on that same birthday from a dear friend."

Paul takes a step back. He pulls his mask down. He stares at me.

I sputter, "What? Do you think I'm crazy? I was hoping to find a dog that looks like my Sasha. She was a small Russkiy Toy puppy, similar to this one, although she can't be pure bred. Do you think I can take her home?" My fingers are glued to her fur. "Are we allowed to do that? Why are you staring at me?"

His eyes begin to fill with tears. He tries to speak, but nothing comes out. He can't stop gawking at me. Then finally he finds his voice. "Antoniya? Nini?"

I look deep into his eyes. How could he know my name? Could this be? I shake my head in disbelief. I can't move. I start panting. The room begins to spin.

Then to make sure I know it is him, he says, "duh VSTRIE-chi. Catch you later."

I sink to the floor and weep. "Pavlov, is it really you?"

"Yes, my beautiful Nini."

He takes the last dog, the one that resembles Sasha, and passes it to another volunteer. He picks me up from the floor with his strong arms and carries me outside to the side of the clinic. He gently places me on the dead grass and takes my face with his warm strong hands. He begins kissing me all over my face. "I always wondered about you. About what had happened to you. Where your family went. I was so sad to learn you were gone."

"Oh, Pavlov. I've thought about you all these years. I've been curious about you and your family. Now, here you are. You've grown up to be a kind, gentle, beautiful man who cares for animals."

We kiss each other more. Then we weep again. I can taste his salty tears running in my mouth. The best thing I ever savored in my entire life.

"How did you end up in New York?" he asks.

"We left the same day as the explosion. We stayed with my aunt. You?"

"We left a few days after you. I too have relatives in New York. They thought it would be best to change my name to Paul. 'More American.'" He does air quotes with his fingers before he picks me up again and gives me a big squeeze. "How's your family? They must be so proud of you."

I wipe my tears with the back of my hand. "Pavlov, I lost them all due to the explosion here. I'll tell you later. I don't want to talk about that now. It's enough that I've found you."

He places his warm hands on my cheeks and uses his thumbs to wipe away the tears that won't stop streaming down my face.

While trying to catch my breath, I stare into his beautiful dark brown eyes. I should have recognized those eyes. "I remember your shiny dark eyes and your adorable dimples." I place my finger into one of his dimples.

He strokes my hair. "I've never forgotten your gleaming blue eyes and long wavy hair. You're so pretty. How did I not know it was you? I always knew you would grow up to be striking. I had such a crush on you when we were kids, and here you are. My true love."

"I love you, too."

Thirty-Five

Later that same evening, we go to our first little café for dinner. We both can't stop talking and reminiscing about our childhood in Chernobyl. I can't keep my eyes off him. He's so steamy looking. My stomach churns with butterflies. My little Pavlov, all grown up.

"We have one last day tomorrow. What do you want to do after we check on the last of the pups and cats?" he asks.

"Remember when we were kids, we were gonna go to the amusement park? I'd like to go there and explore. The only time we saw it was when I was being followed by that wolf."

"We can do that if you want. I'd also like to go see our old neighborhood."

I hesitate. "I'd like that, too. I'm a little worried, though. It might stir up some bad memories. I miss Sasha and my brother, Aleksei, so much."

"It might be good for you. Cathartic. It

may help you get through those wounds."

We finish our dinner and take a long walk down the beautiful streets lit up with twinkle lights. We're all talked out. We just hold hands and enjoy each other's company. On our stroll back to the hotel, just before we arrive, Pavlov gently pushes me up to the side of the hotel wall and covers my mouth with a hot, wet kiss on my moist lips.

"Can I be with you tonight, Antoniya?" he whispers. His hand crawls down the front of my shirt.

My breath is coming faster and fasters. My chest quickly moves up and down. I arch my neck back and look up at the stars.

Pavlov kisses my neck with his wet lips, a brush of his tongue on my neck.

Is Pavlov the one? The one man I've been waiting for my entire life? I can only tell him, "Yes."

We walk to his room, he opens the door, and lifts me into his arms. He's kissing me before the door closes. I wrap my legs around his waist. "Where's your roommate?"

"I don't have one."

He carries me to the bed. My arms wrap behind his neck. I bite lightly down on his lip. My stomach aches like whirling doves. I want our love making to be perfect. He gently sets me down. We maintain perfect eye contact as we slowly peel each other's clothes off. He removes my last piece of clothing—my pink lace bikini. He pulls it down to the floor. My hands rest on his strong shoulders. When we're both naked, we take the time to look at each other, every inch. He lightly touches my face. I smile and run my fingers through his chest hairs, brushing his nipples which stand erect. He pulls me close to him by placing his hand to my back. My breasts touch his strong chest.

"I want you, Antoniya."

"I want you, too, Pavlov." We crawl under the covers, and he begins stroking my face while we kiss. We don't close our eyes but remain focused on each other. I don't want to miss a thing. He lays his slender body over mine. I enjoy his weight on me, his body crushing mine. I quiver with the thought of him eventually being inside me, but I am enjoying his hands racing up and down my body from my face to my thighs. His touch is glorious. I'm already wet.

He begins stroking my nipples with his tongue. My back arches and I moan.

I look down at my breasts, and my nipples are hard and erect. I catch him watching me. My reaction turns him on, and a grin makes a dimple pop. I massage his back with my hands, and they eventually make their way south to his lovely ass. I bite the flesh of his shoulder trying not to break the skin.

He leans over just enough for me to touch his penis. It's swollen and throbbing. I quickly stroke it up and down, and he lets out a gasp. He pushes a finger inside me. I take in a deep breath, and it's my turn to gasp. As he plunges his finger in and out, I hear how wet I am. It sounds like gentle waves lapping on the shore. I can't control myself. I moan several times and then explode. My toes curl and legs quiver.

He slows his pace. I take deep breaths. He waits like a gentleman for me to collect myself while he puts on a condom. Then he opens my legs wider so he can place his knees between my thighs. He looks at me.

"Yes. I want you. I want all of you," I whisper. I can't get enough of him. I can't wait. The agony is killing me. My body is crying out for him. The he does it, finally, gently sliding his penis inside me.

I haven't had sex in a long time, so it stings a little. I let out a moan. Our hips crash each other like bumper cars. Then he simultaneously strokes one of my legs.

He rises to his knees and lifts my leg to the side of his face. He kisses the arch of my foot. I massage his strong chest with both hands, squeezing my breasts with the inside of my arms. He releases my leg and comes back down. I wrap my legs around his waist and squeeze him in further.

I watch his face. A bead of sweat from his forehead drops on to my neck. I love it.

He lets out a huge moan, and his heart rate begins to slow. His arms buckle, and he collapses on top of me. He crumbles like sand.

I enjoy his weight. I don't want to stop. I continue kissing his warm neck. I'm ready to go again. I can't get enough of his touch. I don't care that I'm sore and tired. I want him to make me ache all over again.

He rolls on to his back, still breathing heavily.

I curl on my side under his arm, resting my arm and leg on top of his heaving body. "That was the best. Can we do it again?"

He chuckles. "Already? Are you sure? Round two?"

"Yes," I say as I crawl on top of him.

He pushes my hair back and his fingers brush over my lips.

I sit on his thighs with my legs apart facing him. I begin to make him hard again. He hands me a condom. I roll in on his already-throbbing penis. I take my other hand and massage his balls. I watch him lie still enjoying it, breathing deep. Then he takes his hand and massages my pussy with his knuckles. I let out a groan, closed my eyes, and sway back and forth. It's wonderful.

"Are you ready," he asks.

"Yes, yes. I can't stand it anymore." He places his thick erection inside me. I ride him for several minutes which feels like hours. Right before we climax, I crawl close to his strong body and lie on top of him, pressing my lips hard on his. Our tongues twirl together. Then

I let out a wail, and he grabs my hips for one last push before his orgasm. He lets out a sigh. Our breathing comes heavy and sporadic. We can't stop panting. We sound like the wild dogs.

I look up at his face. He's grinning from ear to ear. I trace his lips with my finger. I lie on top of him with his penis still inside me. I don't want him to remove it. I want him inside me forever.

After a few minutes, I peel off him, get out of bed, and walk to the bathroom. I look in the mirror. I look different. Is this happiness? Am I finally gonna be happy? I look peaceful, I feel safe. I love Pavlov so much. I can't believe we found each other.

I return to bed, and he takes his turn in the bathroom. He crawls in bed with me. I rest my head on his chest, and we fall asleep.

We wake the next morning in each other's arms.

"Good morning, darling," I say as I lean up to his face and plant a kiss on his moist lips. He takes my face and returns my kisses. I lean over to look at my watch from the nightstand. "Oh, my gosh. Look at the time. We overslept. Everyone must be waiting for us downstairs." I get up and dress quickly. "I'll meet you downstairs."

I rush to my room. Alice has left a note on my bed. "I hope you had fun last night. See you at breakfast." I quickly brush my teeth and wash my face. No time for a shower. I stink of sex but don't care. I have the scent of Pavlov's manliness on me and want to smell it all day. After applying some makeup and brushing my hair, I rush downstairs. We arrive at the same time. Yep, everyone is staring at us. One of the vans has already left. We grab a muffin and pile in the other van.

Pavlov drives. I sit next to Alice who can't stop giggling. I look over at Dr. Walsh. She squints her eyes at me while her face turns hot red. If looks could kill…

Alice whispers to me, "I'm assuming you had a wonderful evening."

"It was wonderful. I have so much to tell you."

"Are you in love?"
"Yes."

Thirty-Six

When we arrive at the clinic one last time, we're all a little sad. Darci is weeping. Our final briefing is short. Dr. Best thanks us for our efforts this month and wishes us well. "No surgeries today. We're just checking on the last ferals in recovery and setting them free. We need catchers outside to walk the grounds to make sure the pups and cats are healing well. Then come back and help the rest of us clean up. The afternoon is yours to do whatever you want. Dr. Bonder, Dr. Walsh, and I would like you to join us for one last dinner.

Pavlov and I check on the last animals that had surgery.

"Tell me again why I can't take this dog?" I pick her up and hold her close to my face, stroking her head and running my fingers over her heart-shaped birthmark. I'm certain she's from Sasha."

"Remember, these animals are full of

radiation. That's why we spay and neuter them and set them free. We want them to die naturally. Eventually, they'll all be gone."

A tear floats down my cheek.

Pavlov swipes it with his thumb. "I'll get you a new puppy when we get back to the States. I promise."

We place the remaining animals in their crates and drive them back to the plant.

Pavlov can feel my pain. I know he can. "When we finish, we can go to the amusement park for a walk and then go find our old neighborhood."

When we arrive at the plant one last time, we let the animals go. The little one I believe is a descendent of Sasha slowly walks away. She keeps looking back at me with big, sad eyes. I walk back to the van and look down. There she is at my feet. I pick her up one last time and give her a slight squeeze. She let out a tiny whimper, and I place her on the ground. She knows she must leave. I watch her catch up with the other pups. She turns, lets out a bark, and then moves slowly away. I begin to weep.

Pavlov comes over and gives me a long hug.

We drive back to the clinic. Everyone is ready to leave. We drive back to the hotel, and everyone scatters. Pavlov and I drive to a café for sandwiches and beverages to-go and head back to the ghost town. We eat our sandwiches in the car and talk about the accomplishments of the Clean Futures Fund.

"Do you want to do this again with me next year? We still have lots of animals to catch and fix," he asks.

"Oh, yes. This was the best experience of my life. And, of course, being with you."

"Are you ready for our walk?"

We get out of the van, he takes my hand, and we walk toward the amusement park. When we arrive, we can't believe how it is in such disarray. Some of the go-karts are flipped upside down and rusty. The yellow Ferris wheel cabins are also rusted and chipped from years of inclement weather. The entire Exclusion Zone looks sad. It's dead and gray. No life except for the animals left behind.

We're taking pictures with our phones when suddenly I hear a growl. "Shh," I whisper.

Pavlov is in front of me. He turns back. "Nini, don't move. That wolf is back, right behind you."

I can smell him again. He must be very close.

Pavlov picks up a dead branch from a nearby tree. He reaches his hand to me. "Come this way, slowly."

I bite my lip and taste blood. Can the wolf smell it? I lift my hand toward Pavlov. Our fingers touch, and our eyes lock.

He pulls me close to him. "Get behind me

and walk backwards to the food trailers."

I do exactly as he says.

The wolf follows us, crouches low, his ears back. A strip of fur along his back stands straight up. He growls the entire way.

As we reach one of the trailers, Pavlov tries to pry the door open.

Suddenly, five of our larger dogs appear from nowhere. They scream at the wolf and show their teeth.

The wolf stands tall, as if he's contemplating taking them on.

The screaming, howling, and growling goes on for several minutes. We stare in disbelief as the precious pups help us escape the big bad wolf.

The wolf reluctantly gives up and runs off.

We bend down, and the pups come running up to us wagging their tails, standing tall with pride.

"Thank you, boys," Pavlov says, "You saved our lives." We pat each one, then he addresses me, "We should get back to the van."

We run back holding each other's hand.

"That was scary," I say.

"Yes, I should've known better. I'm sorry to have put you in danger." He picks up my hand and kisses the back of it.

I turn to the window twirling my hair with my right hand so he can't see. What if something happens to Pavlov? Can I sustain another loss? My stomach starts to churn. Lunch doesn't settle well. I quickly drag my head back from the clouds. "Do you think you can find our old neighborhood?"

"I have a good idea where it is. I'm driving to the bridge where we used to walk, and then we'll know. Only we're not walking. Not after that incident. We'll drive."

We drive to the bridge that faces the plant. We can kind of see what used to be a rock road, now reduced to dirt. It leads us back to where we grew up. We creep through the tiny neighborhood. It's all dead. Houses stand with doors open, patio furniture turned upside down, cracked or broken potted planters littering crumbling front porches.

"There they are." Pavlov points to our homes.

At the sad sight of our houses, tears fill my eyes.

We look at each other. He parks in between our homes. He takes my hand, and we walk slowly up to my house. It's unlocked. We walk in and scan the living room. The furniture left behind is a mess. It appears to be stained with animal waste and water from a crack in the ceiling. This may be where some of the pets who were left behind take refuge. Maybe even Sasha waited for me to come home.

The entire house stinks of mold. Plugging my nose from the stench, I make my way through the house. I find my bedroom. The door is open. The only things recognizable are the arnica curtains, torn and faded, that Mother made me. I walk to the broken window, the window I snuck out of with Sasha on that fateful night. My body shivers. I touch a piece of the glass. It's loose and crashes to the ground and shatters. My eyes meet Pavlov's. "This was the window I snuck out of the night of the explosion."

He stares at me but says nothing. He lets me have my moment of memories as I glance out the window. We return to the kitchen where my favorite memories occurred, me sitting at the kitchen table with Father, Mother, and Aleksei. Precious moments when we talked about our day, what was most eventful. What I wouldn't give to have those innocuous conversations again. "We're all right, Antoniya," I hear in a whisper. I look at Pavlov. He didn't hear it.

I let the tears fall unabashedly. "Let's go to your house."

We join hands and walk next door.

"Nini, do you mind if I go in alone?"

"Of course not."

I watch as he pries the front door open with a thick tree branch and goes in. I stand out front like I'd waited for him when we were kids. The front window is broken, and I can still see the sheer white curtains, torn and ragged, hanging haggardly. Only they aren't white anymore. They're gray and dirty. They remind me of his father's beatings. I used to watch them while waiting for Pavlov to come outside. I let out a sigh. How fortunate he turned out so wonderfully. What a kind gentleman he is.

After a few minutes, he comes outside, grabs my hand, and rushes back to the van. He doesn't say anything, and I don't press him. He opens the door on my side and waits for me to jump in. Our drive back to the hotel is silent. I glance at him a couple of times and see his face a little flushed and tears in his eyes. He's doing everything to hold back those tears. He keeps looking away, so I won't see his pain.

Here I was worried about my reaction to coming back, but I never considered the scars Pavlov has from his upbringing. His memories are nightmares.

I no longer feel the need to twirl my hair. My anxieties are nothing compared to his. Should I say something, or should I leave him alone and let him process? I decide to leave him alone, but I reach over and squeeze his hand to show I'm here if he needs me. I receive a light squeeze in return. I hold his hand the entire drive back to the hotel.

Back at the hotel, it's almost dinner time.

"I'm gonna go upstairs and shower before dinner," I say.

He just looks at me. He grasps my hand and leads me to his room. He closes the door, presses my back up against the door, holding my arms above my head, and gives me a hot, slippery kiss. I gasp for air. What's going on with him? Were the memories too much? It's as if he needs to control me like when we were kids.

He picks me up in his arms and carries me to the bathroom. He turns on the shower. He holds my face with one hand with a firm grip, squeezing my breasts tight with the other. His actions are raw and primal, his kisses hard and urgent. My lips will probably bruise. I take his harshness, knowing they're about the ghosts of his father, not about me.

He tears his clothes off and then mine all the way to my naked body. He checks the temperature of the shower, grabs my hand, and pulls me in. He places me firmly against the cool shower wall and buries his hands deeply into my hair. He pushes against me as if he can't get close enough, like a baby kangaroo tucked into its mother's pouch. I know he'll keep me safe, warm, and be with me forever.

He pulls the shower curtain so hard that it crashes to the floor. We don't care. He starts kissing me again. Our tongues flutter against each other. I gently push his face away and kiss him softly on the lips. I start with innocent pecks but quickly grow ravenous. I suck hard on his lips and hear a deep moan escape him. He's enjoying this.

His arm grips me tighter and pushes me harder against the wall. I feel his cock pressed against my thigh. My hands move lower as I caress his strong body until I find what I want and begin stroking. I part my legs, thinking he's going to take me there and now. Not yet. He grasps my booty and rubs it hard as if rolling and kneading bread dough. He takes my right breast in his mouth, sucking so hard I moan with the pain and pleasure. Where does one end and other begin?

I lean in and feel the beads of the water cascading on my back and down my legs. His hands move from my ass to my vagina. He pushes my thighs wider and makes itself at home between my pussy lips. With one hand, his fingers roughly swish and swirl inside me.

Too rough. I'm not sure I like this, but for now, it's about him and the years of pain he took from his father. I'm panting so loud it echoes from the three walls of the shower. I want him to stop, but I feel his pain. Literally. He needs to let it go. I know I can take it. Finally, when he finishes, my legs are like rubber, and I slip to the floor. I start to get up, but he holds me down, pressing on my head. The old shower tiles are small and cracked, their irregularities scrape my knees, causing pain. I don't care. I just want to make him happy.

Next, he takes his swollen cock and shoves it in my mouth. I'm not ready and cough. I look up. His eyes are closed, and his mouth gapes open. He doesn't hear me. I slowly suck his cock, squeezing with my lips tightly on the shaft and head. He leans against the wall, eyes closed, and lets out a huge groan. I hear him chant, "Nini, Nini. Don't stop." I take him in as deep as I can without gagging. His hands entwine in my hair, steering my head in a back-and-forth motion, controlling me, making me take him in deeper and faster. As I'm fighting my gag reflex, I put my hands on his thighs and lightly push away a bit. I can only breath through my nose, it's difficult to catch my breath. I look up. He's so out of control, he doesn't even notice. And then it happens. I hear a gasp. His cock hits the back of my throat, and the warmth of his cum rushes in my mouth and down my throat.

He slowly slides to the floor and leans against the wall, his legs apart, still panting, holding his head with one hand as it rests on his knee. He begins to cry.

Down on all fours, I lean forward and kiss him on the lips. He looks up at me with his dark wet eyes, gives me a peck on top of my head, and turns me around, placing me between his thighs. "I need a minute," he says with a sigh. He lets it all out. Sobbing as if he were child who's fallen off his bike and whose knees are now bleeding.

I lean against his chest.

His heart pounds like a roar. We sit for several minutes. He gives me a hug and whispers, "I'm sorry if I hurt you."

I turn slightly so I can whisper in his ear.

"It's okay, my love. That was years of sorrow you just dealt with. We can stop."

"No, I want to make you happy."

Next, he opens my legs and presses a thumb on my clitoris and begins stroking. My chest raises, and my breasts protrude. He takes his other hand and massages them. I cup my hand under his chin and let out a moan. It's my turn. With his thumb still stroking me, he inserts a finger inside me. I pant hard. I join his motion. The cracked tiles sting my buttock. I don't care. His fingers feel so good.

Then it happens. I let out a gasp. My legs begin to quiver. I can feel myself gushing like the Volga River. He slows his motions. I close my legs, and he pulls me to him, turning me halfway so my head rests on his chest. He holds me tight.

We don't notice the shower has gotten cool until I begin to shiver. Struggling to find my land legs, we get out and towel each other off. He picks me up and sets me on the sink. The sink is cool on my ass, but I don't care. He takes my face, holds it for a moment, gazing in my eyes.

"Thank you, Nini. I know you understand."

"Of course, I do, Pavlov. I'll always love you and protect you from your demons."

He lifts me down. "It's almost dinner time. I need to get dressed. I haven't even started packing yet."

"Me neither." My body aches, inside and

out. I know I'll be bruised tomorrow, but I don't want him to feel badly. He needed this. "Do you mind if I spend tonight in my room so I can pack and spend some time with Alice. I feel a little bad I haven't been hanging with her."

"No." He lifts my chin and pecks my nose. "I'll meet you at dinner. We can go for a short walk afterwards and then I'll see you in the morning."

Thirty-Seven

Alice was packing when I get to my room. "Hey, girl," she comes over and gives me a big bear hug. Only this time she isn't chuckling. She has tears in her eyes.

"Are you okay?" I ask.

"Yes. I'm just going to miss everyone and this program. What a great experience for all of us."

"I know. I feel the same way. Plus, I met the man of my dreams." I jump on the bed, then cringe a little from my sore ass. I hope she doesn't notice. "You're not going to believe this, but I grew up with Paul."

"What?"

"Yes, Paul's from Chernobyl, too. We were best friends and hung out almost every night."

"Oh, my gosh, No!" Alice says with a gasp.

"Yes, we parted the night of the explosion, and it turns out our families moved to America, to New York, and we didn't know it."

"Oh, that's sad. However, things turned out for the best. You see," she says. "It's serendipity. You found your love. I'm so happy for you."

"Let's get ready for dinner. I'm going for a walk with Paul after dinner and then I'll come back and pack. We can chat more then."

I put on a pair of white jeans and a soft pink blouse and wear my hair in a ponytail. My face is slightly bruised, and my lips swollen, so I apply my makeup a little heavily. Too much passion, if such a thing exists. I check myself in the mirror one last time, and then Alice and I head down to meet the gang.

We pile in the van and drive to a nice restaurant. The team shares two long rectangular tables. I sit between Pavlov and Alice. Dr. Best and Dr. Walsh sit across from us. Once again, the snarls from Dr. Witch. I'm guessing Pavlov will get rid of her when we get back to New York. At least I hope so.

Dinner is wonderful. Pavlov and Dr. Best stand up and thank everyone for coming and caring so much for the animals. We arrive back at the hotel. I remind Alice I'll be back. Pavlov and I go for a short walk, holding hands down our favorite street with the twinkling lights.

He looks down at me and squeezes my hand. "One last glass of wine?"

"Yes, please." We enter our preferred

café and sit at our special bistro table. We sip our wine and hold each other's hands across the table.

"Nini, I'm sorry if I was too forceful with you today. I hope you can forgive me."

"Don't worry ... I can handle you." I give him a wink and a smile. "Positive thoughts from here on. I just want to be with you, Pavlov."

"Me too. I want you to be my future, my forever, my serendipity."

"That's what Alice always says. Serendipity. I guess that's what we are." We lean across the table. Our lips meet, and we kiss softly. We finish our wine and begin to stroll back to the hotel with an arm wrapped around each other's waist. Suddenly, I hear howling. It sounds close. I stop and look at Pavlov. "What's that?"

"That's the wolves and the dogs." He chuckles.

"I don't understand. Why are they howling, and why do they sound so close? We're at least ten miles from the clinic."

"Well, howling is their means of communicating. That's how they let each other know where they are or if predators are nearby. Perhaps they know we're leaving and are saying goodbye. They sound close because there aren't a lot of obstacles between us and them. Their voices don't have anything to bounce off like tall buildings and mountains, so their howls go further."

"Wow, I bet they are saying goodbye to us. That's sad. I'm gonna miss them and this place."

"Until next time." He leans in for a kiss.

We make it back to the hotel and he walks me to my room and gives me one last goodnight kiss. It's hot, wet, and sensual. I want to go to his room so badly, but I still need to pack. "I'll see you in the morning."

I unlock the door and turn around. I watch as he walks away. I turn back and close the door behind me. I let out a gasp. I scan the entire room.

It's been ransacked!

I hear someone in the bathroom. The door is partially open. I tiptoe over there, half afraid of what—or who—I might find. But it's just Alice sitting on the floor between the sink and the toilet. Her face is red; she's crying.

I step in. "What the hell happened here?"

"I'm not sure. When I got back, our door was partially open. I saw that our room had been broken into, so I rushed to some of the other teammates on our floor, and their rooms are fine."

"Who do you think did this?"

"I'm guessing Dr. Walsh. She left dinner before the rest of us. I don't know how she got in, though. Your side of the room is the worst. She destroyed your sketches and tore your clothes."

"I'm so sorry, Alice. This is entirely my fault. This is about Paul and me, not you."

"That's okay. I'm just glad you're back and you're safe. Let's start cleaning up and go to bed."

I walk to my side of the room. My sketches are unrecognizable, torn into tiny bits and scattered on the floor like the snowflakes I saw falling from the sky the night of the explosion. As I bend down to pick up each piece, my thoughts are carried back to when my family was driving to the train station and Aleksei whispered in my ear what the flakes really were. The blood in my veins are hot. I can feel my face, ears, and entire body get warm.

"Are you okay?" Alice asks. "You're all red."

"Yes, I'm just upset. Jealousy raised its ugly head tonight, I guess."

Alice walks to my bed and picks up my lacerated clothing. "I guess you'll be wearing the clothes you have on your back on the plane."

"Yep. That's okay. At least she didn't physically hurt anyone."

"Are you going to tell Paul?"

"Yes, in the morning. Thanks for helping me clean up."

Alice gives me a big bear hug.

Whether our flights were early or late, we all meet for breakfast downstairs to say our official goodbye. Most of the women are weeping and making sure we had each other's contact information. Lifelong bonds of friendship are made here. Pavlov rearranges our flights so we can fly back together.

Dr. Best comes over to me and whispers in my ear. "Thank you for coming. You did a great job, and congratulations regarding Dr. Paul. You two are adorable. I hope it works out for you."

Josh drives five of us to the airport in the van. We say our goodbyes. Pavlov and I head to our terminals and wait to embark on our flight. While we wait, I share with him what happened to our room.

His face turns red. "I'll take care of her when we get back."

They finally call our row, and we get comfortable in the first-class seats Pavlov arranged as a surprise.

Before we take off, a flight attendant approaches me. "Hello, dear. Do you remember me? Did you find what you were looking for on your travels?"

She's the same flight attendant from my flight here. "Oh, hello. Yes, I believe I did, but I couldn't take her back with me. However, I did find my childhood friend. This is Paul. We grew up together." I clutch one of his hands with mine and place it on my lap.

"Looks like you got a better deal," she says as she smiles and winks at both of us. "Buckle up. I'll get you both a Mimosa to celebrate your reunion."

She brings our drinks.

We look at each other with tears in our eyes. Our glasses touch.

"To you, my love, my future, my Nini."

Reviews

"A five star novel. I could not put the book down! This is a powerful story as it depicts the journey of a Russian girl who had to leave her country due to the nuclear accident. Her life journey is incredibly challenging and rewarding. However, throughout her sadness, she becomes a beautiful strong woman with a wonderful ending that you will love."

Olivia C. Ralston

"A hauntingly beautiful story of a young woman's healing journey: a tragic tale in its beginning, peeling back layers of both immigrant and adolescent upbringings. This novel demonstrates true healing and love of self-reaps true happiness. I could not put this book down once I started. I was crying, laughing, and blushing, not to mention gasping at a truly unexpected twist towards the end. This is a must read for anyone who loves a captivating tale that redefines the term "soulmates." What an exciting read!"

Danielle Viens-Payne,
Founder of Stilettos in the Boardroom

About the Author

Lynn is a hopeless romantic and animal lover. Her stories will pull at your heartstrings and delve deep into her characters' psyche. The plight of our four-legged friends is evident in all her works. Her readers are genuine animal lovers.

Lynn has a doctorate in Educational Leadership and works in higher education. She volunteers for animal advocacy groups and enjoys writing stories about her animals and experiences.

Lyla Lynn is a proud award-winning author. She shares her home with two beautiful cats who have cerebellar hypoplasia. Some say she loves and has a tender heart for handicapped animals.

To reach the author, contact

Lylalynnbooks@gmail.com